Anne-Marie

Hello! My name is Anne-Marie. We—me, my father, stepmother, brother and wife and child—oh yes, plus the maid and her husband (the gardener)—live in a big house in Hampstead. I know that most people would say that I'm very lucky, and I guess I do have more things than other girls my age—except freedom or friends or boyfriends! You know, the *little* things in life! Yes, yes, I know I should count my blessings! I'm quite pretty even though I don't have a model's figure, and I don't have to work for a living. My family love me, and I do, truly, appreciate that, although it can be stifling! We're quite close, really. Now and then I hear Dad and Mumpets (that's what I call my stepmother; it's Stepmum backwards; her real name is Marge) arguing—I think mostly about me. I wish they wouldn't.

Sometimes I think I'd rather like to have a job, but Dad thinks girls of my class should be at home welcoming guests and making sure the maid does the beds properly. That's what he tells me, but I suspect there's more to it than that. *I* think he just likes people to know that he's rich. Anyway, I have oodles of free time, so I read lots of books, I paint with watercolours and oils, and I have just learned how to bronze things—oh, and I window shop, of course. The trouble with shopping is, I always have to take someone with me. Dad just says the world is full of bad people and someone might try to hurt me. I keep telling him, if I had a dog then the dog would protect me. I love animals, but Dad and Mumpets won't let me have a pet; I think it might be because they're worried about the carpets. People who don't like animals have no soul. I used to have a kitten when I was a child, but it died. Oh, didn't I say? I'm twenty-three. No! I hear you gasp, and I suppose I am young for my age; but that's hardly *my* fault! I have the dreams and urges of a grown woman. I have to admit it, I would like to find Mr. Right.

That's not very likely to happen when I'm not bloody well given any opportunities to meet anybody!

My brother Micky—short for James Michael Smythe the Third—is seven years older than I am. He doesn't want us to have a dog in case it should attack his three-year-old daughter. Jenny is okay now she's growing up, I guess, but God did I hate her when she was born! All she did was cry and wet herself. It just seemed like every time I wanted to hold her, she would scream. Now, animals are nicer; *they* don't cry. Anyway, as I was saying: Micky is a musician. He plays double bass with the English Philharmonia. He loves his job but it does mean he has to go on tour a lot. He always liked touring until he had a baby, and then he hated it until Jenny became a toddler. He said he didn't like to leave Jenny and her mother alone, but they were hardly alone, were they? I mean, just think about it! It's not as though they were living by themselves in a little house in the middle of nowhere. Micky knows I for one would do everything in my power to save them, if the house caught fire, or burglars broke in, or anything. I think he's just plain paranoid.

Micky's wife played in the English Philharmonia too, until she got pregnant. She used to have a good figure but she's never managed to lose the extra weight she put on with the pregnancy. Netty (how do you get Netty from Vanessa, I ask you!) is nice, but she's a little bit boring. Music is all she knows about, and only classical music at that. She and Mumpets are great friends. They're always comparing orchestras and

Blood Love

Inspector Gravitt Follows a Trail of Deadly Passion

by Ann Cherry

PublishAmerica
Baltimore

First printing

At the specific preference of the author, PublishAmerica allowed this work to remain exactly as the author intended, verbatim, without editorial input.

ISBN: 1-4241-1264-8
PUBLISHED BY PUBLISHAMERICA, LLLP
www.publishamerica.com
Baltimore

Printed in the United States of America

Disclaimer:

Any resemblance of any of the characters in this book to any other persons, be they extant, extinct or fictional, is purely coincidental. In fact, I have taken great pains to ensure that no one can say, "Is that whodjamaflick?" The answer is no, it isn't.

Thanks to Timothy Morris BSc DO LicAc for help with technical matters.
Thanks also to my husband Paul, to my sister Kelly Cherry, to John Griffiths and to Franki Rubenstein.

Part 1
(In the Year 2003)

conductors. God, it's such boring stuff! Mumpets studied music when she was a little girl, but her family were poor (she says middle class, but it sounds to me like they were poor! Okay, I know I'm a snob!) and she had to take a practical job. She worked as an administrative assistant in a hospital which, as you can probably imagine, didn't pay well at all. But she's bright, and so she was given a chance to develop some computer skills. She found herself suddenly in much demand—the way she tells it, it was an overnight miracle! But I'm sure it took her some time to learn her way around baffling spreadsheets and relational database programmes. She's not *that* bright, after all! I mean, even *I* don't understand Excel beyond the basics! Anyway, that's how she met Dad; he went to the hospital every day when Granny was dying, and he met her and almost immediately offered her a job as a data processor in his company. Dad publishes books. You've probably heard of him: Smythe's Publishing House. He's one of the more successful publishers in England specialising in non-fiction works. Oh, I guess I like Mumpets. At least she doesn't get in the way. My real mother died when I was five. I only remember her a little bit.

I've got to run now; Dad's not been feeling well the last few days and I'm looking after him.

*

Chapter One

"Oh Dad, you look just awful!" Anne-Marie gasped. Her father looked old and frail, not at all like his usual self. Normally he was full of energy and fun, always ready to have a lively discussion on any topic, always on the move. For him to be lying in bed, his hair unwashed and his hands shaking, was quite frightening. Anne-Marie's voice trembled with emotion. "Are you taking your medicines? Is there anything I can do to make you more comfortable?"

"No, nothing," croaked Smythe, wincing at the effort it took to utter even those two words. "Stomach pains. Hurts, rather."

Anne-Marie pulled her eyes away from her father and looked around the familiar bedroom. It was very grand: large and old-fashioned, with the high Victorian ceiling proudly displaying the original centre rose and chandelier. The walls were covered with a rich navy and gold floral design, once gaudy but now faded into tastefulness. The late morning sunlight penetrated the floor length curtains partially drawn across the two large windows, revealing a busy ballet of dust motes. The furniture too was Victorian, a massive wardrobe with matching dressing table and bed. It was because of this room and Smythe's rigid moral code that Anne-Marie, as a teenager, had dubbed her father Prince Albert the Second. She felt that no matter how straight-laced Queen Victoria and her husband were, her father could give them a run for their money! To Anne-Marie, full of the joys and superior knowledge of youth, the old-fashioned grandeur was rather oppressive, to say the least.

As she turned back to her father, she noticed the undiminished number of tablets lying on the bedside table. "Dad, for goodness sake! You haven't taken the pills Mumpets left out for you. Here, let me help you sit up."

"I don't think they're doing any good." Smythe gritted his teeth and managed to pull himself into a half-sitting position. His wheezing was worse with the effort of shifting his body. "I don't want to take them," he protested grumpily. He was ill; he felt he was allowed to be cranky.

"Yes you do." Marge appeared in the doorway. She had overheard her husband's complaints and was firm with him. "I don't think these pills are doing you much good either, but they can't be doing you any harm. The Natural Health Clinic said they should settle your stomach." She poured some fresh water into a glass and helped her husband swallow two tablets.

"Arrgh," was the response from the bed. "Everyone's against me! It's hard to swallow those things. You're all just waiting for me to choke to death!"

"It's what you get for refusing to let me call a doctor," Marge scolded, but the rebuke was lessened in severity by the tender look on her face. She tried not to show it, but her concern was growing. James had been poorly for quite a few days. In fact, he had been getting progressively tired for a long while, far too tired for a man of only fifty-five. And all this pain! In her work at the hospital she had seen lots of patients in varying degrees of discomfort, but none worse than this. She was afraid her husband's condition was serious, yet he steadfastly refused to consult a doctor. "You make me feel so helpless, James," she complained. "I can't bear to see you like this! What am I supposed to do, just waltz around having fun while you suffer? Forget it!"

Anne-Marie trembled. "*Please* don't get the doctor!" she pleaded with her stepmother. "He'll put Dad in the hospital, I know he will! They're scary places—and lots of times…" She stopped short. She was remembering how Granny never came home again after the ambulance took her away. "I can take good care of him," she urged. "Natural medicines work more slowly than ordinary ones and you said yourself that at least these tablets can't be doing any harm. A little love and attention is what he needs." She moved nearer to her father, like a lioness protecting her cub.

The two women glared at one another, each determined to have her own way. James was important to both of them, and Marge understood that, even if her stepdaughter didn't. Marge also felt that she understood Anne-Marie's desire to look after her father personally. After all, he had been her only parent for many years and she would be lost without him. Oh God, they would both be lost if anything happened to him!

"Well, we'll see," Marge replied placatingly. "Meanwhile, Anne-Marie, I'd like a word alone with James. Would you mind seeing if Netty and Jenny have returned from the park?"

Aloud Anne-Marie said, "Of course; I don't mind at all," and smiled at both parents as she left the room. But inside she was seething, ready to do further battle for possession of her father. He's *my* father, she thought (but was sensible enough to keep this thought to herself.) I've known him longer than *you*.

Marge listened to Anne-Marie going down the stairs and then settled herself on the side of the bed and snuggled up to her husband, her soft brown curls mingling with his thick darker brown hair. "James darling," she said softly, "I love you so much! I really can't bear seeing you in this much pain." She pressed his hand to her heart. "I am going to ring the doctor. You can moan about it as much as you wish, but you won't stop me. I can be as fierce as the toughest matron, you know!"

James looked lovingly at this woman he had married after knowing her for less than a year. His friends had predicted it wouldn't work, but he had been happy for four years now. She was practical and intelligent and really—in his eyes anyway—quite beautiful. "Oh I'm scared, I'm scared," he replied, trying to make light of the agony in his stomach, the throbbing in his head. "My little termagant, you can be as ferocious as you like; you don't frighten me a bit."

12

"That's good, because I won't stand by any longer doing nothing. You are not getting any better. I am ringing the doctor."

"What's this I hear? Why are you lying in bed ill without getting permission from me first?" Dr. Elliot Winston entered his old friend's bedroom like he owned the place. He certainly made the room smaller; his size was as big as his personality: six feet high and two feet wide. A receding hairline with the remaining hair, now almost pure white and tied at the back in a long ponytail, helped to make him look like a caricature of an ageing hippie.

"Doc Elliot, you old windbag, it's good to see you!" James was delighted to discover that his wife had decided to call his regular GP, now semi-retired, instead of the younger and more popular doctor in the surgery. His friendship with Elliot went back thirty years. Elliot had helped him through the terrible months following his first wife's death, and he had been there for Elliot when his wife suddenly left him for another man. These days they got together on happier occasions, such as fishing trips and 'business' lunches. They chatted about the good times while Elliot checked James' blood pressure and reflexes. Elliot tried to keep his growing worries to himself, but James knew him too well.

"What is it, my friend? Give it to me straight."

Elliot frowned. "Frankly, I don't really know. It could be a stomach ulcer, or a hernia or God knows what else. Have you been taking anything for the pain? Who's been looking after you? Marge? She's nobody's fool. You're in good hands there."

"Marge and Anne-Marie share the burden," James replied. "I've only been taking the homeopathic tablets they got for me. Nothing else."

"Show me the bottle." James pointed to the bottle on the bedside table. "Well, they look harmless enough. I need to ask you a couple of questions, if you don't mind." Elliot asked James about his eating habits and his appetite; was swallowing difficult? And how did the food taste? He asked a few more questions of a similar nature and then stood back, pondering the replies. Finally he spoke. "Well, you said you wanted straight talking, so here it is: I don't like the way you're breathing, and the loss of appetite together with such a tender stomach could be symptoms of several problems. I'm going to put you into the hospital for some tests." Elliot picked up the phone and rang for an ambulance. He ignored James' protests, instead shouting for Marge and telling her to pack a few necessities.

"I want to get some x-rays and run a few tests," he explained to Marge. "And I want James where I can keep an eye on him."

Anne-Marie appeared in the doorway so quickly that it was obvious she had been listening from the next room. "I'll go to the hospital with Dad," she said. "I'm perfectly happy to sit with him and keep watch."

"No," replied Elliot in a voice not to be argued with. "Your father needs peace and quiet, not the chatter of a silly young girl. The nurses will keep him under observation. And that goes for you too, Marge. No fussing allowed."

Anne-Marie looked petulant, but Marge only nodded. "The ambulance is here," she said.

James

While I was in the hospital I began to feel better. Doc Elliot finally admitted that he had suspected me of having a carcinoid tumour, but the tests proved negative. What did show up were traces of arsenic. Too much arsenic for me to be ingesting naturally, but just enough to be killing me slowly.

Why would anyone want to kill me? I'm not perfect, God knows, but I have always tried to be fair in my business dealings. My father started our publishing firm with more goodwill than pence and it has grown through the recommendations of satisfied customers. And I am a faithful husband—not necessarily the best husband in the world, because my working days are long—but I have never cheated on my wife or refused my children any reasonable request.

I loved my first wife, Katherine, deeply. She was somebody special on this earth, giving her time and energy to anyone who needed help. Not a do-gooder but definitely a good-doer. She died so young! I wanted to die too. I can't stop my tears, even now. I'm so sorry; it must be my weakened condition. I love her still and she will always be a part of me. Katherine died of pneumonia. She knew she was dying and begged to stay at home rather than enter an impersonal hospital. Elliot

15

had oxygen brought into her bedroom and Greta stayed with her for much of the day. Greta is our live-in home help. Katherine's passing was hard on Micky, then an impressionable twelve years old. He noticed every change in his mother, every new weakness, the blue lips…He tried not to cry in front of me, but I could hear him sobbing in his bedroom when he thought no one could hear. Anne-Marie was only five and didn't understand anything. I caught her pulling Katherine by the arm and screaming because her mother wouldn't get up and play with her. Of course, five is a particularly selfish age and Anne-Marie was quite a tomboy then; she would pull the legs off spiders and laugh as she watched them try to get away, eventually feeding them to the cat. That stupid cat would eat anything! In the end eating spiders seems to have killed it. Micky was furious, but Anne-Marie was too young to understand. Now, of course, she's a woman and just as pretty as her mother was. I'm afraid, however, she's still very selfish. My fault probably; I've spoiled her.

But I digress. When I met Marge I discovered that it was possible to love again. It's a different kind of love, a love built on experience. Perhaps that makes it stronger. Marge was so alone when we met and I hadn't had a steady relationship with a woman since Katherine died. It was a cautious affair to begin with, then something magical seemed to happen and we became much more than lovers. Neither Micky nor Anne-Marie was particularly happy to see another woman in the position their mother had occupied, but eventually they came round. Netty seems to be genuinely fond of Marge.

I wanted Micky to go into the family business, but he said it was too boring. He's a gifted musician and plays with one of the finest orchestras in the world, so I guess he made the right choice. Sadly that means that if the firm goes to any member of the family, it won't be a direct descendant. I could leave it to Harry, my deceased sister's boy; he works for me, in the advertising department. But he's an odd fish and is no good when it comes to dealing directly with people. Frankly I don't want him to have my company. Anne-Marie has the brains to learn publishing, and even though I don't like the idea of her becoming a business woman, I have to admit that she has the intelligence to run the company. But, like Micky, she prefers artistic pursuits. At least no one knows what's in my will, and that, thank God, would seem to absolve my family of any suspicion of attempted murder.

Dear God! Who hates me this much?

Oh, God! Forgive me for my sins, for I have not committed them knowingly. Forgive me for any unhappiness which I may have given to another, for I have never desired to cause pain. If there has been a tear shed because of my ineptitude, know that it was not intentional. Please guide me through this Hell.

Chapter Two

The entire family was gathered in the sitting room awaiting James Smythe's return from the hospital. They had all been horrified to learn that someone had been slowly poisoning him. Marge sat on the antique three-seater sofa beside Netty, Jenny asleep in her stroller in front of them. Anne-Marie sat across from them in the matching armchair, and Micky chose to stand.

"There must be a mistake," Marge said softly. "He's such a kind man. I can't believe anyone wants to harm him."

"Not harm, Marge, kill. Don't belittle someone's almost successful murder attempt!" Micky burst out. He was looking particularly distraught. Micky had left for a small tour the day after his father went into hospital, and then he had to make his excuses and leave the tour two days early when Marge rang and informed him that his father was seriously ill, and not accidentally so. His position in the symphony was precious to him and much coveted by other, probably equally competent, bass players. It was the one drawback to what otherwise was a dream job: no job security. Marge started weeping at his tone of voice. "Oh for God's sake, don't cry! I'm sorry," he said. "I just have a lot of things on my mind at the moment."

Marge smiled tremulously at him but said nothing. She noticed Anne-Marie's interest in the little contretemps between herself and

Micky and sighed, wondering if the four years of hard work she had spent trying to be a part of this family had just been wasted effort.

"We're all worried sick and we're certainly over-reacting," Netty put in. "Perhaps we should remember that whoever tried to murder James hasn't succeeded, after all."

"And unlikely to try it again either, because we'll all be watching for him—or her," interrupted Anne-Marie, glancing meaningfully at her stepmother. Marge flushed and opened her mouth to tell her stepdaughter a home truth or two when the door opened and James walked in accompanied by Elliot and another man which none of them knew. Anne-Marie and Micky rushed to embrace their father while Netty and Marge waited their turn. James appeared to be glad to be home, but there was a hunted look in his eyes. He put his arm around his wife while he introduced the third man to his family. "This is Detective Inspector Gravitt from New Scotland Yard. He is investigating my case."

There were murmurs of apprehension and surprise. Why hadn't it occurred to any of them that the police would be involved? Scotland Yard? My God, it must be true then! Someone really *had* tried to kill James. Each sized up Gravitt in his own way: Micky saw a quiet man far too young to be handling a murder—even attempted murder—case. Netty saw a pleasant-looking face with unruly blond hair, someone you could trust. Marge hardly saw him at all, her eyes never left her husband, but she liked his cultured manner. And Anne-Marie felt an immediate attraction for him and thought to herself, this will be a challenge!

"Are you going to arrest us all on suspicion of murder, Inspector?" Anne-Marie blinked rapidly, knowing it would make her eyes moist and alluring (she had practised this repeatedly in front of the mirror.) Gravitt ignored the flirtatious gesture but kept the light-hearted tone.

"No, no, just one of you will be sufficient. Any volunteers?"

"Perhaps the butler did it," suggested Netty. "The trouble is, we don't have one."

They all laughed, a welcome outlet for the tension. The laughter stopped when Gravitt said he would like to talk to each of them separately. Unofficially today, but they would be required to make a formal statement on the morrow.

Marge offered him the use of the study and volunteered to be first. DI Gravitt closed the door firmly behind them. Fifteen minutes later Marge reappeared, looking as if she had gone for a walk on a treadmill. She sent Micky in next and went to find Greta and her husband Bill, who were also wanted for questioning. By the time she returned with them, Netty had had her interview and had gone upstairs to put Jenny in her cot, and Anne-Marie was with Gravitt. Greta and Bill were with him rather longer.

Gravitt asked only two questions: Where do you keep the arsenic? and, Who would benefit from James' death? He asked the questions over and over, wording them first one way and then another. After he had seen them all he returned to the sitting room and asked to see James' bedroom, and in particular the homoeopathic tablets. No one could find the tablets. Marge said she hadn't realised they weren't in the bedroom any more. Anne-Marie said she hadn't been in her dad's room since he had gone into hospital; Netty and Micky and Bill said they hadn't had any reason to go there either; and Greta said she had not noticed the pills when she cleaned. Elliot said he had looked at the ingredients listed on the bottle the day he sent James into the hospital, but of course he had not taken any away for analysis because at that time he was not looking for anything suspicious.

Gravitt said he would return the next day with another officer and get formal statements, and he asked for permission to search the house at the same time. "I need to locate the source of the arsenic." He waved their attempts to remonstrate aside. "Or I need to be able to eliminate this house as a possible source. I can get a search warrant if you like," he offered, but all agreed it wasn't necessary.

"None of us would want to hurt Dad," Anne-Marie stated firmly. "It must be some nutter in the publishing business," and everyone nodded in agreement.

After Gravitt left and the rest of the family had returned to their normal tasks, Marge encouraged James to lie down for a while before dinner. "Only if you come with me," he responded with a suggestive smile, and they made their way upstairs entwined in each other's arms. They were jerked awake two hours later by a loud rapping on the door.

"Dinner's ready," called Greta. "I've made a lovely garlicky shrimp gumbo, especially for Mr. James, but if he doesn't hurry it will disappear before he's even downstairs!"

Greta's shrimp gumbo was a treat not to be missed! They hurriedly dressed and found everyone else already seated at the table being entertained by Jenny.

"Grandpa! Grandpa!" she shouted when she saw James. He picked her up and put her on his shoulders.

"How is my favourite giant?" he growled in a troll-like voice.

"I'm a *big* giant!" Jenny growled back at him.

"And I'm the mean dragon who's going to eat all the gumbo if you're not sitting in front of your plate by the time I count to five," cut in Greta. The family counted together.

"One." James lowered Jenny to the floor and they looked at each other, feigning disinterest.

"Two." They each took half a step towards their chairs.

"Three." Another half step.

"Four." They scrambled quickly into their proper places.

"Five!" shouted the two miscreants together.

The meal continued in the same carefree vein. There was hot boiled rice and peas to go with the gumbo and just for James, as he said he really liked traditional Cajun cooking best when it was served in the Italian manner, a small pot of finely grated Parmesan cheese to sprinkle on top. The wine was a refreshing Chablis, making the dinner, said Anne-Marie, traditional International.

James excused himself before dessert. "My stay in hospital must have been more exhausting than I thought. I'm feeling quite sleepy." Marge stood up to go with him. "No, don't bother, dear," he said. "You stay and enjoy the rest of the meal."

James left the room and Marge sat down again. She was just about to help Greta make room on the table for dessert when there was a loud thump from the floor above. She raced upstairs, the rest of the family on her heels. James, partially undressed, was bent over on the floor vomiting violently. As he vomited he wet himself; ominous red stains appeared on the carpet.

"Oh my God," Marge breathed. "He's bleeding internally. Call an ambulance, hurry, hurry!"

Micky grabbed for the phone. James started thrashing about, his limbs convulsing wildly. Foam gathered around his mouth. Netty and Anne-Marie tried to hold him, to keep him still.

"Let him go!" cried Marge. "You can't stop the convulsions like that!" And then suddenly he quit moving. The ambulance arrived but it was too late. James was dead.

Ha ha ha ha. Better watch out—there's a killer about!

Chapter Three

Inspector Gravitt arrived shortly after the ambulance. The uniformed officers had already cordoned off the house and the technicians were hard at work. This was the time commonly referred to in police jargon as the 'golden hour'—the time immediately following a crime when most clues were discovered.

When he heard of a sudden death in Reddington Gardens, Gravitt knew immediately that the victim was James Smythe and that death would not be accidental. He cursed himself mentally for having allowed Smythe to return home when he knew that someone had been trying to poison him. But in truth there was no way he could force a man to stay away from his own residence. And he had thought that knowing a full-scale investigation was starting would keep the murderer at bay for a little while. It had never occurred to him—stupid, short-sighted copper!— that the murderer would decide to complete his task immediately.

He surveyed the scene in front of him. Mrs. Smythe—Marge—was leaning over her husband's body, sobbing and saying over and over, "James, James, no no, no, James, no." They seemed the only words she could find. Smythe's daughter was in a hysterical state and was being held tightly by her brother whose face was also tearstained. The other Mrs. Smythe, Vanessa, was clearly in a state of shock. She was transfixed by the happenings, unable to move, her eyes widened in horror. Greta and Bill were just outside the bedroom; Greta was crying audibly while Bill kept whispering to her, "Shh, shh." Gravitt always dreaded this stage of an investigation. He felt unequal to the task of dealing with such intense emotions.

"Please go and make some strong tea or coffee," he said to Greta and Bill, "and get some brandy as well, if there is any. Take it into the sitting room."

He cleared his throat loudly. "Ahem! For God's sake, stop behaving like extras in a low budget film studio and let the police get on with their job. Move away at once!" He turned to Netty. "Who's looking after the baby?" he asked rudely, shocking her out of her paralytic state and sending her scurrying downstairs, suddenly fearful for her child. Early on in his career Gravitt had discovered that a firm dictatorial voice was more effective than sympathy. It worked with everyone except Marge. He pulled her gently away from her husband and was disconcerted when she threw herself into his arms and sobbed uncontrollably. "There, there," he said in the time honoured way of all embarrassed policemen. He managed to catch Micky's eye and ask silently for help. Micky deposited Anne-Marie, now more or less in control of herself, on a chair and took Marge in his arms.

"Please go into the sitting room and wait for me there," Gravitt demanded. "I shall want to talk to you all."

When the family members were finally out of the bedroom, Gravitt waited for the photographer and fingerprint experts to finish their work, although he felt he already knew the results: the prints would include most, if not all, of the residents of the house. He routinely checked the approximate time of death with the pathologist—although the time could be confirmed by the telephone call for an ambulance— and that death occurred by poisoning, probably arsenic. He would have guessed that as well. The pathologist would tell him later how much arsenic had been administered and how long it would have taken Smythe to die. They were lucky in this case to have such specific information about the time of death; arsenic preserves body tissue unnaturally and it can often be difficult to pinpoint an accurate death time. Meanwhile he had to try to figure out how the poison had been given to the deceased.

He left the bedroom to the Scene of Crime Officers and went downstairs. When he reached the sitting room he noticed that the doors to the dining room were open and he could see the unfinished meal still on the table. Greta was fretting because she had not been allowed to clear the dishes. He asked her who had eaten what. Everyone had eaten the gumbo and the rice except Jenny, who had chicken with her rice because she was too young to appreciate so much garlic; all but Jenny had shared the wine; and James had retired before dessert.

"There was the Parmesan cheese," added Greta. "Only Mr. James ate that, it's a favourite of his." Greta explained that she had only grated a little and he had eaten it all. Fortunately she had not yet washed up the bowl, and Gravitt ordered an officer to bag it and to take samples of all the food. He thought the poison was most likely to have been in the cheese, but he also thought it oddly clumsy of the killer not to have washed or removed the bowl if that were the case. This was a villain clever enough to have almost succeeded with the previous attempt on Smythe's life. Why leave detectable traces lying around this time?

He returned to the sitting room and asked, as he had that morning, "Where do you keep the arsenic?" He turned to Micky and repeated the question.

"You asked me that already," Micky said. "I don't know anything about arsenic. Isn't that the stuff used in rat poison? For God's sake, man, I've never even set a mousetrap! And by the way," he continued, his voice taking on a condescending quality, "aren't you a bit young for this job? My father was an important person. The Force should have sent a more experienced man."

Gravitt was used to receiving hostility from suspects and the family of the victim and he ignored the jibe. He asked Bill if he kept rat poison and Bill said yes, but it was locked up in the garden shed. The key? Hanging on the key rack just inside the back door of the house.

"It's there now, Inspector; I noticed it just before dinner. Greta and I have our meal in the kitchen while the family has theirs in the dining room."

"You see, *Detective Inspector?*" Micky put heavy sarcasm on the last two words. "Now you'll probably arrest Bill for murder, Bill, who has worked for this family for years. But if the key is in the kitchen, the truth is anybody could have taken it." Gravitt gave Micky a long cold look which had reduced many big men to babbling idiots, and enjoyed watching him squirm.

"Shut up, Micky," ordered his wife. "Please forgive him, Mr. Gravitt. He's not normally so rude. He was very close to his father."

"Never mind, I understand. Were you close to him too?"

"We became closer after Jenny was born. James loved being a grandfather. And before you ask, yes, I did know where the key to the shed was kept; and no, I didn't know there was rat poison there."

"I did and didn't likewise," offered Anne-Marie. Lord, thought Gravitt, she is quite beautiful when she's not trying to be! Her soft blond hair fell to her waist and the smudged mascara did nothing to detract from the perfection of her pink cheeks. He felt his heart beat a little faster and pulled himself sharply back to the business at hand.

Turning to Marge, Gravitt said, "I do need to see each of you individually. May I use the study again, Mrs. Smythe?"

Marge nodded, once more offering to be first and getting up to lead the way. This time an officer was present to take notes. There were the normal questions—where were you when and who was with you—but as he knew the family was together at the time of death most of this was a formality. He was really interested in knowing who had access to the cheese before the meal.

Marge blushed and told the Inspector that she and her husband had not been alone with each other, "since before he went into the hospital, and we…well we…we went upstairs until Greta called us to dinner."

Gravitt made a mental note to find out exactly when the Parmesan had been grated. Then he said, "This is quite an unusual case, where all the suspects are also the alibis. Off the record," he gestured to the officer to quit taking notes, "I would like you to give me your personal opinion of the other members of the family. I know, I know," he interrupted her objections, "but somebody here is a cold-blooded killer. Somebody here killed your husband, Mrs. Smythe. He or she needs to be stopped before it happens again. Please help me."

Marge reluctantly agreed. Okay, she said, no holds barred. "On the surface we're a happy family; but there is an undertone—though actually I'm sure there are undertones in every family. In a pinch we would stick together, I'm sure." She told how the children had baulked at having a stepmother thrust upon them; how Micky had accused her of marrying his father for the money, and only Netty's sensible behaviour had finally brought him to realise that James was still a vigorous man with his own life to live, especially as his children were grown. She and Micky had long since made their peace. "But Micky's in a bad mood all the time lately; something is obviously wrong, but I don't know what. He wouldn't tell me, of course."

She told Gravitt how Anne-Marie worshipped her father and he, her. They were unusually, she sometimes felt abnormally, attached. But she probably felt that way because she herself was never close to her own father. She thought Anne-Marie must look like her mother, who had died young, and perhaps that's why James was so protective of his daughter. Marge said she felt no jealousy of Katherine because she realised that there are many different ways to love, and she knew that James truly loved her. As for Greta, she had been with the family for years, she would never hurt "Mr. James." Bill, she hardly knew; he kept himself to himself, but she liked him well enough.

Gravitt asked Marge what she had been doing that morning before Mr. Smythe arrived home. She replied, not much, just female vanity stuff.

"I'm a middle-aged woman, Inspector; it takes me a little longer to look good than it used to. I didn't want to disappoint my husband." And she began to weep again.

Gravitt escorted her to the door and asked Greta to come in. Greta was visibly shaking with nervousness and her face was blotched with tears.

"You think I did it, don't you? You think I killed Mr. James." Gravitt was unable to stop her tirade. "You think I poisoned his food. Well, I didn't! As if I would, me, who's been in this house for thirty years. I keep a clean kitchen, I do, you could eat off the floor if you wanted. And you leave that nice Mrs. Marge alone, too. You got no right to make her all upset." Gravitt let her continue until she finally realised how badly she was behaving to an officer of the law. Then he had to wait while she waded through heavy-going contrition. Eventually she calmed down enough for him to ask a few questions without getting his ear blasted. He explained that taking food samples in a case of poisoning was a routine matter.

"It certainly looked like a tasty meal," he complimented her. "I wish I had been invited to share it. Is shrimp gumbo one of your regulars?"

"It's a special favourite of Mr. James. I don't prepare it too often because it's an all day job the way I do it, which is nicer than the short cuts the books suggest. I use only fresh ingredients." This last comment was uttered defensively.

"It must be incredibly tricky, doing all the housework and the cooking as well. How did you manage to organise it today, what with all the excitement of the homecoming?"

Greta was softening under Gravitt's gentle handling. "Well you see, I planned it all last night. I grated the cheese then, because that will keep nicely in the fridge. And I mixed the dry ingredients ready for adding today. Once breakfast was over I did the beds and hoovering, and we only had sandwiches for lunch so that was no bother."

"Mr. James was a good guv'nor?"

"The best. Like my own son, he was, and treating me like one of the family. If he had callers and I was in the room he would introduce me by name, not as the maid or housekeeper." Greta was talking freely now and needed little prompting from Gravitt. "I came here when Mrs. K— Katherine, that is—had just given birth to the young master, Micky. She was beautiful, Miss Anne-M is the spitting image of her except Mrs. K's hair had more red in it and her eyes were blue, not brown. When she died the whole family was torn apart. Mr. James buried himself in his work and Mr. Micky started having nightmares and wetting the bed. I'm sure you won't let on to him that I told you this. He was twelve you know, such a difficult age for a boy. Thank Heavens, Miss Anne-M was too young to understand much of it. Her pain was more stretched out, if you know what I mean; after a day or two she began to ask where her Mummy was and then she started having tantrums because her mother wouldn't come home and play with her. Oh it was a bad time, a real bad time. But we got over it."

"I understand Mrs. K died of pneumonia?" queried Gravitt.

"That's what the doctor said, but it seemed like more; she had black-out spells as well, and she just didn't have the energy to fight the sickness. Her mother died the same way."

"Is that why Mr. James was so protective of his daughter? Fear that she would also suffer from the same problem?"

Greta frowned. "Well yes, certainly that. It's odd, now you make me think about it. Both of Mrs. K's children had fainting spells when they were young. The doctor said he thought they'd got too tall, too soon, if you know what I mean. Anyway, they seem to have grown out of it." Gravitt waited patiently as Greta sank into her memories. "Miss Anne-M was a terror as a child. You get them like that sometimes, children who don't know good from bad naturally, they have to be taught the difference. She was always in trouble in school. But she grew up just fine. You wouldn't be able to recognise the lady she is now as the same brat. She's taken an interest in art and everyone says she has real talent."

"Does she go out much with friends?" Gravitt tried to convince himself that he had no personal interest in the question.

"She has a few casual friends, mostly people who like to go to art galleries. Her father didn't like her to go out alone. It's a rough world for a pretty young woman."

"Micky Smythe seems moody; is he always like this?"

"Mr. Micky has always been a serious kind of person. Since Jenny was born he's been worse, I think it's because his job takes him away so much."

"I understand that he was close to his father. He must have been upset when Mr. James married again."

"That he was sir, he was indeed." Greta remembered the day well, the day James announced he was going to get married. Everyone knew James had been seeing a woman, but no one expected him to marry her.

Micky and Mr. James had quite an argument about it. You could hear them a mile away! Micky called his father a 'senile old fool' and Mr. James tried to hit him. It was Netty who finally managed to calm them both down. Anne-Marie had also been shocked. When the row between her brother and father was mostly exhausted and Netty seemed to be getting them to see how stupidly they were behaving, she suddenly screamed at her father, "I hate you!" and ran out of the room. But eventually they all got used to the idea, and life returned to normal. When Mr. James brought his fiancée to meet the family, they had behaved like angels. Well, mostly.

It was now approaching midnight and Gravitt wanted to go home. He felt he had absorbed all he could for the moment and he needed some thinking time before interviewing the other members of the family. He suggested that Greta, who looked ready to drop from grief and fatigue, should go to bed. He then told the Smythes he would return the following morning when he would expect to find them all at home. They were not to try to enter the sealed rooms, but neither were they to feel like prisoners. He would leave an officer, Detective Constable Bateman, with them overnight to ensure their safety.

After Gravitt's departure, nobody moved. It was as though time had come to an end and they were all in suspended animation. Finally Marge rose and went to sit by Anne-Marie on the sofa. She took her stepdaughter's hand in her own and held it tightly. "We will have to support each other," she said in her soft voice.

Anne-Marie sank gratefully into Marge's arms, glad of the warmth and comfort. "Oh Mumpets," she cried, "I don't think I can stand it! It must be hard for you, too"—this last statement was almost an afterthought. But better that than nothing at all, Marge thought, feeling hopeful.

"Very touching," Micky said with an ugly sneer in his voice. "Aren't you forgetting, dear sister, one small fact? Nothing like this happened before Marge joined this family." He wrenched Anne-Marie off the sofa and held her tightly. "I'll look after my own flesh and blood," he said to Marge. "It's safer."

Netty gasped. "Now you've gone too far!" she said to Micky, her voice shaking and shrill. She noticed that the officer, seated at the other end of the large room, was keeping a close eye on them.

But Marge didn't care who was watching. "How dare you! How dare you!" she shouted back at Micky. "You are disgusting with your constant moping and moaning and carping, trying to blame everyone else for your bad temper. You're a thirty-year-old man and you behave like a moody teenager. I'm sick of your snide little innuendos. *I* didn't kill James, but maybe *you* did! Maybe you *all* did!" she added, including the others in her accusation. She ran out of the room sobbing hysterically and slammed the door to the spare bedroom where she was forced to sleep while the police kept her joint bedroom with James sealed. I don't even have the right to sleep in my own bed, she thought. Marge felt very sorry for herself, very alone, and very scared.

Meanwhile, tempers continued to flare downstairs in the sitting room. Anne-Marie also turned on Micky. "You're not Dad! I don't want your protection. You stay away from me or you'll be sorry!" she warned him childishly. And she too ran upstairs to her bedroom, which was on the second floor, just above the room where Marge was staying the night. She too slammed her bedroom door loudly.

Netty and Micky were alone now, except for the policeman. "I want to know what's the matter with you," she demanded. "You've been grizzly and short-tempered for months now. If there is something wrong, tell me and maybe I can help you to put it right. If you're in some kind of trouble, we can face it together. But I can't do anything if you won't tell me what the problem is."

"Oh drop it, won't you?" Micky was exasperated. "There's nothing you can do. For God's sake, leave me alone, woman! I'll sleep in the study tonight so you can be rid of my 'teenage' moods. Who needs you anyway?" He went into the study and completed the pattern set by his sister and stepmother by slamming the door.

Netty gaped after him, shocked by his words. What had happened to the charming young man she had married? What difficulty was he in?

Was he worried about money? His job? They had always faced problems together. Why wouldn't he confide in her now? Slowly she trudged up the stairs, worry making her legs heavy, to the third floor. She and Micky and their daughter occupied the whole of this floor, which made them, except for the lack of a kitchen, self-contained. She went into their bedroom and quietly closed the door.

Detective Inspector Alex Gravitt felt like a limp dishrag. Lord, how swimming through a sea of emotions wore him out! Sadly he was not going to get much sleep tonight; he had to go through his notes, make sure he didn't overlook any salient points. He had never had a case quite like this one, where all the suspects were able to vouch for each other's whereabouts. I don't suppose they were all in it together, he wondered idly, almost immediately dismissing the notion. They hadn't really seemed very fond of each other, despite Mrs. Smythe's assertions to the contrary.

The telephone rang. It was the lab, not yet ready to give him a full report, but letting him know that there were traces of arsenic in the cheese dish. Gravitt made a note to be sure to ask who had access to that dish the night before the murder; he remembered that he hadn't known the cheese was grated so far in advance when he talked to Marge.

The choice of dinner was most interesting! Garlicky shrimp gumbo. Did Greta know that the mouth of someone who's ingested a large dose of arsenic smells like garlic? Was she hoping to disguise James' breath with the gumbo? He needed to know more about her. What did she do before she went to work for Smythe? He would ask Bill, her husband, that question. Bill's interview must be well planned! He had the easiest access to the shed, but what could be his motive? It seemed too easy a solution anyway, Gravitt decided.

He would have to look into Katherine's death. And Anne-Marie's school record, especially regarding relationships. And Micky's job. He would run a police check on all of them, but particularly Bill.

And he mustn't forget that this was not the first attempt on Smythe's life. If Dr. Winston had not insisted that James be admitted to hospital, the slow poisoning would probably have succeeded, and might even have gone unrecognised for what it was. He shivered at the idea of such a cruel killing going undetected. How was James being poisoned? Was the arsenic in those homoeopathic tablets? And where the hell were they, anyway? Probably flushed down the toilet long ago.

His thoughts drifted to Anne-Marie. Yes, she was selfish; her father must have loved and cosseted her very much. But who could blame him? Gravitt put his pen down and allowed his mind to drift. He imagined himself taking care of Anne-Marie, how he would cherish her, buy her little trinkets…He brought himself back to reality with a jolt. That beautiful creature could be a sadistic murderer.

Gravitt rose from his desk to prepare for bed, but he couldn't get his mind off Smythe's daughter. It wasn't just the unusual combination of golden hair with brown eyes, or even her well-developed body. Oh, no; he could recognise her faults, the too thick waist, the slightly crooked nose. It was all of those things combined in an aura of frailty and helplessness that made her so desirable, appealing to man's instinct to defend womankind.

It's been too long since you had any female companionship, Gravitt said to the image looking back at him from the bathroom mirror. Here I am, talking to myself when really you—I—you—oh damn it, *we*! should be talking to an armful of the opposite sex. He finished brushing his teeth and went to bed. For the first time in over a year he forgot to say a silent goodnight to Sarah, the girlfriend who had deserted him because his police work kept him too busy.

Chapter Four

The next morning Inspector Gravitt arrived at the house in Reddington Gardens at 9.30, meeting DC Bateman, whose replacement was already ensconced in the chair inside, on the doorstep.

"I'm glad you arrived before I'd gone, sir," Bateman said. "Bit of a wing ding here last night." Bateman had an excellent memory and was able to give Gravitt an accurate accounting of the evening's volatile events. Well, well, Gravitt thought to himself; perhaps the suspects would solve the crime for him. Bateman also volunteered the information that the pathologist and technicians had approved removal of the body.

Gravitt rang the bell and Greta arrived to welcome him. "Good morning, Detective Inspector. The family are still at breakfast. Have you eaten?" she offered. Gravitt said he would like a coffee and followed Greta into the dining room. Everyone was there except Marge. Only Jenny was talking and clearly no one was listening to her. Looking at the black faces, Gravitt thought they all probably welcomed the child's chatter, obviating the need to be civil to each other. He asked if Marge was up yet, trying not to let his growing fear for her safety show.

"Yes, she's awake but says she has a headache," Greta answered. "I took her a tray half an hour ago."

"What's in store for us today, Inspector?" Micky asked. For once he was speaking with a voice that held no hostility. He looks tired, Gravitt thought. The arguments with his wife and sister must have taken the fight out of him. Gravitt even felt some sympathy for this attractive young man who seemed to have the weight of the world on his shoulders and no idea of how to handle it.

"I talk to those of you I didn't see individually yesterday, and there needs to be a search of the house and grounds in daylight. Any questions?"

"I don't think so, Inspector. Is it okay if we begin funeral arrangements? Dad's friends and colleagues keep ringing up to ask when the funeral will be and I don't know what to tell them. Actually— don't take this comment the wrong way—but I think they really ring out of morbid curiosity. Because of the press coverage, you know."

Gravitt said he had no objection and, having obtained the name and telephone number of Mr. Smythe's solicitor, settled himself once again in the study. The solicitor, Frederick Collins of Collins, Collins, Harris and Collins, upon being strongly urged to do so, finally agreed to stop by that afternoon with Smythe's last will and testament.

Anne-Marie appeared at the door, and Gravitt blushed as he recalled his earlier thoughts about her. She noticed his embarrassment and guessed instantly the reason for it, and her own cheeks also turned warm. There was an awkward silence lasting in reality for only a few seconds, but to the young man and woman looking at each other, a lifetime.

"I wondered if…" Anne-Marie's voice disappeared and she had to start again. "I wondered if I could have the first interview today." What's wrong with me? she asked herself. She felt breathless and faint.

"Of course, that's no problem," Gravitt responded. "Do you have something important to do this afternoon?" God, what a bloody stupid thing to say, he thought. Where were his brains?

"Not really, but I'd like to work on a painting I've started and I need to be free of distractions. Do you want to see my studio? "

"Yes. We can talk now and afterwards I'll have a look in your workroom, and then you can be left in peace for the rest of the day." The technicians would already have searched the room, but Gravitt liked, whenever possible, to carry out a little search on his own; it helped him to get to know the people involved better.

He pulled up a chair for her, called the officer in to take notes, and said, "I'd like you to tell me about your mother. Your real mother, Katharine."

Anne-Marie was surprised. "I hardly knew her! She died when I was only five. I can't really tell you anything." But with careful manoeuvring Gravitt did get her to recall incidents from her childhood. She remembered that her mother spent a lot of time in bed but at the time she hadn't understood why. Of course, when she got older she did realise that her mother had been ill. She remembered the golden red of her mother's hair, and that her father was with her mother "all the time." Again, when she grew up she understood why. She remembered her father's pet name for his wife: Kitty; and she remembered that she had wanted a pet name for herself. She had even named the cat 'Kitty.'

"Dad and I became very close after Mama was gone. He worried about me, and even when I got older and started to grow up, he didn't like me to go out alone. In fact, until I went to art school and met other people interested in paintings, he would insist on accompanying me to galleries himself rather than let me go on my own. Oh, I'd forgotten this! After Mama died we started going to church every Sunday and he would give me what he called Morality Lessons on Wednesday evenings. They were fun! We would take turns playing the good guy and the bad guy, you know, in little skits. The good guy always won, of course. Dad was strict in his beliefs about good and bad. He made up a little limerick for me about honesty; it went like this:

"There was a young lady named Smythe
who lisped when she tried to tell lies.
She learned to be good,
as a young lady should.
And was truthful until her demise.

"Only you have to say it with a lisp:

"There wath a young lady named Smythe
who lithped when she tried to tell lieth.
She learned to be good,
as a young lady should.
And wath truthful until her demithe."

They laughed together, enjoying the camaraderie, the brief intimacy. Gravitt was impressed with Anne-Marie's quick intelligence and decided that her father had worried needlessly; she would be able to extricate herself from any uncomfortable situation, he was sure. He noticed a tear running down her cheek—a real one this time—and changed direction before one tear turned into a hundred.

He asked the usual questions about her movements before the murder, asked what she knew about Marge and Netty's movements, and about Micky's and Bill's. He was going to get the same answers from them all, he could see. Everyone had access to the cheese dish and the shed. No one could be readily eliminated from suspicion. And no one seemed—not yet, anyway—to have a motive.

He asked about her general likes and dislikes and managed to get her talking about her early school days.

The classes were okay, Anne-Marie replied, but the play periods were hell. "I was good at all the subjects, and a lot of the students were jealous of me. They called me horrid names like Egghead and Brainbox and so in the play periods I beat them up. Even the boys. They soon learned to call me names from a distance! I was kept in detention most days and Dad had to take me to and from school. That led to more name-calling, of course! Spoiled brat, and Daddy's girl."

Middle school was slightly better than the primary grades, but Art school was a different matter altogether. There she met people who were intelligent and ambitious, who liked to go to galleries and museums and who didn't waste time on stupid emotions like envy.

"Would you like to see my studio now?" she asked.

Gravitt said he'd like that very much and followed Anne-Marie to the second floor. She took him into a large well-lit room facing southeast and so catching the morning sun.

"I used to have my studio on the top floor where there is a skylight, and this used to be Micky's room; but when he married and then had a child, he and Netty asked to have the whole of the top floor. They wanted to be self-contained and I could hardly refuse." She forgot how she had raged and cried at the time, how she had felt almost physically abused by the injustice of being pushed out of her sanctuary.

The Inspector did his search, looking for anything and missing nothing, half hoping to find something and half hoping he wouldn't. He picked up jars of paint and looked inside, scrutinised brush cleaners, looked behind piles of canvasses. He noticed a pair of bronzed baby shoes and asked Anne-Marie about them.

"They're Jenny's first shoes," she explained. "I'm not very good at bronzing yet, but I'm getting better. I find cleaning the shoes the hardest part. All the old wax and polish has to be removed—that's what the alcohol here is for." She pointed to a bottle of denatured alcohol. "Then you have to prepare the liquid bronze; you have to get a 'feel' for the consistency."

Gravitt picked up the container of bronze powder and studied the ingredients. They included a small quantity of arsenic. "I'd like to take this," he told her. "The amount is so little that it's probably not important, but I think the lab should see it anyway."

Anne-Marie flushed. "I've never even looked at the ingredients," she protested. "I didn't kill Dad, whatever you think." But she felt guilty, all the same. It was his low voice, his non-accusatory manner that did it, and his smile—that smile that must have encouraged a hundred women to confess! Only one thing was wrong: she knew she had not poisoned her father. "Do take it," she said sweetly, now on her guard. "And why not take the shoes as well?" She smiled and left the room.

Gravitt completed his search and went to find Greta. He wanted a coffee. In the kitchen he met Bill and asked if he would come into the study and have a little chat.

Bill followed grudgingly, muttering, "I don't know nothing, nothing at all." But little by little he unwound under the Inspector's mixture of friendship and encouragement, combined with an air of helplessness which made Bill feel needed, like a father guiding his son. Bill told how he met Greta, fifteen years ago; he had knocked on the door looking for odd jobs and especially gardening work. He had never had a proper education, but he loved plants.

"We understand each other and they grow for me," he explained. Greta had asked Mr. James to give him a try, and Mr. James had liked his work and recommended him to the neighbours, and now he worked the whole area. "None of the gardens around here are very large; no one wants a full-time gardener. But I'm kept busy six days a week. When Greta and I wanted to get married, Mr. James offered to let me move into the basement flat with Greta. And that's how it's been for years. I wonder what we will do now?" He was plainly distressed.

When asked what Greta did before she began working for the Smythes, Bill wasn't sure. He thought she'd always done domestic work.

At that moment Greta opened the study door to let the Inspector know the station was on the telephone and wanted a word with him. She peered closely at Bill but he looked happy enough. If that policeman upset her man, she would have something to say to him, she would.

From the phone call Gravitt learned that the police checks on Bill, Greta and Micky were completed and had turned up nothing. Katharine Smythe's death was as they had been told, pneumonia. One bit of interesting information about Marge Smythe though: before marrying Mr. Smythe, she had worked in the administration office of a large research hospital. They were carrying out experiments on patients with a highly pernicious form of leukaemia known as Acute Promyelocytic Leukaemia, or APL. What substance were they experimenting with? Arsenic. "And by the way, Inspector, we visited a natural health clinic as you suggested, and apparently some homoeopathists prescribe arsenic to cure stomach cramps; although the amounts would be too small for our purposes, I think—practically undetectable, I'm told."

While Anne-Marie and Bill were having their interviews, Marge was lying on the bed. Her grief made her feel dull and listless; her breakfast lay untouched on the bedside table. What was life without James? Did he know how much she loved him?

Marge

Oh, James Are you there? Are you somewhere where you can hear me? Yes, I know you're with me, I can feel your presence. Oh James, James, did you know how much I loved you? You were my life, my everything. I wasn't alive until I met you.

When we were married and you brought me here, to your home, did you know how hard it was for me at first? I hadn't felt so much emotional strain since before my father disappeared. To jump from half a lifetime of just the two of us, Mom and me, to a family with two children and even a grandchild was more than I sometimes knew how to cope with.

I still don't know how to cope with it. Not without you. James, oh James! There's so much I never told you. How my father deserted us when I was twelve. It was good that he left; I know you're not supposed to say things like that, but it's the truth. He was an alcoholic and on drugs, and he abused my mother regularly, both physically and sexually. He would shout for me to go to him and no doubt would have raped and beaten me as well, but I used to hide in the closet until he passed out. Once he left, my mother and I were much happier. She saw to it that I had all the advantages that other girls had, even music lessons

41

and school trips. I loved my piano lessons. Music opened a whole new world for me, a wonderful world full of fantasy and magic. When Mom became ill with terminal cancer I had to take a job, and that was the end of my never-admitted-to-anyone dream of becoming a music teacher. It was a struggle just to make ends meet. I worked in several different factory jobs, but I loathed them all; the hours were long and left me with little enough time to look after my mother and no time for anything else. I was determined to keep Mom at home with me for as long as possible, and I like to think I made her last years comfortable ones. When she had to go into permanent care, I managed to get a job in the same hospital. That was where I was given some computer training. At last! Something to stretch my mind. It was exciting!

And that's where we met, James, do you remember? Your mother was very ill, like mine, and we found we could share our grief. We had so much in common! Not just the sadness of our dying loved ones, but good things too, like literature and music. When my mother died, I felt lost. After all, she was my only true friend, the only one who knew what we both had been through. You helped me so much! A new direction, you advised; break the old mould and start a new life. The job you gave me in your company allowed me to develop better computer skills and for the first time in my life I felt truly useful. You gave me self-respect, James—the most precious gift of all! Our friendship grew and little by little we were swept into something beautiful and exciting, and yet...and yet a little bit frightening because of our intangible recognition that this was no ordinary affair.

I hope you can hear me. I hope you know how much I love you. I hope you know how much you did for me! What should I do now, James? What would you like me to do? I feel like you would want me to keep the family together, but I wonder if my being here, as Micky said, is what has caused this dreadful split.

I know how much you loved your daughter. I would like to be closer to her, but every time I think we're forming a solid relationship something goes wrong and I realise that I haven't gained her affection at all. It's probably my fault, my own shortcomings. I've had no experience with children and my own childhood left much to be desired. Anne-Marie has always had it easy, and I suppose I am a little jealous of that; well, jealous of her opportunities to study the arts and never having to worry when the next meal will be. And perhaps I am also jealous that she has known you all her life and I but for a few short years. I know she reminds—reminded—you of your first wife. I would like to have known more about Katherine, but I would never intrude on your privacy. She died very young, I know. Were you afraid of losing your daughter as well? Is that why you were so protective of her?

Instead…

It was obviously a shock to your children when I suddenly appeared in their lives. Netty was the only one who welcomed me with open arms. Micky was definitely suspicious; I'm sure he thought I married you for mercenary reasons. And Anne-Marie was downright rude at first. But I think we learned to accept the new life; and now here we are, left only with each other. And I'm the one who must try to find a way forward for us all. Oh James, I need your wise advice!

I fear for the future.

Chapter Five

"Marge, can you spare me a moment?"

Marge turned to face the voice, her eyes flashing, ready to defend herself against another verbal attack from Micky. He held up his hands in a gesture he might have used to protect himself from an opponent and said quickly, "I come in peace. Please, Marge." Marge held back the retort she was about to utter but retained the stony look. Micky took her by the arm and ushered her into the back garden where they would be undisturbed.

"I'm so sorry, Marge, I really am. I don't know why I behaved like that last night. I'm not usually such a monster, and I've managed to alienate both you and Netty." Marge didn't move. "Anyone could tell you really loved Dad; I know you didn't kill him. Please forgive me." He held out his arms in a supplicating manner and she took his hands.

"You know Micky, I think the world is upside down." Her tears stated to flow." I just don't understand anything that's happening. None of it makes sense. None of it. Who could have hated James so much?"

They stayed talking until lunch was ready, both wanting to be friends again. They talked about James, Micky sharing silly stories about life in the family between Katharine and Marge. They talked about music. They talked about flowers. But they never talked about

Micky's current problems. He wanted to ask her advice but he didn't know how.

Shortly after lunch the solicitor arrived with Dr. Elliot Winston.

"I asked the doctor to come with me this afternoon because he is concerned in these proceedings," Collins explained, introducing himself to Inspector Gravitt. "Harry Franklin—that's Smythe's nephew—is coming as well. He's one of the beneficiaries." Frederick Collins gave no indication of his disapproval at being asked to present himself at a client's home, 'like a paper boy,' he thought to himself. Normally he would never consider leaving his plush and comfortable office; but this was not a normal situation. Murder! Collins felt a frisson of excitement.

When Harry arrived everyone gathered in the study. Collins said he didn't propose to read the will in its entirety, as he would be sending copies to the beneficiaries in any case. He was there because this was a murder case, very tragic, and Detective Inspector Gravitt had requested this meeting.

Collins paused for dramatic effect. He had always wanted to be another Perry Mason but alas his work as a senior partner in Collins, Collins, Harris and Collins gave him very little opportunity to exhibit his theatrical abilities. He had to grab the moments as and when they presented themselves! He was gratified to see every eye upon him. Collins pulled on one end of his rather large and messy looking moustache before continuing.

"There are a few nominal sums to charities totalling just under a thousand pounds. Dr. Winston will receive fifty thousand pounds; Greta Norman will receive seventy-five thousand; and Harry Franklin, one hundred thousand pounds. Fifty thousand is to be placed in a trust fund for Jenny's future." Collins cleared his throat and sipped a bit of water, enjoying the sensation of his own importance. "The main beneficiaries are the direct family. One half of the remaining estate goes to Mrs. Marge Smythe, and I'll read this: 'to let her know that I did appreciate her willingness to accept a life with my ready-made family.'" Again the solicitor indulged in a timely pause, interested in seeing the effect of his words. Marge looked as though she would cry. Both Micky and his sister looked surprised.

"Were we difficult?" Anne-Marie asked sweetly, turning in her chair to face her stepmother.

"Also," Collins hurriedly continued, recognising that a longer pause might result in his losing the spotlight, "the house goes to Marge for as long as she lives in it. If you decide to move, Marge," Collins said to her, "then the proceeds from the sale will be split three ways, between you, Micky and Anne-Marie." Collins turned to face the brother and sister. "The other half of the estate is to be equally divided between you two."

At this point he did pause long enough to give an opening should someone wish to speak, but as no one moved or commented on the will, Collins carried on. "The named executors of the estate are myself and Dr. Winston. James felt that as there is quite a substantial sum involved—he was a wealthy man—it was better not to ask a family member to act as an executor."

Micky asked the size of the estate.

"Well, we'll have to get the business and the house appraised, but I would estimate that the business will sell for at least ten million; various investments must amount to another million. Marge, the house was already in your joint names, so there's no difficulty in putting it in your sole name, but we will have to get it appraised for the records and also in case you decide to sell. A four-storey house with a self-contained basement flat in this area ought to fetch a minimum of two and a half million." He looked around the room carefully before his next statement. "I guess I have to say this, but it is said without prejudice: a person guilty of a criminal action cannot benefit from that crime. And these legacies are naturally dependent on the usual condition, that in order to benefit an heir must fulfil the 'shall survive me by thirty days' clause. If one of you dies within a month, that person's legacy is returned to the James Smythe estate." He picked up his briefcase and headed for the door.

There was an immediate muttering of protest. Inspector Gravitt's voice could be heard above the general disapprobation.

"One moment, please, Mr. Collins. I'd like a word with you before you go." He crossed the room to where Collins was standing and ushered him into the sitting room, closing the door firmly behind him.

"That was a damn fool thing to say!" Gravitt exploded.

"It's the law, Inspector. And the 'thirty days' clause is in the will." Snobbery and iciness dripped from the solicitor.

"I don't give a shit if it's in the Ten Commandments! What you have just done is tell the killer—*if* one of them *is* the killer—that they should commit the next offence within the month. And you have put the criminal on his guard and everyone else at risk."

"Then you had better do your job properly, hadn't you, Inspector? Catch the offender."

"And you had better prepare your defence in case I cite you for obstructing the police in the line of duty!"

"Hah! I wish you'd try that." Collins walked out in all his dignity. He had enjoyed himself immensely and he wasn't going to let any shirty bobby spoil his day.

Upon returning to the study Gravitt was surprised and gratified to find things much calmer than he expected. Netty was making light of the events by mocking Collins' mannerisms.

"And the way he tugged his moustache!" she was saying, "for all the world as if he were Hercule Poirot. And him with that scruffy brush on his lip!"

"I don't propose to read the will in its entirety," mimicked Doc Elliot, assuming a pose like a proud emperor, his nose in the air, and his accent too-too uppercrust. There was appreciative applause.

Greta handed Gravitt a cup of coffee. "You'll be needing this sir, if that's what you have to deal with in your line of work."

Micky said, "We were about to discuss the funeral arrangements, Inspector, since we're all here. We're all happy to have you part of this discussion. We haven't known you long, but we're getting to know you—or perhaps I should say, you're getting to know us—rather well. You are practically part of the family now."

Gravitt started declining. He was well aware of the dangers of becoming too involved with people he met when on a case. But Anne-Marie cut his refusal short. "We call you Gravitt, we call you DI Gravitt, we call you Inspector. Greta calls you 'sir.' At least, these are the things we call you to your face," she teased. "Do you have a first name?"

He was totally disconcerted. "Well, I…Well, it's…It's not really…" He looked at Anne-Marie's upturned face and felt his knees begin to wobble. "Alex," he blurted out hoarsely.

"Alex," she repeated, turning the sound of his name into a caress. Gravitt sat down beside her, hardly knowing what he was doing.

Everyone agreed that the funeral should be kept small, family and close friends only. They would hold the ceremony in the crematorium and Micky would arrange for a string quartet to provide the music. The funeral party would return to the house for cold refreshments, as Greta and Bill would of course attend the service. Throughout the discussion Gravitt watched the body language, taking mental notes. He saw that Marge was fighting a losing battle with tears. He saw that Micky had the look of a beaten man and also that his eyes never left his wife. Netty, on the other hand, never looked at her husband. Gravitt would have to find out what the difficulty between them was; it might be relevant. Dr. Winston appeared sad, but he was also surveying the scene closely. Harry was yawning with boredom. Greta was fussing over the coffee and tea. And Bill looked most uncomfortable to be sitting as a guest with his employers. As if he heard this thought, Bill stood up and excused himself, muttering about weeds that don't stop growing, no matter what. Harry took the opportunity to depart as well. He had not contributed to the day's events at all, Gravitt realised. He supposed he would have to look into Harry's movements over the last few days.

One by one the family left the study until Gravitt found himself alone with Anne-Marie. She asked him to walk with her in the garden.

"I really should continue with the interviews," he answered. But he let himself be talked into the walk anyway. In the garden she took his arm and squeezed it.

"I'm glad you're here to help us," she said. "Have any of your other cases been like this one, Alex? You must lead a very unusual life! When do you get any time for yourself?"

Somehow—how did it happen?—he found himself telling her about Sarah, and about loneliness and empty nights. He hadn't meant to talk about these things, but it had been so long since anyone had shown a personal interest in him. Especially a young woman. Especially a beautiful young woman. He noticed almost idly that he was holding her hand. When had that happened?

Anne-Marie touched Alex's cheek lightly. "Poor Detective Inspector Alex Gravitt," she said softly. "Always sorting out someone else's life and never sorting out your own." He covered her hand with his own and bent to kiss her on the cheek, but at the last moment she turned her head and the kiss landed on her mouth. She slipped her arms around his neck and pulled him closer.

"You're so beautiful, so beautiful," he breathed into her ear, "but we really shouldn't be doing this," Alex murmured, not pulling away. But Anne-Marie was enjoying the fire that ran through her and pressed herself into his body. Then as he became more passionate she pushed him away and freed herself from his embrace.

"Oh, Alex! I'm afraid. Is this love? I've never felt like this. You know so much and I don't know anything at all. What am I supposed to do? How am I supposed to behave? You'll have to tell me because I...I don't...I've never...I don't...oh, I can't even talk!" and she burst into tears.

Gravitt felt awful. Here he was, on a murder case, frightening one of the witnesses or a suspect—or even a possible future victim—with his advances. "Oh my God," he gasped, "what can I be thinking of? I'm so sorry, little Anushka, please forgive me. I promise you, it won't happen again." If I can't control myself better than this, he said to himself, I'd better get myself removed from the case. How on earth can I explain this to the Super? His stomach tightened as he thought of the bollicking he was sure to receive.

"Anushka? What does that mean?" At last she had a pet name. She stopped crying.

"It's Russian for Anne. I meant it as a term of endearment. I didn't mean to scare you, really I didn't. I'll call you by your proper name from now on." Gravitt's day was getting darker and darker. He started to turn away, to go back inside.

"Please, Alex. Please let me talk. I just need time to find the right words." She took his hand and held it, not speaking for a long while. Gravitt waited, but he couldn't look at her. He felt miserable and he was ashamed. Oh, so very ashamed.

"I'm twenty-three. I know girls my age get married and have babies. But when my schoolmates were playing Post Office, I was studying. And when they were buying wedding dresses, I was buying canvasses. And then, while Dad never actually forbade me to date, he never encouraged me either. I'm very self-oriented. I mean, what I'm trying to say is, yes, okay, I've kissed a man before—but I've never kissed a man like we…like you…like just now." She felt her face growing hot. "Alex, I think maybe I…I'm falling in love with you. But you need to give me time."

'Alex I think maybe I'm falling in love with you' echoed in her head after she had said the words, taunting her, mocking her. What a stupid little prig she was! No man could possibly be interested in such a goody-goody like her. What he wanted was a *real* woman.

Gravitt put an arm around her and whispered, "I don't want to rush you into something you might regret." He put a hand under her chin to lift her face and kissed the tip of her nose. "Will you be my friend?" he asked.

"Willingly!"

"May I take you out to dinner tomorrow evening?"

"I thought I was confined to the house."

"You'll be in police custody."

"That's an invitation I can hardly refuse. No doubt you'll arrest me if I do!"

"You can count on it." They both laughed, relieved that the awkwardness was behind them. They never saw the face in the window, watching them.

Gravitt decided not to complete the interviews that day. Instead he went to the station to see his Superintendent. They discussed the evidence to date and considered the possibility that the crime had been committed by someone living outside the house.

"All in all, sir, it seems a fairly normal family; they flare up at each other but it's soon forgotten." He told his boss about the solicitor's visit and about the way the family turned Collins' dire warnings into a joke. As he talked about the individuals involved, he failed to notice the Superintendent peering at him more and more closely.

Ah, so that was it, a young lady. Gravitt has it bad, he thought. It's time he got over that other girl, what was her name? Sophie? No, Sarah. But he shouldn't get involved with someone concerned in a case; that was out of order.

So the Superintendent was not surprised when Gravitt asked to be removed from the case. If he agreed, however, people would speculate and rumours would fly all over the place. Rumours could be even more damaging than facts; Alex's father, Commander Gravitt, would hear them and he would certainly have to take disciplinary action against his own son. Damn Alex for putting them all in such a tricky position! Sighing inwardly, the Super decided to pretend ignorance. After all, Alex hadn't actually voiced his reasons for wanting to be taken off the case. He hoped a few strong words would be enough to snap Gravitt into reality.

"Forget it," he said sternly. "If you can't finish what you start you shouldn't be in the Force at all. You go back tomorrow and finish the interviews. Try and find out what's bothering the son and his wife. I'll send someone else around to speak to Harry and Dr. Winston, if you like. But I want you in that house as much as possible. I want you to eat and breathe Smythes until you know everything about them, their personal habits, their table manners, *everything*. My gut feeling tells me this is a domestic crime." And with that he dismissed Gravitt.

Alex Gravitt left the station and made his way to the small flat he called home, stopping long enough to buy a fish and chip from the takeaway and a bottle of cheap white wine. DC Bateman was once again on night duty in Reddington Gardens, so his immediate fears for the members of the household were reduced. But he knew the Yard could not afford twenty-four hour surveillance for much longer. He had to find the murderer soon.

He drank the whole of the bottle and crawled into bed. He cried.

Chapter Six

The next morning Gravitt arrived at the Smythe residence promptly at 9.30. A quick word with Bateman informed him that the evening had been uneventful, although Micky Smythe had once again slept in the study. Bateman said that after he got some sleep he was going to visit first Harry and then Dr. Winston, as requested by the Superintendent.

"Mind if I tag along?" Gravitt asked. Bateman felt honoured. It was not every day that an important person the stature of DI Gravitt showed an interest in his work. He was up for promotion soon and was hopeful of being made a Detective Sergeant. Bateman offered to collect the Inspector after lunch. Smythe's Publishing House was in Ongar, just east of London. Bateman said he knew it well as his wife was a keen gardener and there were at least two respectable nurseries there. Gravitt entered the house, said hello to Bateman's relief officer whom he had never met, and made his way to the kitchen. Breakfast must have been early this morning; he found only dirty dishes and the remains of bacon and eggs to greet him. He turned to retrace his steps and nearly bumped into Anne-Marie.

"Searching the house again, Detective Inspector Gravitt?" she asked coolly. He was surprised and disturbed by her tone of voice and mumbled something about looking for Micky when he noticed she was peeping at him through her long eyelashes, her eyes twinkling, and a smile playing about her lips.

"Minx," he replied under his breath, and she laughed out loud. The DC looked up, wondering what they were saying.

Her face grew serious. "Micky is in the study helping Mumpets write a press notice about the funeral, suggesting that people send donations to charity instead of flowers." She offered him a coffee while he waited and they sat in the kitchen together talking, eager to grab every opportunity to get to know each other better.

Marge appeared, apologising for keeping him waiting. "Whom do you wish to see today, Inspector? Micky is in the study now. Netty has taken Jenny to the park; poor child, she's not having much fun these days. I hope that's okay; Officer Bateman said you wouldn't mind. They'll be back soon."

Gravitt put down his cup and stood up to shake hands. "You are all perfectly free to come and go as you wish; the most I can ask is that you don't leave the country. But it would be a kindness if you let me know where you're going. I asked the station to keep an officer on duty here primarily for your safety. There's a killer still at large." As he finished the last sentence, he felt Anne-Marie slip her hand in his, and he blushed.

"It's all right, Inspector; Anne-Marie told me that you have invited her to dinner tonight. I'm pleased that you are getting her away from all this sadness for a few hours. This has been a terrible ordeal for her."

"And for you too, Mumpets." Anne-Marie held out her free hand to her stepmother who took it and in turn held out her other hand to Gravitt, who had no option but to take it, looking for all the world 'like children playing Ring Around the Roses,' he thought. He extricated himself from this extremely embarrassing position quickly, hoping the officer had not been able to see them clearly.

"If Micky is in the study, I'll start with him," Gravitt suggested and left the kitchen.

"Inspector. I've been expecting you. Come in." Micky motioned Gravitt towards the most comfortable chair in the room.

"This is an official interview, sir. The Constable will take notes, so if you don't mind, we'll use the desk." Gravitt beckoned to the officer and pulled up a second chair for himself.

Gravitt noticed Micky's nervousness, the telltale fidgeting, the restless twisting of his hands. As he had before, he felt sorry for this unhappy young man; but he would have no pity for him if he were the murderer. He decided he would give Micky the scare of his life.

"I find it interesting," Gravitt said coldly, "that you left on tour the day after your father went into hospital with arsenic poisoning. When did you plan this tour?"

"Well, I don't remember exactly," Micky hesitated.

Gravitt cut in. "You don't remember *exactly*? What do you remember *in*exactly? Did you plan it the day before? Two days before? Or did you plan it when you first started administering the poison to your father, knowing that you would be away when he died? It must have been a terrible shock to you when you found out he had survived your first attempt!"

"Now wait a minute, Inspector!" Micky tried to speak, but Gravitt wasn't ready for that yet. He was shouting now.

"How did you do it? Was it through the homoeopathic tablets, substituting arsenic for the original powder? Or did you sprinkle it in his whiskey, knowing he always had a nightcap?" Micky was looking bewildered and very scared. Gravitt didn't relent. *Tell me how you did it!"*

"I didn't do it, I didn't do it, do you hear me? I . did . not . do . it!" Micky jumped up angrily and spaced the last words out for emphasis. The officer rose to his feet menacingly. Micky slumped back into his chair, the loser in the shouting match, a beaten man. "I didn't do it," he said quietly.

"Okay. Then let's find out who did."

If Micky was surprised by Gravitt's change of tone, he didn't show it. He merely nodded. "The whole orchestra is required to go on the international tours, but the shorter tours are largely optional. We form small ensembles. I like them because they give me a chance to play some jazz. But I haven't accepted many of these gigs since Jenny was born and consequently I don't get invited so often. In my business if you say no too many times, people quit asking you. I thought Dad had a stomach ulcer or maybe appendicitis. I didn't know someone was trying to kill him."

"Why did you think Marge had done it?"

"What? Oh, you're referring to the scene in the sitting room that first night." And he asked sarcastically, "Do you have spies everywhere, Gravitt? That was a personal family discussion not meant for anyone else to hear." The Inspector merely looked at him quizzically. Micky's voice calmed down again. "I don't really think Marge killed Dad. I don't think she could hurt anyone. To be honest, I think she was brave to take us all on. She wasn't responsible for my bad temper. I have other things on my mind."

"What other things?"

"None of your business."

"Right. In that case we can continue this interview at the Yard. Officer, put the cuffs on Mr. Smythe and escort him to the car, please."

"No you don't! You can't do that. Am I under arrest?"

"Let's just say, you are helping the police with their enquiries."

This was not Micky's day. "You win again, Gravitt," he conceded. "I'll talk if it's private and off the record."

Gravatt signalled to the officer to leave. "Okay, Micky, it's just the two of us now. Tell me what's got you so worried."

Micky looked at the floor. He spoke slowly and falteringly. "My marriage isn't too good, Alex. It hasn't been for a very long time." He put his elbows on his knees and lowered his head into his hands. "I love my wife and daughter. People think musicians—particularly touring jazz musicians—live a wild life, but it's not true. I met Netty in the orchestra, she ought to know that. When I'm on one of the jazz tours, I work bloody hard: sometimes two gigs a day, travelling in between, and often there's an evening gig that doesn't finish until 1 a.m. Of course the pay is good and the music is great. I liked my family living here while I was away, I liked knowing they were safe. But Netty wants us to move; not just now that Dad is gone, she's been after us moving for ages. She loved it here at first, but now she says it's not private enough. I think…I'm pretty sure…I think she's having an affair."

Micky took a big breath. "I had arranged for a private detective to watch her while I was touring this time, but I cancelled him when I had to come back early. It made me feel sleazy, putting a private dick on my wife. But she hasn't made love with me more than half a dozen times in the last year. I don't know why I turned on Marge; maybe it's because Netty is so close to her."

There was a long silence. Finally Micky asked, "You weren't really going to arrest me, were you, Alex?"

"I don't know," Gravitt answered truthfully.

Gravitt accompanied Micky to the door. He asked the officer to fetch him a coffee and Netty Smythe, in that order. When Netty arrived, looking like the unshakeable sophisticated woman that she was, he decided instantly to adopt a formal manner.

"Thank you for giving me your time, Mrs. Smythe," he said politely. "I'm sure you appreciate that in a case of this sort, I need to know everyone's movements."

"Of course, Inspector. I had the same opportunities as everybody else to put arsenic in James' food, but I didn't do it."

"I'm delighted to know that," Gravitt replied, without an ounce of sarcasm in his voice. "But I still have to ask the questions." Once again he went through the 'where were you when' routine, and when she was relaxed and off her guard he changed his approach to a more personal one.

"How long have you been married to Micky, Mrs. Smythe?"

"Six years."

"Was it"—he took a shot in the dark—"your first marriage?"

"No." She began to look uncomfortable.

"Tell me about it, your first marriage."

"There's nothing to tell; I was very young."

"Was your first husband also young?"

"No."

"Come, come, Mrs. Smythe, please give me fuller answers."

Silence. Finally she said, "If you must know, I was eighteen; he was forty-two."

"Did you divorce him?"

"No, he died. Of a heart attack, not poison." Netty said this wryly. Gravitt asked his name and their former address.

"Why did you marry a man old enough to be your father?"

"Why else, Inspector? I loved him. He treated me well."

"Is your marriage with Micky a good one?"

"Really, Inspector Gravitt, I fail to see any reason why I should answer such personal questions!"

"Oh don't you? Well, I will tell you why. A murder has been committed. A heinous, premeditated murder by someone so determined that when the first attempt failed, it was immediately tried again. Someone so depraved and sadistic that inflicting pain on the victim gave him—or her—pleasure, probably of a sexual nature. Someone so egotistical that the second attempt was carried out practically under the noses of the police. And I believe that someone is in this house. *That's* why I'm asking you these questions, and *that's* why I expect you to answer them!"

Netty was quite shaken by the Inspector's outburst. She said, "The murderer is like that? All those things? But then it can't be anyone here, in this house; we all have our faults, but none of us is like that."

Privately Gravitt agreed with her. But the detective who had been asking questions at the publishing house had so far found nothing amiss there either. "Please tell me about your first marriage."

"I went to a girl's boarding school. The only men I met were elderly, so I was more comfortable with, shall I say, mature men. Ronald was my violin teacher. He was artistic looking, tall, with black hair just greying at the temples. We performed the Bach Double Concerto together at my school in my final year, and after the concert I asked him to marry me. I never regretted it."

"What attracted you to Micky? He's the same age as you, is he not?"

"Actually I'm a year older. Micky courted me; I had never been wooed before and I liked it. But young men are not really trustworthy, I'm afraid."

"What do you mean? Is Micky untrustworthy?"

"He goes away fairly often. He tells me he's on tour, but I still have friends in the orchestra and they don't seem to know about the 'tours'

Micky is doing. And he's moody; Ronald was never moody, he'd grown beyond that stage. And Micky doesn't seem to want my company anymore, if you know what I mean."

She almost whispered her next comment. "I'm sure he's having an affair."

Chapter Seven

On the way to Ongar, Gravitt brought Bateman up to date, impressing upon him the information they wanted from Harry Franklin. They needed to check for opportunity and motive, that went without saying; but they also needed to know what kind of person Franklin was. Was he capable of such a cruel crime? Did he know about the rat poison in the shed? They were lucky with the traffic and the journey was gratifyingly quick. Harry was waiting in the reception area and ushered them to a small storage room where they could be private. Gravitt had not particularly looked at him on their previous meeting, but now he gave Harry his undivided attention. He saw an unprepossessing youth, pale, with limp posture and facial scars, the result of bad acne. He had ink stains on his face and jeans. Harry noticed Gravitt's scrutiny and turned red. "Been working," he mumbled.

Bateman took the opening. "What exactly do you do here?" he asked in a friendly tone.

Harry stared at he floor while he described his job designing adverts for the books they publish. "I always read the book first so I can come up with something appropriate. I've even been allowed to do a jacket," he added. As he talked about his work, he became almost lively.

"I'd like to see some of your designs," encouraged Bateman.

"Really? There are some here, I keep my portfolio in this room." Harry pulled a large album off a shelf and explained each advert. "This was for a book on early American history; this was a nature book; this was a chemistry textbook." Gravitt and Bateman glanced at each other.

"You read all these books? That must take some doing! Do you understand the textbooks? I don't think I would understand a word of this chemistry book!" Bateman let Harry see his admiration.

Harry bristled with pride. "I'm giving myself an education," he boasted. "I never was able to go to university, but I know more than most people who did. Because I read."

"But not all the time, surely. What do you do in your spare time?" It was a bad question. Harry once again became the inelegant, gauche person they had met in the reception area. Gravitt decided it was his turn to ask a few questions.

"James Smythe was your uncle, wasn't he?" Harry nodded, once more talking to his feet. "How did you become one of his employees?"

"Isn't it obvious? He's my uncle, so when I wanted a job he gave me one."

"I understand that you live with your father. Is that right?"

"Nah, not anymore. He kicked me out a few months ago. Said I'd been working long enough to have some savings and I should 'leave the nest.' His words."

"Presumably your inheritance will take some of the financial strain off your back. What will you do with the money?"

"Dunno. Haven't thought about it."

"Harry, you know your uncle was murdered, don't you?" A nod. "Have any of the books you've been reading been about criminal investigations?" Another nod. "Then you understand that we have to ask you a few questions."

"Yeah. Where was I the night of the murder. That's usually the first question, isn't it?"

Gravitt motioned for Bateman to take over. "Usually, yes. But we'd like to know about the week before as well."

"Really? I wonder why?" The police had kept the attempted slow poisoning out of the papers, and they weren't about to tell Harry about it. If he truly didn't know, it helped to eliminate him from the list of suspects. "Doesn't matter. I don't go out much, I read most evenings. If it's nice outside I might take a walk."

"Girlfriend?" Harry shook head and smiled crookedly. He knew he was no beauty. Anne-Marie had told him that when he had tried to kiss her two years ago. 'Hideous' was the word she used.

"Where do you go when you take your walks?"

"Nowhere in particular. There are lots of fields around here. You can walk for hours and not see a soul. I like it."

"But it leaves you with no clear alibi, doesn't it?" A nod and a shrug.

"How often did you visit with the Smythes?"

"Uncle gave me a standing invitation for Sunday dinners, but I didn't go very often. I haven't been over for a couple of months or more. I saw him at work of course, but not often. I'm responsible to the head of the advertising department. And I'd better get back to work now." A final question about the key to the shed brought only a blank stare and a bewildered, "What shed?"

The two policemen thanked him for his time. Because they were in the area, they drove to Harry's flat and knocked on neighbouring doors in an effort to ascertain his movements. It was a fruitless quest: few of the neighbours were in, and of those who were, almost no one knew who Harry was. Knowing that the uniformed officers would carry out a more thorough door-to-door enquiry, they headed back to London for their interview with Dr. Winston. While Bateman drove, Gravitt made notes of their meeting with Harry.

"He hasn't got an alibi," offered Bateman. "And no matter what he looks like, he's nobody's fool." Gravitt agreed.

As they approached Dr. Winston's house, they saw Mrs. Smythe— Netty—leaving. "That's interesting," commented Gravitt. "I wonder what she's up to?" He put that question to the doctor. "Oh, she came to pick up some gripe water for her daughter. Jenny's got another tooth coming through." Gravitt asked in the most innocent voice he could muster if Netty often dropped by to pick up medicines.

Elliot peered at Gravitt closely trying to tell if that remark was as trivial as it appeared. "From time to time. I'm sort of retired now so an appointment with me is quicker than going to the surgery." He offered them coffee; Gravitt, who was addicted to the brew and was beginning to suffer from withdrawal, would have loved a cup; but before he could accept it he heard Bateman saying, "No thank you, sir. This is not a social visit." Gravitt sighed; he would have to have a word with Bateman about coffee.

Elliot said, "Why don't we skip the formalities, and I'll tell you about my relationship with James. I'm getting to be an old man and I like to talk. When I'm done, if there's anything more you want to know, ask your questions then."

Elliot talked about his long friendship with James and about Katharine's illness. "Funny thing, her illness. There seemed to be another problem as well. Oh, it was the pneumonia that killed her all right, but she had unexplained bouts of forgetfulness, times she couldn't remember. They were probably a result of the pain or the painkillers, but they may also have been indicative of another problem. Anyway, I don't suppose it matters now." Elliot talked about Marge and the close relationship between her and James. "And you know about the rest, the discovery of arsenic. Now I have a question for *you*, Inspector: that day we brought James home from the hospital, you knew there was a murderer around. Why did you leave James unguarded that night?"

Gravitt flinched. He had asked himself that question so many times! "You don't know how often I wish I had stayed myself. I misjudged the villainy and the desperation of the poisoner. I thought that knowing the police were involved would stay their hand, at least for a little while. Poisoners are usually cowards."

Elliot nodded. "I accept that."

"Now I have a question for you, Dr. Winston. Why was Mrs. Smythe collecting gripe water when there is a nearly full bottle in her bathroom?" Elliot looked askance. "I saw it when I searched the house."

Elliot let out a loud guffaw. "You don't miss much after all, do you Inspector? All right. You know she and Micky are having some difficulties; I know you know because she told me that she told you.

She needs a confidant. That's me. I'm a substitute father to her. No more, no less." Why didn't he say that in the first place? Why lie? "Micky's temperament is unstable, Inspector, you must have noticed that. Netty is afraid that if he learns she visits me, he will misinterpret it."

Gravitt had just enough time to go home, shower, shave, and down two mugs of Nescafe before picking up Anne-Marie. As he stood on her doorstep he realised that he was nervous. God forbid that he should do anything to upset her! He should have brought flowers, but he hadn't thought about it. Oh, well, she would just have to accept him for the inconsiderate bastard he was. He rang the bell.

Micky answered the door and stood aside to let him in. "Is this one of the perks of your job, Inspector? Dating the suspects? I wonder if your superior knows you are here tonight." Gravitt looked uncomfortable. Micky pressed his advantage. "I take responsibility for my sister's well-being now Dad's gone. If you lay a finger on her or upset her in any way, you'll answer to me!" Gravitt was tongue-tied; he felt like a teenager on his first date meeting a concerned and disapproving father. And Micky was right. He shouldn't be here socially.

"Micky!" said Marge repressively. "Do come in, Alex. Anne-Marie will be down in a few minutes. Would you like a drink while you wait?"

"No, thank you," Gravitt replied hoarsely.

"You had that coming to you, Inspector." Micky's voice was softer but still icy.

"Yes, I did," Gravitt agreed.

Anne-Marie came down the stairs. She was wearing a silk dress, dark brown to enhance her rich brown eyes and golden hair. It was tight over her full breasts and then flared gently over her hips. Gravitt's eyes softened when he saw her and he felt an unaccustomed tightness in his chest. He forgot Micky and Marge were there. He forgot he was in the middle of a brutal murder case. He forgot he was a policeman.

Detective Inspector Alex Gravitt was in love.

He took her to a little French restaurant in Camden Town, the only place he knew of where the chef properly understood a fluffy omelette. She charmed him with stories of Degas and da Vinci, and he shared with her some of the sillier moments in the life of an officer of the law. And as the evening went on, Alex fell more and more under her spell, and her eyes glowed with pleasure and triumph. Their legs touched under the table. Was it an accident? Neither pulled away. When he asked her if she'd like a coffee she said, "Yes, but not here. You've seen my house many times, but I've never seen where you live. I'd like you to make me coffee." She swept away his protests of mess, of clothes on the floor. "If it weren't for Greta, I would live in a mess as well."

They drove the short distance to his two-roomed flat and Alex put the kettle on, surreptitiously kicking dirty underwear under the settee. As he was putting the instant coffee in the mugs, she put her hand on his arm and said softly, "Alex?" He turned to face her. "Alex, will you kiss me, please? You haven't kissed me all evening."

He took her in his arms and held her gently, afraid that he would frighten her. She pressed her body close to his and he groaned in an agony of desire. She whispered, "Make love to me, Alex; make love to me!"

Afterwards—when he had time to think about it—Gravitt felt surprised. Oh, he enjoyed it, make no mistake about that! But he was surprised; surprised at her passion, at her knowledge and apparent experience. He had been afraid that she was a virgin, and he was relieved, he admitted to himself, that she was not. But he had not expected the demure, seemingly inexperienced girl he kissed in the garden to come on to him like a professional hooker! He decided, with the sexual conceit of the male of the human species, that she simply couldn't resist him. He liked that thought. He cradled her in his arms and cooed softly, "Dear, sweet Anushka, I love you, I love you. Please don't ever leave me."

She purred with pleasure. She had proved herself a real woman tonight. "How could I ever leave you when I love you so much?" she responded, and was startled as she realised she meant it.

Alex got Anne-Marie home by midnight. Micky was waiting up for them.

65

Chapter Eight

On the third morning following the murder, Gravitt reported to his Superintendent. He wanted to talk to him about the interviews with Micky and Netty, and how each accused the other of adultery. "Even if they are both having affairs, I can't see that it has any bearing on the case. It might be a motive for killing each other, but not James."

"You'll check into this touring business, of course," advised the Superintendent.

"I'll get on to it today. Harry Franklin is the ugly duckling, the person one would like to find guilty. A hundred thousand pounds is a powerful motive, or would be except for the fact that Smythe had already given him something more valuable than money: self respect. Harry likes his job, that's obvious. With Smythe gone, he could be in danger of losing it."

Gravitt continued, "The meeting with Dr. Elliot Winston was unusual. Bateman and I saw Netty Smythe leaving his house as we arrived, and Winston lied about it." He described the interview, commenting on the fact that Winston hadn't been at all bothered about being caught out in an untruth; in fact, he had been amused. "It naturally occurred to me they—Winston and Netty—might be sleeping together; but again that doesn't give a motive for killing James Smythe. And it was Winston who saved his life during the first murder attempt.

If he hadn't insisted on sending Smythe to hospital so promptly, he might have died without anyone's recognising it as homicide."

"In fact, what you are saying is that nobody had a motive. Or at least, not an obvious one. Winston was all right for money?" Gravitt nodded. "As I see it, that leaves two roads to explore: Netty's reasons for wanting to move house; and Micky's touring. Have you any reason to think the murderer will strike again?"

Gravitt shrugged. "As I don't even know why he or she struck the first time, I don't know what to think. It does seem as if someone was particularly out to get Smythe."

"Yes, that's what I think—but it is possible, especially since you haven't uncovered a motive, that we may be dealing with a serial killer. I want Sergeant Wilcox, from the Hampstead station, to work regularly with you now. His other case has finished."

"A fresh mind will be welcome," Gravitt admitted. "I'd also like to keep Constable Bateman. We work well together." The Superintendent agreed, but not before giving Gravitt a stiff lecture for having made no progress. He hadn't even progressed through elimination.

DC Benjamin Bateman was chuffed when he learned that Gravitt had specifically requested his presence on this case. Detective Inspector Alex Gravitt was something of a hero among the lower ranking officers. His almost meteoric rise in the Yard was often talked about in the canteen. Of course, Bateman thought, it had been relatively easy for Gravitt as the son of a detective who was the son of a detective. It seemed at times as if the Yard was their family business! Three generations of Gravitts, but none was as respected as the present one. Most people believed he could rise to the top if he wished, but Bateman had seen enough of Gravitt in operation to know he liked what he was currently doing and was not eager to move upwards just yet. Bateman had also seen the way Gravitt looked at that girl, the daughter of the murdered man. He was afraid his hero was about to make a fatal mistake; fatal to his career, that is. Personal involvement with a suspect was taboo.

Bateman himself was ambitious. He was already as old as Gravitt—thirty-two—but he knew he would soon be made a Sergeant. His father had been a schoolteacher and consequently Benjamin had received a solid, well-rounded education. Angela Bateman, his Missus, was sensible and level-headed. She was also ambitious for her husband; she wanted her children's future to be secure.

Gravitt asked Bateman to contact the orchestral manager of the English Philharmonia about Micky's tour schedule. The manager promised to have it ready by the time someone arrived at the EPO offices in Brixton to collect it. He was clearly curious and when Bateman arrived did his best to wheedle information from the officer, but Bateman was not interested in satisfying the man's morbid thirst for ghoulish gossip.

"In desperation he tried to threaten me with Smythe's dismissal for being absent from work," Bateman told Gravitt later. "I told him that wasn't any concern of mine, but I advised him to be careful he didn't leave himself open for an 'unfair dismissal' charge!" What Bateman didn't know was how the manager had laughed inwardly at this threat; there was, after all, no binding contract to be broken. But he felt it was probably best not to cross the police and kept this knowledge to himself.

While Bateman was attending to the errand set him, Gravitt drove into Hampstead. He wanted to get Micky's personal diary to compare with the orchestral schedule and he wanted to let Anne-Marie know he would be out of town for a couple of days. He was eager to see her! Marge let him in, greeting him warmly. He noticed how haggard she had become; the loss of her husband had aged her considerably.

"How nice to see you, Inspector. Have you made any progress in solving the case?"

"Yes and no," he replied noncommittally. "I came by to have a quick word with Micky."

Marge went to fetch him, saying, "Anne-Marie is in her workroom; I'll let her know you're here."

Micky entered the sitting room a few minutes later. "What do you want, Gravitt?"

"I want to see your diary, sir."

"My diary!" Micky was surprised. "Whatever for?" He folded his arms across his chest in a defensive manner.

"Routine, Mr. Smythe, just routine."

"And if I refuse?"

"Then I suppose I can get a court order."

"I could, of course, destroy it meanwhile."

"That would be inadvisable. You can get in a lot of trouble by destroying evidence in a police matter."

Micky threw up his arms in defeat, inviting the Inspector to accompany him to the study. "Take it with you, take it with you," he insisted, handing over the diary. "I know what I'm doing for the next two or three weeks." Micky walked out.

Anne-Marie walked in. "Hello, Inspector," she said shyly. "Mumpets said you were here." She was wearing an old pair of jeans under a paint-smeared smock, her hair piled untidily on top of her head. Gravitt's heart skipped a beat.

"Anushka," he said softly. "You continually surprise me. I've never seen you looking so...so gorgeous!" He reached for her hands, but she pulled away. Gravitt was genuinely surprised and more than a little worried. Was she sorry about last night? Was she going to end their relationship almost before it began? She had said she would never leave him. Oh dear God, how he hoped she meant it! He said, his voice shaky with concern, "My darling little Anushka, I hope you don't have any regrets about last night! It was wonderful."

"My name isn't Anushka!" she yelled at him. "It's Anne-Marie! Anne-Marie! What's so special about last night? It was just an ordinary night!" She burst into tears and fled upstairs.

Gravitt stared after her. He didn't understand at all; if she didn't want to see him again, all she had to do was say so. He would never understand women. He stood for some time, unable to move. Finally he sat down and just looked at the floor. Poor, hurt Inspector Gravitt.

He was still in that position when Micky walked into the study half an hour later. Micky sized up the situation accurately, poured out a large brandy and put it in Gravitt's hand. "Drink it!" he ordered. When

Gravitt had emptied the glass, Micky said, "I can't explain it to you. She's very young for her age. Inexperienced. And she has too much artistic temperament for her own good, if you know what I mean. She'll blow hot and cold and she'll lead you a merry dance. Are you strong enough to take it, Alex?"

"I don't know."

"Then my advice is, get out now."

"Well, I have to get out for a couple of days anyhow. I have to go out of town for a while, but I will be back in time for the funeral. Sergeant Wilcox will be around tomorrow to talk to you all; can you make sure everyone is here?" Micky nodded. Gravitt wrote down his mobile phone number and told Micky to ring him if there were any problems whatsoever. Then he left.

Chapter Nine

Sergeant Wilcox, accompanied by a junior officer, arrived at the Smythe residence early on Friday morning, the fourth day after the murder. He considered himself a good-natured fellow who always hoped to discover that no crime had in fact been committed, but who had little mercy for a proven criminal. He was also a methodical man, punctilious in the preparation of his work before the day began and never forgetting to sum up his progress at the end of the day. Yet no man is without a secret vice; Wilcox's vice was poetry. He read it and he wrote it and he told nobody about it. He was afraid it would destroy his macho image. He had read the notes on this case carefully and knew exactly what questions he was going to ask and how he was going to ask them. In his opinion Gravitt and Bateman had been sloppy and disorganised in their approach. Hunches and gut feelings were as foreign to Wilcox as was the notion that a detective should get to know the suspects beyond relevant vagaries. He believed in maintaining a distance between investigator and investigated.

He introduced himself to Greta, who answered the doorbell, and asked that the members of the household assemble in the sitting room, and he also asked that the study be made available to him. He had never been in the house before, but in reading the reports he had conceived a pretty good idea of the layout. He was pleasantly surprised to see Greta had laid on refreshments. There was one thing he did have in common with Gravitt: coffee.

Before beginning the discussion Wilcox studied the faces in front of him. Bill was easy to pick out, he was in his work clothes. Wilcox assumed the person sitting next to Bill, the lady who had admitted him, must be his wife, Greta; she was a slightly podgy and comfortable looking woman and reminded him of his mother. The other middle-aged woman had to be Marge Smythe, wife of the deceased. She looks tired and completely clapped out, he thought to himself. He presumed, correctly, that the youngest female was the daughter. She was something to look at, all right! The younger Mrs. Smythe was obviously a well-bred woman, but her husband looked almost as knackered as his stepmother.

Wilcox said he would like to start by asking some general questions while they were all together. As four days had lapsed since this atrocious tragedy had occurred, he hoped that a joint discussion might help to kindle memories.

"How long had James been suffering, getting weaker and generally losing energy before he was admitted to hospital?" He looked at Marge.

"I'm not really sure," she replied. "It was a gradual thing. I thought he was coming down with a cold, or the flu. He refused to see a doctor; he always said doctors can't do anything for colds. And he was right about that, of course."

Wilcox looked at Micky. "I work every day. Even when I'm not on tour I don't get to spend much time here, at home. I don't know the answer to your question."

Netty said her three-year-old daughter was a full time occupation and she really couldn't say. Bill said he works outside and doesn't have any idea of what goes on indoors. Greta said she'd noticed Mr. James was eating less but attributed it to his getting older.

Anne-Marie said, "I was very close to my father. He'd been in bed for about a week before going into hospital, but this cold he had—and an upset tummy, too—had been hanging around for a few weeks." She wasn't sure exactly how many.

Wilcox said that perhaps the next question would help to answer the first: "Who bought the homeopathic tablets?"

Marge said she and Anne-Marie had bought them together. "As I said, James wouldn't see a doctor. We thought he ought to have something to increase his appetite; you know the saying, 'feed a cold and starve a fever.' The Natural Health Clinic recommended them. They were supposed to settle his stomach, not kill him." She started crying. That seemed to be what she did best these days.

Wilcox said sharply, "What do you mean? Are you trying to say those tablets killed him? And that you and your daughter are responsible for his death?" He knew about the tablets, naturally, it was all in the report. But this was almost sounding like a confession!

Everybody was speaking at once. "Silence!" bellowed the Sergeant. I want to hear Mrs. Smythe answer the question."

"Marge, don't say a word. We'll get a lawyer," said Micky.

"Silence!" repeated Wilcox. "Mrs. Smythe, if you don't mind?"

"Inspector Gravitt said the tablets might have been tampered with, that someone might have changed the powder inside for arsenic. If I hadn't bought them in the first place, then no one could have tampered with them." Marge covered her face with her hands. And Wilcox thought, damn the Inspector; why didn't he keep his mouth shut?

"But that makes me guilty too, that way of thinking," objected Anne-Marie. "And anyway your thinking is lopsided. We bought those pills because he was ill, not the other way around. Don't you see, Mumpets? Dad was sick and *then* we bought the pills."

"And don't forget," reminded Netty, "Inspector Gravitt was unable to verify his suspicions because the pills disappeared."

Wilcox turned to Anne-Marie. "Just exactly when did you buy them?"

"You see, Sergeant, I don't go out to work so one day is much like another. It was a week or two after Dad started wheezing and sniffling." Marge was unable to pinpoint the time any better than her stepdaughter.

"Now please take your time over this: I want you all to think back to the weeks before Mr. Smythe went into the hospital; who visited the house—for any reason?"

Greta said the postman had come to the door. She remembered because he brought a recorded delivery letter and she had to sign for it; but he didn't actually come inside. Micky said the paper is delivered every day, but the delivery boy doesn't enter the house either; the newsagent is paid weekly when he—or someone else—goes to the shop to settle up. Anne-Marie said she had received a package two or three weeks ago; but again no one came into the house. What was in the package?

"Oh, just some bronzing powder." And she blushed as she recalled that Gravitt had taken it away for analysis. Wilcox saw her embarrassment and made a mental note; he didn't understand why bronzing powder should make her blush, but he would find out. It couldn't be guilt, he knew, because the lab report had cleared it.

"No one else called? No friends? No playmates for your child, Mrs. Smythe?" he asked Netty.

"I wouldn't let Jenny have her friends over while there might be flu germs around. Instead I took her to their houses, or we went to the park."

"What time was dinner last Monday?" At the blank faces he added, "That's the night Mr. Smythe died." Really, he thought, can the whole family be as vague as this? He didn't believe it. He began to suspect they were all in collusion.

Greta spoke up. "Dinner is at seven every evening, sir. Lunch is at one usually, except that particular day because we weren't sure when Mr. James would be arriving. I made sandwiches and left them on the dining table so's people could help themselves when they liked." At last! A definitive answer! Wilcox wasn't sure how it helped in solving the crime, but it did at least tie up one loose end.

"During the meal did anyone leave the room?"

They all looked at each other and shook their heads. Micky responded. "No one got up from the table until my father said he was feeling tired and sleepy. That was just before dessert."

"No one went with him? He was after all just returned from hospital." No, no one. Marge had offered, but James said he needed no help.

74

"Were you aware of the contents of the will before it was read on Tuesday afternoon? Marge?" No. Micky? No. One by one Wilcox singled them out, and each gave the same answer. "Really, you're a most unusual family!" he exclaimed. "Weren't any of you curious?"

"You understand, Sergeant, we've been taken care of all our lives. My sister and I, anyway. We knew Dad would provide for us in his will." Micky was patient, quite an accomplishment for him.

"Will you sell this house, Mrs. Smythe?"

"We haven't discussed it yet, but if that's what most people want, then I will. I'd be happy, though, if we all stayed together, like now. I think James would have wanted that, and it would certainly make me happy."

Anne-Marie smiled, relief showing on her face. "I'd like to stay with you, Mumpets."

Micky said, thank you. Greta asked, did that offer include her and Bill? Of course it did. The only person who didn't respond positively was Netty. Her face was a closed book.

Sergeant Wilcox said he had finished asking the questions he felt were important for group discussion and was ready to see people individually.

"Please have a sandwich first, Sergeant; and you, too," said Marge, including the junior officer in the invitation. "What is your name?"

"I'm DC Miller, ma'am; Gordon Miller. And thanks, I missed breakfast this morning."

Anne-Marie joined them. "I've never met anyone named Gordon before. It's an unusual name. Have you had it long?"

They laughed. "Not long," he answered, "only since I was born." The two of them drifted to the far end of the room, talking like old friends.

Netty approached Wilcox who was glowering after Miller. He would have to lecture the DC on the importance of keeping distance when working on a case.

"The young know how to make friends so quickly, don't they Sergeant? Please don't be angry with the officer. A chance to talk with someone her own age is just what Anne-Marie needs." Netty didn't approve of Gravitt; she thought him too experienced for a girl who had been so very sheltered all her life. She had watched from the house when Gravitt had kissed her sister-in-law in the garden.

Wilcox was ashamed of himself; he should not have let his disapproval show. Netty waited a moment and then continued. "Why don't we follow their example? My first name is Vanessa, but everybody calls me Netty. I hope that you will call me by my nickname."

Is she coming on to me? wondered Wilcox. Her, a married woman, and under the eyes of her husband? He decided she was probably just trying to make conversation. Some people seemed to need to talk; he wasn't one of them of course. Before he could reply she said, "Now you are supposed to tell me your first name, Sergeant, and your nickname if you have one."

"My name is John, Madam, but under the circumstances it would be inappropriate for us to be on a first name basis. Just under the circumstances," he repeated not wanting to appear rude.

"You're quite right, of course, Sergeant, but I imagine you are usually right." She was flattering him quite openly; he appeared to accept her admiration as understandable. "You seem to be the kind of person who considers words before speaking. An admirable trait indeed! And one most of the rest of us lack." She smiled ingratiatingly. Wilcox decided she wasn't such a bad sort and hoped she was not guilty of the crime. Netty, meanwhile, was starting to enjoy herself; she would get through this pedantic man's armour or bust! Micky, watching, was amused; he had seen his wife in action before and his money was on her.

"But what do your friends call you, Sergeant? Johnny?" He nodded reluctantly. "Yes, I can see why. You have the cutest dimples when you smile, just like a baby." Wilcox was gob-smacked, there's no other way to describe it. No one talked to an officer of the law like that. Especially to him! While he was thus dumbstruck she took him by the arm and led him into the garden, saying, "I want to show you something, Sergeant. I think you will want to see this." They walked to the bottom of the gently sloping lawn until they reached the garden shed. "This is where the rat poison was kept. It's gone now of course. The police took it away." Wilcox was relieved. He had been worried when she first led him away from the safety of numbers, but now he could see that she was only trying to help solve the case. She was probably not very intelligent which explained her odd behaviour. "From the house you can't see the shed. Anybody could have taken rat poison without being seen." She gave a shudder and gripped his arm more tightly. "I'm afraid, John; I'm afraid for myself and for my daughter. I'm afraid that if the murderer isn't arrested soon, there may be another attack." She put her head on his shoulder and cried softly.

He handed her his handkerchief, glad of a reason to move away. He headed back to the house saying, "If I'm going to catch the perpetrator, I'd better get on with the interviews."

She followed quietly, dabbing at her tears. Not bad, she thought, for her first attempt at diverting a copper from his duty. Anne-Marie and the young officer had had a little time together away from the Sergeant's hawk eyes.

Sergeant Wilcox settled himself in the study to begin the individual interviews. He asked to see Marge Smythe first. "I believe you worked for a while at the Walton Hospital, is that right?" She nodded. "When was that, please?"

"Well, let me work it out. James and I have been married for four years and my mother died nine months before our marriage. She was in the terminal ward for four months. That means I started working there just over five years ago. You see, my mother and I were very close; we had only each other to depend on for many years. I kept her at home with me for as long as I could, but eventually she needed more help than I could give her. When she was admitted to the hospital, I took a job there to be near her."

"She had cancer, I believe?"

Marge was surprised. "Yes, and it was spreading. How did you know that, Sergeant? Is my mother's illness important to you?"

"Everything is important at the moment. The Walton Hospital is a research institution, is it not?" She nodded. "What diseases are of particular interest to them?"

"I believe they look into many different problems. I was just a general dog's body, I'm afraid. You would have to ask the Registrar if you really want an answer to your question."

"Come now, Mrs. Smythe, I think you can give me a better answer than that! What exactly was your mother's condition?"

"She had a form of leukaemia known as Acute Promyelocytic Leukaemia. It has a very low survival rate. The Walton is the only hospital that I know of that carries out research into APL."

"Then you were lucky to get her admitted. What was the basis of their study?"

Marge stood up. She was angry. "Let's quit playing games, Sergeant Wilcox. I'm sure you already know. The studies were based on arsenic. My mother responded well at first but later relapsed. At this stage in the research a relapse is almost inevitable, but it did give Mother a good month. One good month only, but that's better than no good month. And yes, while working in the hospital I did get to learn quite a lot about the studies. And no, I did not have access to the arsenic; all the poisons are kept locked up and I didn't have a key!" She turned to leave.

"Sit down, Mrs. Smythe. I'm not finished yet." Marge reluctantly returned to her seat.

Wilcox was not really interested in whether or not Marge had access to the hospital's cache of poisons; the lab report had already confirmed that the tin of rat poison from the shed was the source used. He was, however, extremely interested in knowing how much she knew about the quantities needed for both slow killing and immediate death.

"You said your mother had cancer and now you say she had leukaemia. Forgive my ignorance, but are they the same thing?"

"Sergeant Wilcox, I am not medically trained. If you want to know about a disease in depth, you will have to ask someone else." At his frown she added, "There are something like a hundred different types of cancer. All I can tell you is that it is caused by abnormal cell growth."

"Did you ever help with administering treatment to your mother— or anyone else for that matter?"

"I worked in the office. I am not a registered nurse. I was not allowed to give out medicines."

Wilcox said he would confirm her statements with the hospital. Marge said, fine, and left.

Anne-Marie entered the study. She was dressed once again in her painting smock, hoping to get in some work while the light lasted. Wilcox gestured for her to be seated.

"I want to know your movements on the day of your father's death, Miss Smythe, and also on the night before."

"The night before? I don't think I did anything noteworthy, just helped Netty bathe Jenny and then watched a little television."

"What was on the telly?" She couldn't remember.

"Did you see Greta working in the kitchen?" Oh yes, she recalled seeing Greta when she went to the fridge for a coke.

"Did you happen to notice if the Parmesan cheese was in the fridge?" No, she hadn't noticed.

"Do you ever help in the garden?"

"No, Sergeant, I prefer painting flowers to growing them. If this is your roundabout way of trying to discover if I had access to the shed, the answer is yes. I occasionally set up my sketchbook in the garden, but the light is not great. I don't think I've ever been in the shed, but I can't prove it."

"How long have you been bronzing?"

"Not long. Detective Inspector Alex Gravitt has already pointed out that there is arsenic in the powder, but I gather it's only a minute amount." That's interesting, thought Wilcox; she had blushed when she mentioned Gravitt. Now, why would that be? He probed, "Gravitt gave you a hard time about it, did he?"

"I suggest you ask him that yourself; you *do* confer with each other, don't you?" she gibed. "If you're finished with me, I'd like to get back to my studio."

When she was gone, Wilcox turned to Miller and said, "Snotty little bitch." Miller kept his mouth shut. He thought she was wonderful.

79

Micky was next in the firing line. He wasn't particularly worried. Nothing could possibly be as harrowing as his interview with Gravitt had been. Oddly enough, he liked Gravitt in spite of the nasty manner he had chosen to take in their interview; or maybe he liked Gravitt because of it. Micky approved of people who tried to do their jobs thoroughly.

"I just want to ask you a couple of questions, Mr. Smythe; I won't keep you long."

"Fire away, Sergeant."

"What were you doing on the evening before your father returned home from the hospital?"

"Practicing."

"Pardon? Practicing what?"

"Stravinsky's *Rite of Spring*, actually. It's a pig. Do you know it?"

"I do, sir," responded DC Miller, who hitherto had not said a word during the afternoon sessions for fear of riling his superior. "It's one of my favourites!" He turned towards Wilcox. "Stravinsky—Igor Stravinsky—was a very unusual man; did you know…"

"That's enough, Miller," interrupted the Sergeant, who had heard of very few composers indeed. And, if the truth be known, Wilcox didn't like being the underdog in any situation.

"Did you go into the kitchen that evening?"

"I dare say I had a cuppa at some point, but I can't be specific about the time."

"Can you recall seeing the grated cheese?"

"Of course not. Who can think about cheese when your head is full of glorious sounds and difficult fingering?"

"Have you been in the garden this week?"

"Certainly. We all have. The sun has been shining on England for a change."

"You were out of town, I understand, while your father was in the hospital. How did you learn about the attempted poisoning?"

"Marge rang me on my mobile and told me to come straight home. So I did."

Wilcox thanked him and let him go.

It was Netty's turn to talk with Wilcox. She noticed he was looking at her warily as she approached the desk and laughed inwardly. She said to him, in the most demure tone she could muster, "You're not going to be as rude as DI Gravitt, I know. You're a kind man, anyone can see that."

"I won't keep you long, Mrs. Smythe." This he said in his most formal voice. Then, before Netty could say anything which might be embarrassing, he continued, "Were you on good terms with the deceased, James Smythe?"

"Oh yes, everyone got on well with him. There's no earthly reason for anyone to kill James. I can't believe he has—had—any dark secret." Wilcox could tell she was speaking from her heart, no matter how silly a ninny she might be.

"Are you in a position to give yourself, or for that matter anyone in the house, an alibi?"

"No. We established that when Gravitt was doing the questioning. We all had opportunity; but none of us has a motive."

"Money?"

"If you know the contents of the will, then you know that we all were treated well. In addition, none of us has had to pay for food or lodging. James supported us. Micky and I have saved a tidy little nest egg, and I imagine Anne-Marie has as well."

"Do you really like living so closely together? Doesn't it seem rather claustrophobic?"

"Yes and no. It's a big house so we aren't squeezed. On the other hand, there isn't really much privacy. It's no secret that I would like to move. But I wouldn't kill to do so."

"Did you have access to the cheese? And the shed?"

"Yes to both. But as I said, I didn't kill him. He was like my own father."

"Thank you, Mrs. Smythe. You can go now."

Netty smiled coyly at Wilcox. "Will I see you later?" She watched

Wilcox go red. Then, "Bye for now, Johnny." And she quickly left the room, throwing him a kiss, but afraid she might really have gone too far this time.

Miller burst out laughing. Wilcox's red face, however, had changed to purple. "That bloody woman!" he expostulated. "Where does she get off with that kind of cheek!"

"She has the hots for you, sir. It's her way of flirting."

"She'd be better off looking after her husband. And that reminds me, Miller; *your* behaviour leaves something to be desired." He gave Miller the long overdue lecture on fraternising too closely with suspects and witnesses. Miller didn't enjoy it but he did have some consolation: he was positive that for all his blustering his superior had found the attentions of 'that bloody woman' flattering.

Part 2
(In the Year 2002)

Dean woke up early. He wanted to get to school as soon as possible so he could make sure his drawing was just right. Today was Visitors' Day, and after lunch parents and relatives would come to see the children's work. There were going to be displays in art, science, story writing—you name it, if it was taught at the school there would be a display about it. And Dean's drawing would be hanging on the wall! He had drawn a picture of the school, and everyone said it was the best drawing in Year 4. Dean thought it was better than most of the Year 5 pictures as well, but he didn't say that to anyone except his Nan. They taught him in RE that it was wrong to boast. But how could it be boasting when it was only the truth? They also told him not to lie, didn't they? It was all very confusing! So he kept his mouth shut.

It was on special days like this that he wished his mother could be there. Otherwise he didn't miss her much. Well, not too much anyway. She lived in London with her new family. After Pa died, she married again. Dean had a stepbrother who was twelve and a new half-sister just five months old, but he hadn't met either of them. In fact, he hadn't seen his mother at all since his baby sister was born. "I bet," he said out loud (because there was no one around to hear) "if I were a baby Ma would stay with me!" At least he had Nan all to himself. He didn't have to share her with brothers and sisters, although he thought maybe it would be fun to have an older brother. But a sister? Girls, ughh!

He dressed quickly, putting on his school uniform: a dark green sweatshirt with 'Fritts End Primary School' written in yellow letters on the front, black knee-length trousers and black shoes. He packed his satchel, remembering to include his recorder. The recorder group was going to play in the dining hall before the parents were allowed to wander around the school. "Oh, it's going to be a grand day today!" he sang tunelessly at the top of his lungs as he ran down the stairs of his grandmother's old house.

Nan was in the kitchen cooking Dean's breakfast of eggs and bacon. She liked having her grandson around, it made her feel young again and it gave a purpose to her life. He was such a happy child! Shame on his mother—her daughter—for dumping Dean the way she had! How could anybody think an occasional telephone call was a suitable replacement for a mother's touch, a mother's hug when an elbow was bumped? Of course, Dean didn't realise that he had, to all extents and purposes, been abandoned. He was too young to understand these things. She knew, however, that soon he would start asking the difficult questions. He was eight, and he was bright.

Nan set his plate on the table as he arrived. He gave her a hug and a kiss and thanked her for getting his breakfast earlier than usual. "It's a big day for you! You need a good solid nosh to keep you going."

"What time will you come, Nan?"

"I'll be there for the recorder group, don't you worry none," she replied.

"That's 'don't you worry any,' Nan. 'Don't you worry none' really means I should worry lots."

"My, my, aren't they making eight year old boys clever these days! I wish I had of been so knowing when I was your age, but I simply weren't no brainbox!" They laughed at this ritual family joke.

Dean gobbled his breakfast as fast as he dared under the watchful eyes of his grandmother. She was always telling him dumb things like eat slowly, chew your food thoroughly, don't drink your juice in one gulp. He carried the dishes to the sink, prepared to help with the washing up.

"Don't you worry about that today, Deanikins," said Nan, shooing him away. "You get your lunchbox and go on off."

Dean *knew* it was a good day. He didn't have to help clear up breakfast!

Normally Dean would have taken the bus to school but he decided he would walk this morning. It would be quicker. Nan preferred him to wait for the bus, she always said it was safer. But Dean knew he shouldn't get near a stranger's car, and he liked the walk. The area was mostly farmland, and he frequently saw rabbits and squirrels and once he even saw a family of ducks crossing the road. Although he didn't live on a farm himself, many of his friends did. He liked visiting them because he liked animals. Especially pigs. Pigs are intelligent creatures with expressive faces, and Dean felt he could speak to them.

Miss Murphey, the Headmistress, saw Dean from her window and went to let him in. The school was not due to open for another half hour, but she was not one to curb enthusiasm, especially in such a promising lad. She asked him, "Have you come to check that your drawing survived the night safely?"

"Yes, Miss. Is it okay?"

"I guarded it all night!" she promised him. "But I've been in my office for the last fifteen minutes. Would you be good enough to make sure it's still hanging where we left it?"

"Oh yes, Miss! I'll go right now!" and he started running down the hall to his classroom until a shout from the Headmistress reminded him that he was not allowed to run inside the building. He walked as fast as his little legs could manage. Professional athletes would have been put to shame! Until, that is, he rounded the corner and was out of Miss Murphey's sight; then he broke into a run again.

It was still there. He was so happy! He threw his arms around himself and wiggled with excitement. "Oh it's going to be a grand day today," he sang again.

The morning seemed interminable. Because there was only half a day for lessons, each subject was half its usual length. Reading and spelling were easy for Dean; he and Nan read passages from a child's version of the Bible every evening, and there were some very big words in it! Also, his mother had sent him a large print dictionary for his last birthday, and he considered it one of his most treasured belongings. Maths was difficult! Nan wasn't very good with figures and couldn't help him and he had to have extra coaching sessions once a week. He was good at science unless it involved maths. But geography and art and music were what he really loved. As part of the geography lessons, the school arranged outings so the pupils could see for themselves the Frittenden landmarks. When they got back from a field trip, they would compare the local environment to other areas in the British Isles. One day, Dean vowed to himself, he would visit all the places they studied.

At last the lessons finished, and then the lunch break was over, and finally the recorder group was gathered at one end of the dining hall. Dean could see his Nan standing near the front. It made him feel good. The music teacher had arranged a little suite of folk songs which the students played with gusto, if lacking somewhat in finesse.

After the ten-minute concert, Dean pulled his Nan by the arm squeaking, "Come and see! Come and see!" He practically dragged her down the hall to his classroom. "Can you tell which one is mine?" he asked, pointing to the row of pictures.

"Well, let me see. Don't tell me. Now, I don't think it's *that* one, and it certainly isn't *that* one with the horse; I suppose it could be this one— but I don't really think it is. Maybe this one here…"

"Oh Nan! It's *this* one, this one here, of the school!"

"Is *that* one yours? Really? I thought that was by Leonardo da Vinci!"

"No, Nan. That's by *me*! *I* did that!" Dean didn't know who da Vinci was, but he knew it must be someone famous. Oh, he was so proud! He jumped up and down with excitement. What a grand day it was! Now if only he could distract Nan from talking with his teacher about maths…He said, "There's the geography display. Mr. Dilling was telling us about the history of Frittenden and how it's built on an old track used for driving pigs into the forest." And thus the history of the village no longer had anything to do with Jutes or Romans but was totally dependent on pigs. "Why did they drive pigs into the forest, Nan?"

"To keep them out of the house, of course," she answered with a straight face.

"Oh, Nan!"

Dean wasn't able to stop his Nan from talking with Mr. Dilling about his progress, or perhaps it would be better described as his lack of progress, with maths. But it wasn't as bad as he was afraid it would be. Mostly they discussed strategies for interesting Dean in the subject. "Try to relate the questions to pigs," suggested Nan, "pigs and other animals; for instance, how many pigs would it take to feed a herd of cows?"

"None!" chirped Dean. "Cows don't eat pigs, don't you know that, Nan?"

After school activities at Fritts End Primary School included sports such as netball and soccer. Dean enjoyed netball and usually stayed longer once a week to participate. Today visitors were given the opportunity to see the children at games, but Nan needed to return home to prepare the evening meal. She told Dean not to be too late and left him to burn off his excess energy.

Dean set off from school just as the light was starting to fade. He hurried because he had stayed longer than he should have and he knew he would be punished. He didn't even take time to watch the cows returning from the fields. He was half walking, half running along the winding single-track road, his eyes on his feet to avoid stepping in a pothole. Nan was going to be so angry!

Micky was taking the scenic route. The EPO's jazz band had just finished a gig in Maidstone at the Cornway School and it was a resounding success. This large comprehensive school had its own jazz band which was pretty damn decent! The students had joined with the professionals for some numbers, a ploy that had gone down well with the rest of the student body. There had not been much need to talk about the instruments: the students had all the answers; so they talked about the music instead. Micky much preferred that! The band demonstrated Blues (*The Bourbon Street Blues*), Ragtime (Scott Joplin's *The Entertainer*) and Mainstream (Micky liked this best—they played

Dave Brubeck's *Take Five)*; the student band joined them in some Dixieland and Trad Jazz. Hey, two of the students were really outstanding! One was a baritone saxophonist and the other was a guitarist. Both had improvised neat little solos.

Usually the EPO Jazz Combo did two or three demonstration concerts a day on these short tours, but in order to include the Cornway School they had found it necessary to alter their normal routine. Consequently they had the rest of the day and all of the following day off. As Micky always had to take his own car on these gigs because his bass fiddle occupied so much space, he told the others he would meet them tomorrow evening in Tunbridge Wells and set off to enjoy the Wealds of Kent. He thought about ringing Netty and asking her to join him, but he knew she would refuse. She never wanted to do anything with him anymore; he was afraid to ask why.

Micky drove slowly, enjoying the smell of the hopfields and the rare sight of oast houses. His route was erratic; if he saw a road that looked interesting he took it, not caring if he was doubling back on himself. Eventually he saw a signpost to a village called Headcorn and he decided on a whim to see if Headcorn had an old parish church worthy of a look. He was surprised, when he got there, to see that the village boasted not only a church and the essential pub but also a good little shopping area. He found an old pub on the High Street, The George and Dragon, left his car in the parking area at the rear, and went inside. The interior had wood floors and brick walls and was clearly a favourite with the lunchtime crowd. Which reminded Micky that he was hungry. He enjoyed a steak and baked potato but accompanied it with only half a lager; he never drank much when he had his bass with him! A coffee and a chat about the surrounding countryside with the locals, and he was ready to visit the church and walk around the town for a little while before continuing his mini sightseeing holiday. These little villages were so informative of English history! He had learned that Headcorn was not so named because of the cornfields but because it was a deviation of the Old English language: Head was a derivation of 'Huda,' a Saxon personal name, and Corn was a fallen tree. He surmised that once upon a time someone called Huda must have cut down some trees. Well, who knows? It could have been like that.

Keeping in the same vein and being in no hurry, Micky decided to go in search of more corn history. Now, he tried to remember, when exactly were the Corn Laws established? Some time in the mid-fifteen hundreds, he felt sure. Bloody Mary's time. The publican at the George and Dragon had told him that the big corn scandal in southeast England had occurred in Maidstone; a miller and his wife, locals of the Frittenden area, were found guilty of undercharging for their corn and were taken to Maidstone to be burned at the stake. The fact that they were Protestants may have had some bearing on the matter...

Micky didn't really want to return to Maidstone, he preferred to visit the smaller villages. So instead he made for Staplehurst where he had been told he could find a memorial to the two corn martyrs. The light was beginning to fade and his day's meanderings were coming to an end; with any luck he would find a comfortable inn at Staplehurst.

The trees looked spooky in the failing light and Micky began to brood over his unhappy marriage. In his eyes Netty was beautiful and he didn't mind that she hadn't lost the weight she had gained when carrying Jenny. In fact, he preferred her this way, with a bit of meat on her bones. What was happening to their marriage? What if she really was having an affair? What could he do about it? If he sued for divorce, he'd lose his daughter. Micky loved Netty but he had no illusions about her: she was a hard woman. If he initiated the break up, she would take him to the cleaners.

What was that shadow in the road? Micky's heart leapt into his throat. My God! It's a child! I'm going to hit him! He slammed on the brakes.

Screech!

"Shit!"

Thump!

And silence...

For one horrible moment Micky couldn't move. Then he heard someone crying and he scrambled out of the car saying, his voice trembling, "Oh my God, are you hurt? Don't try to move!"

"I'm all right, Mister. I think my knees are bleeding, that's all." But his knees hurt something awful, and he couldn't stop crying. The suddenness and unexpectedness of the accident made him cry harder. He had been terribly frightened!

"Let me see." Micky took out his handkerchief and gently brushed and blew the grit off the wounds. He was careful not to do anything to make them hurt more. "It doesn't look too serious. I think you will live. By the way, my name's Micky," he said, holding out his hand. "What's yours?"

The boy took Micky's proffered hand. "Dean. Dean Thompson. I'm sorry, Mister. I hope I didn't scratch your car. I was trying not to step in a pothole and I wasn't looking where I was going."

"The car is fine; it's only a bit bruised, not bleeding like you are. You certainly are a very brave young man!" This gentle talk was calming for both of them. Dean stopped crying and Micky's voice began to steady itself.

"Well, it's a pleasure to meet you, Dean. May I say, I'd prefer to have met you in different circumstances!"

"Me too. Oh gosh! I'm so late, Nan will never let me walk home from school again! She's going to punish me something terrible."

"I'd better take you, I think; those knees look pretty sore."

"I'm not supposed to get in a car with strangers."

"That's very wise, but I think you are allowed to make an exception with those knees. I'm fairly certain Nan will want to meet me." He opened the back door behind the driver's seat as it was the only place a passenger could fit with his bass occupying the front and back of the left side. "You must give me directions, because I don't know the area," he said.

Dean told him, "I live on this road, around the next bend. It's the stone house at the end of the drive, the one with the two big fir trees. I say, mister, you won't tell Nan that I wasn't watching where I was going, will you? She thinks I'm too careless and she worries about me. She'll punish me good, she will!"

"Well, I certainly don't want to get you into trouble, and to tell you the truth *I* don't want to get into trouble either! We'll tell her a rabbit ran in front of the car and we both tried to miss it and so we ran into each other. How does that sound to you? Is Nan terribly scary?"

"Ooh, that sounds good! I'm not really a very good liar. I live with Nan, she's my grandmother. What's this thing in your car?"

"That's my contrabass; do you know what that is? It's a big violin."

"Are you a mugi…magi…mugician?"

"Musician. Yes, I play with the English Philharmonia. Have you heard of it?"

"I've seen it on television. I play the recorder. I played in a concert today. It was Visitors' Day and my drawing was put on the wall. Nan came to see it but she didn't know it was mine. She thought it was by some famous painter, Lee…Leon…da…somebody famous."

"Leonardo da Vinci?" Micky suggested, amused. What a charming child! So bright! "How old are you, Dean?"

"I'm eight. There's my house! Just there, by the trees!"

Micky saw an old stone house made attractive by the climbing roses which covered the front. It had two floors and although he could see, even in the dusk, that it needed repairs, it was obviously much loved. A tidy little garden surrounded it on all sides, although the picket fence was collapsed here and there. Money was, Micky suspected, a problem. He wondered why Dean's father didn't make a few repairs. Or did Dean even have a father?

As he approached the house an elderly woman hurried out to meet them. Her hair was grey, but it was stylishly cut to frame her still attractive face. She had changed out of the suit she had worn to the school that morning and was now wearing brown slacks and a dark blue pullover sweater. She saw Dean in the back seat and the relief that swept through her body was so thick it was tangible.

"I'm sorry, Nan. Please don't yell at me in front of my friend. You can punish me later," pleaded Dean.

Cunning boy, thought Micky. If he can delay the punishment until

Nan cools down, it will probably not be so severe. I'd better do my bit now. "It's my fault, I'm afraid. A rabbit ran in front of the car and I swerved to miss it…"

"And I tried to catch it," cut in Dean.

"And we kind of ran into each other, you see," finished Micky.

"Oh yes, I do see," responded Nan, who clearly saw more than she was meant to. "How badly are you hurt, Dean?"

"Only my knees a bit. They don't hurt anymore." He put on a brave face that proved he was lying.

While they were talking, Micky got out of the driver's seat and opened Dean's door. He picked him up and asked, "Where shall I take him?" He followed Nan into the house and deposited Dean on the sofa, as indicated. "Don't be too alarmed," he said soothingly. "Nothing is broken; but I think his knees will be sore for a few days. Have you any iodine?"

"Oh no! That stuff stings!" wailed Dean.

"Then that will be part of your punishment." Nan was beginning to relax now that she could see Dean was not really hurt. While Micky applied the iodine, she put on the kettle and fetched some fruit juice for Dean. She stayed chatting with Dean about the Visitors' Day until she saw that his eyelids were drooping from exhaustion, then she invited Micky into the kitchen for a cuppa.

"Now who the hell are you?" she demanded forcefully, "and what really happened?"

"Micky Smythe," he said, handing her his card.

"You're not a doctor? You seemed to know how to keep Dean calm and how to clean his knees without giving him too much grief."

"I have a two-year-old daughter who has yet to learn to look where she's going, and my kid sister was a tomboy to beat all tomboys. I've mopped up a bit of blood here and there."

"And what really happened this evening?"

"I was heading towards Staplehurst—slowly, thank God!— enjoying the last of the daylight, and Dean suddenly appeared from the bushes and ran into the road. I braked immediately and turned the car away from him, but he ran into the side of it."

"You're saying it was Dean's fault? Were you truly trying to avoid a rabbit? Because if you place a rabbit's life above that of a little boy, then I'm ringing the police right now!"

"And so would I, in your shoes. No, the rabbit story was just something I concocted for Dean's sake to try to calm him down. He was worried about the punishment you are likely to mete out to him, and he was suffering from shock and guilt. Technically I suppose I am to blame since it was a road accident and I was the road user, and if you wish to report it to the police, please do. I will report it myself, if you prefer. But if you care to examine the side of my car, you will see where he ran into it. Oh, and I think you should know he was reluctant to get into my car; he remembered that you had forbidden him to accept a lift with a stranger. He only accepted a ride because walking was painful."

Nan refilled Micky's cup. "I'm glad to know he listens to me sometimes, at least. It's hard on an eight-year-old boy to be raised by an old lady."

"Where are his parents? Is he an orphan?"

"He might as well be!" Nan spat out. "His father's dead. He was a military man, an American. He died in the Afghanistan Al Queda War last year, a little more actually. Do you know about that? There were only sixty-four Americans killed, and Dean's father had to be one of them. His mother remarried almost immediately—too immediately, I think!—and she's got a baby now. She's all but forgotten Dean, I'm afraid. She rings him most weeks, but she hasn't been to see him for months; more like a year, in fact."

"So in a sense he lost both parents at the same time."

Nan nodded. "My loving daughter" (this was said with a sneer in her voice) "would have placed Dean in a home. Can you imagine that? A mother putting her own child in care! And just so *she* could marry a man with money, a man who wanted her but not her child. Yet *he* expects her to be a mother to *his* son. Phah!"

Micky and Nan stayed talking for an hour. When he realised how dark it was getting to be, Micky stood up to make his apologies.

"I have to find somewhere to stay the night. I was on my way to

Staplehurst when Dean and I crossed paths; the barman in Headcorn recommended it. But if you don't mind, I'd like to come back tomorrow and see how Dean's knees are."

"Dean and I would appreciate another visit. If you really intend to come again tomorrow, you might prefer to stay the night here. I occasionally rent out the guest room."

"I don't wish to intrude…"

"No intrusion, this is strictly business. Twenty-five pounds for bed and breakfast and seven pounds for dinner tonight. I'm a good cook, you won't get a better meal in Kent," Nan added with a smile.

"Agreed. I'll just get my things from the car."

Nan

I had a perfectly normal childhood. It's stupid when people say to you, 'You'll look back on your youth as the best days of your life.' Growing up is painful. I tried to remember that when I raised my own child, and I try to remember it now, while I'm raising my daughter's child.

My parents loved each other, and if there were indiscretions they kept them private. Money was tight, but we kids—there were four of us—always had a warm winter coat and gloves. My oldest brother chose to do missionary work. He never married, preferring to devote his life to Third World families. He died ten years ago. My other brother married a Japanese woman and now lives in Tokyo. They have three children and five grandchildren, all cute as buttons, if photos tell the truth. We haven't met in years, but we correspond regularly. He's my favourite. My older sister lives with her husband in Scotland; she has Alzheimer's Disease and doesn't know me now.

And that leaves me, the baby of the family. I eloped with my young man because I knew my parents couldn't afford a big wedding. I met my husband-to-be when I was only seventeen; it was love at first sight, but we waited two years before running away together. *Those* were the best days of my life! Simon was a carpenter and a good one, so he always had work. We bought this stone cottage when I became pregnant with Doris. It's a lovely spot to raise a child.

Simon fell off the roof of a four-storey building when Doris was sixteen. It changed her. After the first grief abated, she started to attack life instead of flowing with it. She married Dean's father because…because…well, I'm not sure why. Because he was there. She was a good mother, but something, some element, was missing. Doris was still fighting life. Apparently she didn't waste too much time mourning for Greg, as you can see by the speed with which she remarried. Several years of living together as husband and wife were just dropped, as though they never happened. Except they did happen, and a child was born. Hiding Dean in the country with his grandmother doesn't alter the fact that he does exist. One day she will have to face it. One day she will have to face Dean.

I am ashamed of my daughter.

While Nan cooked dinner, Micky and Dean cemented their new friendship through music. Micky demonstrated slap bass while Dean laughed with delight, then Dean played a folk song on his recorder and Micky applauded enthusiastically. Micky said, "let's play some jazz," but Dean replied, "I don't know how!"

"Then it's time you learned, boy, time you learned! See if you can copy this on your recorder." He played a few notes from 'Swanee River' on his bass. When Dean could repeat the tune, Micky said, "Now swing it like I'm doing." That was fun! "And together now!" They played in unison, except Micky cheated: he started playing other notes. So Dean cheated too. Howls of laughter rocked through the house, and Nan was sorry to interrupt the musical thuggery for something so mundane as dinner.

Nan had not exaggerated when she had bragged about her cooking. They dined on shoulder of lamb cooked in garlic and red wine, served with home grown potatoes, broccoli and butternut squash. This colourful meal was accompanied with a bottle of cheap but respectable red wine (milk for Dean) and finished with apple pie and ice cream. "Yum yum," said Micky and Dean in unison, their mouths too full for more conversation.

After Dean went to bed, Nan offered Micky a coffee. When he was settled, she said, "I hope you won't object to what I'm going to say. Dean has really taken to you, and either you're a good actor or you've taken a shine to my grandson. He very much needs a father figure; the only adult male in his life at the moment is his class teacher. I'm a woman, his music teacher is a woman, the Headmistress is of course a woman. It's not good. Just say no if I am asking too much: is there any chance you might visit him from time to time? I can see you're a very busy man and I don't want to impose." As Micky said nothing, she continued, "I've asked too much, I can see. You did say you have a daughter and obviously you want to spend your free time with your family. Perhaps you might bring them with you?"

Micky remained silent for quite a while. There were so many thoughts spinning around in his head, yet he seemed unable to catch any of them. He walked over to the window and stared into the night. Finally he said, "I have enjoyed today more than I have enjoyed any day in the last two years. Never mind why. Thank you for your offer, I will come as often as I can."

The next morning was a Thursday and Dean wanted to go to school, but when Nan saw how stiffly he was walking she felt he should stay home. They were still arguing about it when Micky came downstairs. "What a hullabaloo!" he exclaimed, a smile playing at the corners of his mouth. "This disagreement obviously needs an arbiter; shall I act as go-between?"

"Yes, yes!" shouted Dean confident that his new friend would back him up. Nan was less enthusiastic. She also thought Micky would side with Dean.

"As I understand it, *you*" he pointed to Dean, "want to go to school. An admirable trait. And *you*" he pointed to Nan, "want him to rest his knees, because you love him and don't want to see a painful situation become worse." They both looked at him.

"Tell you what I'm gonna do. I'm gonna make you both happy. I will drive you to school, Dean, and bring you back at midday. I can't leave it longer than that because I have a gig in Tunbridge Wells later. And I will have a word with his teacher, Nan, and make sure Dean doesn't get up for anything except the toilet. Okay?"

This solution having been accepted, albeit reluctantly on both sides,

Micky picked up Dean and deposited him in the car, in the front passenger seat this time; the bass stayed with Nan. Dean directed Micky to the school and, taking his hand, led Micky to his classroom. Mr. Dilling came to meet them. He was a youngish man of about thirty-two or thirty-three with light brown hair and a jovial round face. It was easy to see why his students adored him. Dilling noticed Dean's knees immediately.

"Well, look at you, Dean! What have you been up to? Roller skating on your knees?"

Dean giggled. Remembering his manners, he said, "This is Mr. Micky. He's my friend. He drove me to school today."

Dilling asked, "Are you a friend of Mrs. Yates? I don't believe we've met." He was a conscientious teacher, careful about adults who hang around children. When Micky mentioned that he would collect Dean at midday, Mr. Dilling said he was sure that would be all right, but he'd like to introduce Micky to the Headmistress before he could agree to it.

Dilling put Dean in charge of name-taking while he was out of the classroom and ushered Micky to Miss Murphey's room. Micky saw a pretty dark-haired woman seated behind a large and imposing desk and burst out with, "*You're* the Headmistress? I thought all Headmistresses were gorgons!" He realised how rude this was and tried to make up for it.

"Don't apologise, Mr. Micky, you're quite right. I may not have snakes for hair, but I do know how to hiss, I assure you."

"Actually my name is Smythe; Micky is my first name. Well, actually James is my first name but Micky is what people call me. It's short for Michael, which is my second name. Michael was also my father's middle name, just as James was my father's first name. It was terribly confusing, our same names, so I decided to change mine." He handed her his card. "When I met Dean I introduced myself as Micky; that's why he calls me Mr. Micky."

"I will have to ring Dean's grandmother and get her approval to release Dean to you. I won't be long." She returned after a few minutes sporting a big smile. "She speaks very highly of you; it seems Dean is quite fond of you."

101

"I hope so; I'm certainly fond of him."

"We feel that Dean is one of our most special students. Not necessarily the cleverest child here, but one who clearly evinces talent in certain directions. It's quite unusual at his age"

Micky nodded. "Art and music. I noticed his musical ear last night. We played a bit; I was showing him how to improvise and he was picking it up like a natural."

Miss Murphey led the way to the exit nearest the car park. Naturally, being a man who was not getting his oats at home, he noticed the swish of her skirt over her shapely hips. Whew, he thought to himself, Headmistresses ain't what they used to be when I was in school!

When Micky returned to Dean's house, he decided to make himself useful. In a garden shed which he explored he found some planks of wood, a saw, a hammer and nails, and he set about repairing the garden fence. "I'm not a carpenter like Simon, but hauling a contrabass around the world has developed a muscle or two, so I hope you won't mind strength over beauty," he said to Nan. "I'll come back next week and paint it, if that's okay."

Micky was so happy that day. He picked up Dean from school and after taking him home he made his way to Tunbridge Wells where he met up with the rest of the band for a rehearsal; he played his bass like he hadn't played it for a couple of years. The next week he returned to Frittenden and painted the fence, not forgetting to give Dean his improvisation lesson. It became a regular pattern: when there were no concerts Micky went to Kent. The three of them always had fun, especially the time Micky and Dean decided Nan should be the singer in their combo. "But I can't sing!" she protested. "I don't even know the words."

"Then scat, madam, scat!" Micky replied.

"What's that! What on earth is scat?"

Dean had the answer. "It's what the cat does when you sing, Nan!" Doo be doo be doo! sang all three but not, I must inform you, necessarily together or even in the same key. That had been a most embarrassing moment! That was the day Miss Murphey decided to make an unannounced home visit, a thing she did occasionally to keep a watchful eye on children from broken homes. When the Frittenden Jazz Trio (for that's what they decided to call themselves) looked around, they saw the Headmistress standing in the doorway totally—in the words later used by Sergeant Wilcox—gob-smacked.

"Oh, no!" moaned Nan. "Whatever will you think of us?"

"Just what we need!" gloated Micky. "A piano player! Now we're a quartet." He took Miss Murphey by the arm and steered her towards the piano.

And this Headmistress who was like no other Headmistress took up her position at the keyboard and calmly asked, "How about a little Ragtime?" as she launched into the *Maple Leaf Rag*. "Hooray!" shouted the other three members of the now-named Frittenden Jazz Quartet.

Micky wondered: why can't my real family be like this?

Part 1
(Resumed)

Chapter Ten

A year passed. In all this time Micky never met Dean's mother. It was as though Nan and Micky had a tacit agreement not to mention her, for Dean's sake. She hadn't telephoned for months. Micky didn't even know her name. And then one day she showed up.

Micky was trimming the hedge. She obviously thought he was the gardener; she criticised his work. "You've cut too much off this end," she carped. "It will take forever to grow out again."

"Sorry, Mum." Rather surprised at this verbal assault and then realising that this snotty woman thought he was the gardener, Micky rose to the occasion. He put on his best uncultured accent and decided that he might as well take advantage of his lowered position in society. He looked her up and down slowly, eyeing her shapely figure and staring openly at her breasts. "Aah," he said insolently.

Her face turned a dark red colour and she said, haughtily, "I don't know why Mother hired you, but you can be sure you will never work here again!" She marched towards the house.

Uh oh, Micky said to himself as it dawned on him what her words implied. That's Dean's mother, and I'm buggered. He felt he'd better try to redeem himself and followed her inside. He was in time to hear the daughter—he didn't yet know her name—complaining about his crudity.

"He *leered* at me! Actually leered! And made the most disgusting growling noise."

Nan looked up and saw Micky standing behind Doris looking contrite. "I'm really sorry, but you did have it coming, you know," he smiled. "Just because a man works for a living doesn't mean he's insensitive. I'm not a gardener, as you've noticed, but I am a human being."

That was the wrong approach. It put Doris in the wrong, and Doris didn't like to be in the wrong. Nan intervened before this skirmish had a chance of turning into full-scale warfare. "Micky, dear, let me introduce you to my daughter, Doris Wainthrop. Doris, this is..."

"*Wainthrop*, did you say? Wainthrop, from London?"

"Do I know you?" Doris asked frostily. "Your name is.?"

"Micky. Just Micky. No, you don't know me. You don't know me at all. I, uh, was, uh, confusing you with someone I know with the same name, but I, uh, just remembered they don't live in London anymore." Micky's lies were desperate. He didn't want Doris to know who he was. His wife had often mentioned a Mrs. Doris Wainthrop, a proud, selfish woman trying to disguise her real arrogance behind a façade of charity work.

He caught Nan's eye and tried to convey a message to her. When Doris insisted, "Micky who?" Nan said, "Micky is Dean's friend," and Doris lost interest.

Micky left the two together and made himself scarce. He walked until he found a big tree and sat behind it, out of sight. He let his head fall forwards onto his hands and while on the outside he appeared to be resting calmly, inside he was weeping. He had found a refuge from a frigid, towards him anyway, wife and a frigid life. Oh, there was no hanky panky with Dean's grandmother, although there had been an occasional night with Emma Murphey. But it was the wonderful family life he had found here that brought him back. He loved Dean like his own son. Of course he always knew this idyll could not last forever but did it have to end now? If Netty knew how he was spending his free time, that he was being a father to another woman's son, that he was acting the role of Man of the House in someone else's family, she would never understand it. Why should she? He didn't understand it himself. And God forbid! If Netty learned that he was playing father to the son of 'that bitch Doris Wainthrop' she would probably kill him.

Dean saw Micky from his bedroom window and wondered why his friend was sitting under a tree instead of joining in the family reunion. Maybe Micky didn't like his mother. He could understand that! He had felt quite ill when this woman, reeking of perfume, had hugged and kissed him as though she had never gone away. Dean was nine now, and he understood lots of things, but he didn't understand why she had disappeared for so long. Was he that bad a person? Did she dislike him? If so, that was okay by him, because he didn't like her either. He went to join Micky.

"I don't like her either," Dean said to his friend.

"What makes you think I don't like her?"

"Because you're sitting out here instead of in there."

"I'm sitting out here because it's a family do; you should be in there getting to know your mother. I'll join you in a little while."

"Really? How long will you be? "

"A while."

"No you won't! I can tell! You're going to go away, aren't you?" He threw his arms around Micky's neck and clung to him. "I won't let you go! I won't, I won't!"

Micky held Dean tightly. "I love you," he said softly. "I love you, I love Nan and I love this house. I will never leave you, Dean, I promise. So hush. But you're right about one thing: I don't want to see your mother. You see, I know a friend of hers in London, and I don't want this friend to know where to find me."

"Are you afraid of this person?"

"Yes." God yes; that was certainly true. He was afraid of her reaction when he announced he wanted a divorce. The sad thing was, he loved her and didn't really want a divorce at all. What did he want? A wife who found him attractive; for Dean to be his adopted son; for Nan to live with his family. None of these things were likely to be acceptable to Netty. But God damn it! He would talk to her just as soon as he returned to London. But first he had something to do.

"Dean, I am going to the pub. I will probably get drunk. Tell Nan, if she wants to find me later, that's where I'll be."

Doris watched from the kitchen window as Dean and Micky walked to the end of the drive together. "They look like father and son," she said to her mother. "What the hell has been going on here?"

This was an opening not to be ignored. Nan launched into a tirade about negligent mothers and fatherless children. She didn't pause for breath and she didn't mince her words. When she finished speaking, there was a long silence. Finally Doris murmured softly, "Micky. From London. I wonder if that's Netty's Micky?"

Although the question was addressed to nobody, Nan replied. "I don't know what you are talking about, but I will say this to you, and you had better listen closely. If you do anything to harm that young man, Doris, I will go to the Social Services and inform them that you are an unfit mother; that you arranged for me to look after your child for one month and left him here for two years. I will go to the newspapers and expose you for the uncaring parent you are. I will destroy your reputation utterly."

"You wouldn't!"

"I would."

"You'd do that to your own daughter?"

"If my daughter treated my son like that."

"Your son! My, things have been happening in this Godforsaken piss hole, haven't they!"

Two hours later Nan walked into the pub and found Micky, not quite blotto but definitely well-lit. "It's time to come home now, " she said sympathetically. "The enemy has departed."

"My wife knows your daughter," he explained. "They don't like each other."

"I gathered as much. I'm afraid, Micky, we have to talk. Dean is going to be hurt, I don't think that can be avoided; but it's important we try to minimise the pain. You have been a father to him for a long time now. I know I have been extremely selfish in taking up so much of your time, but it's been so good for Dean. And for me, too. Whatever your problems are at home, please don't just disappear from his life suddenly. I ask only that."

"Oh, Nan! I've ballsed up everyone's life. Yours, Dean's, my wife's, my daughter's, my own. I don't know what to do. I've loved coming here, and the last thing I want to do is hurt you or Dean."

"Well, we can talk about it, and perhaps that will help you find a direction. But I can't advise you; I'm not a disinterested party. Decisions have to come from you."

"I know what I would like. I would like a wife who is warm and loving. I would like us all to live together, perhaps here. But my wife doesn't care for me, and Dean's mother—your daughter—may cause trouble. I do need advice, I think, before talking with Netty." He suddenly stopped talking. Then he continued, speaking slowly and thoughtfully. "And I think I know where to get it." Nan's eyebrows rose in question. "Marge," he responded. "My stepmother. When she married my father, she moved into a house full of suspicious people, every one of us assuming she was a gold digger. I bet she sees us all in our true characters."

The next day Micky began a schools tour with the EPO's string ensemble. It was while he was on that tour that he received the call from Marge asking him to return to London because someone had been poisoning his father.

Chapter Eleven

Detective Inspector Gravitt and DC Bateman were working their way through Micky's touring schedule and his diary, taking particular interest in the discrepancies. They noticed immediately that on certain dates in the diary there was only the initial 'F.' They also noticed that 'F' never appeared on a date mentioned in the schedule. It seemed fairly obvious that if Micky was up to something secret, it must be in a place beginning with the letter F or with someone whose name began with F. To find an unknown town beginning with F in the whole of England was a formidable task. To find an unknown person whose name began with F seemed impossible. They looked for similarities between schedule and diary and noticed that about a year back, when 'F' first appeared in Micky's diary, the EPO Jazz Combo had toured extensively in Kent. The policemen decided to begin their search in the Garden of England. Eventually they found themselves at the Cornway School talking to the Headmaster, who remembered the jazz event very well. "They made a special effort for us because music is an important component of our curriculum," he informed the policemen. "They had to waste a day and a half to fit us in." In answer to the next question he said, "No, I have no idea what they did or where they went afterwards. I do know that their next engagement was in Tunbridge Wells."

As this information tallied with the schedule, they concentrated on the area between Maidstone and Tunbridge Wells, and it was not long before they found themselves in Frittenden, a town small enough for everyone to know everyone else's business. "Oh, the musician," said the publican. "He rents a room in Mrs. Yates' cottage."

Mrs. Yates—Nan—answered the door and realised at once that they were either policemen or private investigators. She had read in the newspapers about the murder of James Michael Smythe, and while she felt sympathy for the Smythe family, a part of her had been relieved to learn there was a reason for Micky's continued absence. The thought that they might be PIs was engendered by her knowing that Micky was trying to come to some arrangement with his wife, and her lack of knowledge as to what, if any, progress was being made on that score.

"Mrs. Yates?" Nan nodded. "I'm Detective Inspector Gravitt and this is Detective Constable Bateman. May we have a word with you, please?"

Nan invited the detectives into the kitchen, "the most comfortable room in the house," and put hot, strong coffee on the table. Gravitt automatically looked around, it was an occupational disease; you can learn a great deal about people from the way they dress, or decorate their homes, or from the car they drive. In Nan's kitchen he saw a mixture of old and new: old-fashioned lacy net curtains, tied back to let the sun in, and the latest in kitchen appliances. Probably a woman who likes to serve an attractive meal but who doesn't want to spend hours preparing it, he thought. He was right, of course.

Nan saw Gravitt looking around instead of questioning her and decided enough was enough. She wanted them gone before Dean returned from school. "You're here because of Micky," she volunteered. All I know is, he was here two weeks ago, and not since. I know he was on tour with the EPO after he left us."

"Who is 'us' Mrs. Yates?"

"My grandson Dean and me."

"How long have you known Micky Smythe?"

"I suppose it's a year or more now." She told them how Dean and Micky met, being careful to put the onus of blame for the accident on Dean. Micky obviously had enough problems at the moment without the worry of an unreported traffic violation. "Micky and Dean took an instant liking to each other. Micky was the father Dean needed and Dean was the child Micky wished for."

"And what exactly is your position in all this, if you don't mind my asking?"

Nan looked disgusted. "To answer your rather impertinent question, Mr. Gravitt, Micky is not my 'toy boy.' He is very much a son to me, as Dean is a son to him. He is a warm-hearted and kind man. I only wish his wife appreciated his qualities; he loves her very much."

"I don't mean to be impertinent, but I'm sure you can appreciate that I need to understand the personalities and characters of all the suspects, Mrs. Yates. Our problem is that everyone in the Smythe family had opportunity and means, but I'm damned if I can find anyone with a motive."

"Then perhaps the crime was committed by someone who is not in the family, or maybe it was an accident."

Gravitt frowned. "I wish it could be!" he said with feeling, "but unfortunately that's not likely. I would like to meet Dean; do you mind?"

"Yes, actually, I do. He doesn't know about Micky's father, and he's beginning to fret because Micky has been away for so long."

"We'll be cool. Don't worry."

As it happened, Nan didn't have time to worry because just at that moment Dean walked in. "Hi, who are you?" he asked. "I'm Dean. That's an American name. I'm half American, you know."

"My name is Alex Gravitt and this is Ben Bateman. We've just come from London."

"*London!*" screeched Dean. "Do you know Micky? He's my best friend. But I don't know where he is. Do you? He *promised* me he wouldn't leave me. He told me he loved me, and Nan, and the house. He told me that."

"Hush, Dean, don't let your mouth run away with your manners," Nan said sternly. She was afraid Dean would get hysterical and she was both worried about him and angry with the police for mentioning London—a ploy, she was sure, to bring Micky's name into the conversation. But Gravitt was deftly bringing things under control. He was talking in his soothing voice, saying to Dean that he had stopped by to see him at Micky's request.

"He was worried that you might be missing him. I promised I would make sure you are all right. Is there any message you would like me to give him?"

Dean cheered up. "Can you wait while I write a letter?"

Of course they waited. While Dean worked on his letter, Nan explained that his father had been a war casualty and for one reason or another it seemed better that Dean should live in the country with her than in London with his mother. Gravitt sensed that enquiring into the reasoning behind that decision would be unwelcome. He hoped it didn't really matter because he had his own emotions to contend with and didn't feel he could cope with much more.

The letter written, the men thanked Nan for her hospitality and made their way back to London. Had this part of the investigation been worth the effort, the time and the expense? They had learned Micky's secret, but where did it get them? They had found no motive for Micky to murder his father. It almost looked as if Smythe's homicide truly had been an accident. But what kind of accident took two attempts, the first one so cleverly disguised? Had Smythe been mistaken for someone else? Yet all indications were that this was an 'in-house' crime. Suicide, made to look like murder? Unlikely. There was no suicide note, and you'd have to be nuts to put yourself through that kind of agony. It was back to square one. Do not pass 'go.' Do not send anyone to jail.

It was time to return to London for the funeral.

The funeral for James Michael Smythe took place in the Golders Green Crematorium off Hoop Lane. It was fitting, Gravitt thought, that Smythe, a literary man, should begin his final journey here, where Rudyard Kipling and TS Eliot had been cremated. The family and one or two close friends arrived in a procession of black cars, but Gravitt had made his own way.

In his will James had left instructions for the service to be simple. He had said that all he really wanted was to have a candle lit to guide him on his journey. The Chapel was prepared with a ring of candelabra and each mourner lighted a candle upon arrival. Members of the EPO String Ensemble played slow movements from the late Beethoven Quartets. It was beautiful.

"'I am the resurrection and the life,' saith the Lord; 'he that believeth in me, though he were dead, yet shall he live: and whosoever liveth and believeth in me shall never die.'" The service had begun.

After the opening scripture readings, a hymn was sung: *The Lord Is My Shepherd.* Then members of the family stood up to say a few words. Marge, looking pale as death herself, spoke of her husband's warmth and understanding. Micky's voice shook as he spoke of the good advice and support his father had always given. Anne-Marie said he had been more than a father, he had been her best friend. And unexpectedly Harry stood up to speak. "He believed in me when no one else did; he was like a father to me. God bless Uncle James."

The ceremony over, there was a general milling about and a few desultory comments; most of those in attendance were in tears. Micky approached Gravitt and said, "I hope you are coming back to the house with us, Alex. We're expecting you. Greta has worked hard preparing a cold collation."

"Thank you. I'd like to join you."

Micky noticed Gravitt's eyes searching the guests and he smiled wryly. "She's over there, by Marge," he said, pointing to the far end of the Chapel. "But I'm sorry to tell you that you have competition. DC Gordon Miller also has his eye on my little sister."

Anne-Marie appeared beside Gravitt as guests were departing. She looked lovely in her black full-skirted dress adorned with lace around the low décolletage and wrists. "Have you come in your car?" Gravitt nodded. "May I ride with you, please? All this grief is making me crazy." A small tear escaped from the prison of her eye and, surprised by its freedom, hovered on the edge of a lash before dropping onto her cheek. Gravitt wiped it into oblivion with his forefinger. As they walked to the car, Anne-Marie tilted her head to look up at him, saying,

"I'm so pleased to see you! I thought you might at least have telephoned me."

Gravitt was confused. "I thought you didn't want to see me anymore. I mean, socially. You have to see me professionally, of course." God! Why is it I always babble like an idiot when I'm near you, he said, but not out loud.

"Of course I want to see you! Will you take me out tonight? We could get a Chinese takeaway and go to your place." She gave his arm an intimate squeeze and a smile which promised the world.

"Oh God, Anushka, you drive me crazy! Oh, bloody hell, I get everything wrong! I didn't mean to call you that; I know you don't like it."

"But I love it! You *must* call me 'Anushka.' It's my pet name."

"But before you said...I thought you didn't want..." She looked at him blankly. Wisely he dropped the subject. "Tonight," he agreed. Does any man ever fathom womankind? he wondered.

The rest of the funeral party was already gathered in the Smythe home by the time they arrived. Marge greeted Gravitt warmly. "Alex! It's so good of you to take time for us when I know how busy you are. I hope you don't mind the informality of first names? Wasn't it a beautiful service? I think James would have been pleased."

Gravitt agreed. "I was particularly moved by the testimonials. Harry's seemed to come straight from the heart. I was surprised he stood up to speak."

"To be honest it was a surprise to us all. He's so shy he hardly ever says a word to anyone. But he spoke well, didn't he? He must have loved his uncle very much. I've convinced him to start coming to Sunday dinner on a regular basis."

"I'm glad of that. Are you aware that his father kicked him out some months ago? He's living alone now."

"Oh, poor child! Knowing Harry, I suspect he probably likes living alone, but I don't believe too much solitude is good for anyone. And of course it's one thing when you decide yourself to leave home, but it's different when you're told to leave."

"My thoughts exactly!" Gravitt and Marge shared an understanding smile.

Gravitt spotted Micky standing alone and, catching his eye, motioned towards the study. They went inside and Gravitt closed the door firmly.

"You know about my other life." It was a statement, not a question. Gravitt said nothing, he just handed Dean's letter to Micky. As he read it, Gravitt noticed that Micky's face softened and a smile hovered on his lips. "Have you looked at this?" he asked. Gravitt shook his head. "Read it." Micky handed him the letter.

Dear Micky (my very best friend),

I miss you. I don't know why you haven't come to see me yourself but I'm glad you sent your friends to say hello. They're very nice, especially the one named Alex.

I have learned a new tune on my recorder. It's called When the Saints. Miss Murphey played it with me. Guess what! My new drawing of the school building is going to be put on the school leaflet!!

If you're too busy to come here, maybe Nan and I can come to you — ? She misses you too—but not as much as I do! And Miss Murphey misses you. But I miss you most of all.

Love,
Dean XXX

Ps. This would be longer but your friends are waiting.

"Do you know how we met?"

"I'd like to hear it from you," Gravitt answered.

"I had a couple of free days in the middle of a tour. Actually," he interrupted himself, "do you mind if I ask Netty to come in? I really do have to tell her about Dean, and it would be nicer not to keep repeating the story." When he saw Gravitt was going to refuse, he urged, "Please Alex. I'm afraid of her reaction; it will be easier for me." He smiled.

"She can't kill me in front of Detective Inspector Gravitt." At Gravitt's nod, Micky fetched his wife. He handed her Dean's letter.

"As I was saying," he resumed, "I had a couple of free days in the middle of a tour. I could have returned to London, and I considered asking Netty to join me in Kent; Marge would have looked after Jenny, and we could have had a couple of nights together, just the two of us. In the end I did neither. Why drive back to London to see a wife who only says 'no' in bed? And she would have refused to join me in Kent. So I decided to indulge in a little sightseeing." Netty bristled but kept silent.

"To cut a long story short, Dean and I met on a small lane in Frittenden. He ran into my car. He wasn't really hurt, but he was frightened and his knees were pretty sore, so I took him home. If you've met him," he addressed this comment to Gravitt, "you know how charming he is. He was only eight, and he was being very brave. I got a right bollocking from his grandmother, who is bringing him up alone. It turned out that Dean's grandmother rents rooms, and as it was getting late by then, she suggested that I stay there for the night. While Nan made dinner, I discovered that Dean has a talent for music. He was far more interested in my bass than in his knees. I showed off to him a bit, I admit, then he got out his recorder and we started improvising. He's very bright! I stayed there the next day as well, helping Nan with some of the things she couldn't manage; she's not a young woman and she can't mend fences, things like that. I got into the habit of going there on my free days, and Dean became like my own son." Micky's face took on a look of contentment, followed by amusement. "After a few weeks of making music, just the two of us, we talked Nan into being our singer and we called ourselves the Frittenden Jazz Trio." Micky's eyes twinkled at the memory. "We weren't very good, but we were loud. That day the Headmistress, Miss Emma Murphey, dropped by—she does spot checks on children from broken homes. She caught us practising. Nan was embarrassed, but Dean and I sat her down at the piano and now we're the Frittenden Jazz Quartet." He laughed. "We still aren't very good, but we're louder!"

"And that's where I go, every chance I get. I'm happy there, I can relax there. Nobody nags at me and nobody shuns me. You see," Micky said, turning towards Netty, "there is no other woman. But there is another child. I'm allowed to be a father to him."

"Where is his real father? Are you his real father?" Netty asked calmly; too calmly, Gravitt felt.

"I only wish I were!" was Micky's response. "His father was an American soldier, killed in action."

"And his mother?"

"She remarried and left Dean with his grandmother."

"You've met her? His mother, I mean."

"Only once."

"If it's this innocent, why haven't you told me about it?"

Gravitt broke in. "The rest of this conversation is between you two. But I have one question before I go: Micky, did your father know about Dean?"

"Not to my knowledge." Gravitt slipped out and left the young couple to talk.

"I'll ask my question again," said Netty. "If it's this innocent, why didn't you tell me about it?"

"All right, I'll tell you why." Micky's voice rose; he couldn't stop himself from shouting as three years of frustration were suddenly released. "I didn't want you to destroy things for me. You never let me have any input to my own child. You won't let me give her music lessons. Yes, yes, I *know* she's only three. But she could be having fun with music even at that age. You've never let me bathe her, or change a nappy, or take her for a walk without you. She's *your* child, not mine! *Is* she my child? *Am* I her father? You sure as hell don't sleep with *me* anymore!"

Netty stood motionless, staring at the floor. Finally she walked over to Micky and put her arms around him. "I never realised how deeply you were being hurt. Forgive me." She held onto his hand but resisted his embrace. "Now I have something *I* have to confess to *you*, something I should have said when we first started seeing each other." Netty's sophisticated aplomb disappeared and she suddenly looked very young and vulnerable. "I'm so afraid you are going to hate me when I tell you this!" She gulped and took a deep breath. "Before we were married, I went for a full medical check-up. I had some gynaecological problems, you see, and I felt I had better find out what it was all about. I was told that I could never have a child, that I would never be able to carry one for the full time."

"You never told me that."

"No, I was afraid to. You had said you wanted children, and I was afraid to tell you that I wasn't able to give them to you. You might not have married me."

"But since you have given me a child, why won't you let me have a place in her life?"

"I don't know. I realise I'm too possessive and Doc Elliot has been giving me counselling."

"I thought you were having an affair with him."

"Me! Having an affair with that old goat, for God's sake!"

"But you don't sleep with me."

Netty started crying. "At first it was because the birth was so painful I couldn't bear to be touched. And then when I felt better, I thought you were sleeping with another woman. I couldn't stand to be touched by someone who was screwing somebody else."

"Oh, Netty, darling sweet Netty. I have never loved any woman but you." Micky held her close, enjoying the sensation of her body next to his. He reluctantly let her go. "I would like to adopt Dean."

"I think I'd like that. Have you discussed it with his grandmother? Do I get to meet him first?"

"To your last question, of course. We can drive down tomorrow or they can come here, if you prefer."

"And my first question?"

"The grandmother agrees. It's the mother who's the problem. I have to tell you who she is. But before I do that, you have to believe me that I only found out recently."

"No more secrets, Micky, please."

Oh well, in for a penny, in for a pound. "His mother is Doris Wainthrop," he said bluntly, and waited for the storm to break.

"Doris!" She began to laugh. "It will give me great pleasure to give that poor abandoned lad a home. I knew she had a child by her first marriage, but she never talks about him. Don't worry, she'll go along with the adoption, I'll see to that."

They stayed talking in the study until the funeral party had dispersed, and then they went upstairs. Together. It was really so much easier to tell the truth. Sad to think that this marriage between two people who love each other nearly ended in divorce.

That was exactly what Gravitt was thinking as he tried to convince himself that he had not wasted his and Bateman's time and the Department's money by tracing Micky's movements in Kent for the last two days. He still had failed to uncover any motive for Smythe's death. Suppose someone, some family friend like, for instance, Dr. Winston, or even Harry, had found out about Dean; could that trigger a murderous response from someone, somehow? He didn't believe it, but he thought it through all the same. Perhaps someone thought Dean was Micky's love child. But even so, why kill Micky's father? Was James Smythe being blackmailed? Threatened with a family scandal? Well, there were a couple of things that belied that. For a start, the police had looked for anomalies in Smythe's financial records and had found none. Secondly, Smythe didn't sound like a man who could be blackmailed. And thirdly, that *still* gave no motive for killing Smythe. Rather the opposite, in fact. It would make more sense for Smythe to kill the blackmailer than for the extortionist to do away with the goose that laid the golden egg. Gravitt sighed. Never had he been so stymied. And yet he thought he was beginning to sense a glimmer of what might be the truth, if only he could find some hard evidence.

Chapter Twelve

It was now a full month since the murder of James Michael Smythe II. The police were no nearer to solving the crime than they ever had been. The case was still open, but Gravitt and Bateman (now proudly Detective Sergeant Bateman) were also investigating another homicide.

Micky and Netty maintained their new understanding and were making plans to apply for legal custody of Dean. The day after their reconciliation they went down to Frittenden, taking Jenny with them. At Micky's insistence, they loaded the car with his bass fiddle, Netty's violin and Jenny's toy xylophone. Netty liked Dean immediately, and Dean certainly liked her. In the middle of a virtually unrecognisable Swanee River, Dean suddenly turned to Netty and said, "I wish my ma were like you," and receiving a nod from both Micky and Nan, she replied, "I could be your mama, if you'd like that."

"Boy, would I! Yippee!" Dean shouted for joy, jumping up and down in his chair with excitement. Jenny didn't understand, of course, but she thought jumping up and down was a good idea.

"Yippee!" she mimicked.

After the children were in bed, Micky, Netty and Nan talked the situation through. The first obstacle was Doris. "If you will let me," offered Netty, "I'll telephone her right now. I'm sure I can persuade her." She wore a mischievous grin. She dialled the number.

"Doris, darling, is that you?" Oh, the accent was *very* snobbish! "It's Netty here, love. Are you well?...You'll never guess where I am...Oh, do have a guess...You can't?....I'm in Frittenden. (Even Micky and Nan heard Doris' screech. Netty had to hold the phone away from her ear or risk permanent otic damage.)...Yes, I'm with your mother...I've been here all day, playing music with your son. He's quite talented, you know...Darling, I was really ringing to ask if you'd like to be on the committee for the Christmas Ball. The Mayor will be there, and his wife is on the committee, you know...You would? That's splendid!...While I have you on the phone, Doris darling, let me talk about something else. It's rather personal...Yes, I know you wouldn't tell a soul...I'm not able to have any more children...Yes, it is terrible; I knew you would understand...Micky always wanted a son...Yes, I wouldn't confide in you if I didn't trust you *implicitly*...The thing is, Micky and Dean have taken a great shine to each other; I know Dean doesn't live with you...Yes, a woman sacrifices *so much* for a man!...I understand perfectly...Doris, dear, I have the perfect solution: why don't you let Dean come and live with us?...Of course it's a huge sacrifice on your part. I know you love him dearly—one is always fondest of the first child...Perhaps you'd like to come for tea one day and tell me all about his childhood; bring photos, too, if you like...You could? That's grand! I'll set the adoption procedure in motion immediately...You're a very kind and selfless person, Doris darling. Ta ra."

When she hung up the phone, Netty doubled over in fits of laughter. "That was too easy, too easy!" She looked at the two gaping mouths. "Why do you both look so surprised? Did you not realise it was an ideal solution for her? She has a husband who doesn't want another man's child and a friend who does. Letting us have Dean absolves her of any allegations of negligence and in fact—in her eyes—enhances her image of generosity. Break out the champagne!" she demanded of Micky. "We now have a son!"

During the celebratory drink, Micky asked Nan if she minded

awfully if, when the adoption was completed, they came and lived with her. "Netty has been urging me to move out of London; in the busy season I will be able to stay nights in my father's—my stepmother's—house." And so the planning began. When Dean's school closed for half term, Nan and Dean would make a trip to London to meet Marge, Anne-Marie, and Greta and Bill.

Meanwhile, Gravitt was getting more and more involved with his Anushka. He may have been in a position in the Force to order his underlings about, but that was not the case in his personal life. He went out with Anne-Marie when she told him they were going out; he talked to her on the phone when she rang him; he made love to her when she demanded it. He learned that when she was painting she denied all personal feelings and relationships, and at these times he left her alone. In short, he was under her thumb and he liked it. In his eyes the relationship was progressing more than satisfactorily.

Half term was approaching and sleeping arrangements had to be made for the impending visit of Dean and his grandmother. It was agreed that Nan would occupy the spare room next to Marge. Micky asked Anne-Marie if she would allow him to set up a small divan in her workroom for Dean. As you can imagine, she was not happy about that idea! She fumed inwardly at the injustice. First, because of Micky she had been turfed out of the upstairs room with a skylight, and now once again Micky was usurping her work area. Had he no respect for her needs? Marge intervened before the situation blew up. "It's only temporary," she reminded Anne-Marie. "And when the adoption comes through they will move to Kent. When that happens, you can have your original workroom again, if you wish."

"I've got used to working where I am," was Anne-Marie's sulky reply. "And I don't want Micky to go to Kent. I want things to stay the way they are! And I don't want a nine-year-old child touching my canvasses."

"Did you know Dean is already showing an aptitude for art himself? You are probably going to find him in awe of you." That was a clever observation on Marge's part. Anne-Marie liked attention just as much as the rest of us. She gave permission for Dean to sleep in her workroom.

Nan and Dean arrived at the Smythe residence on Saturday morning; it was perfect autumn weather, warm in the daytime sun but chilly in the evenings. Marge welcomed them and ushered them into the lounge where all were waiting to meet the new additions to the family. Greta provided Danish pastries and other goodies because, as she put it, "Travelling makes you so hungry!" Dean quite agreed with her and helped himself to the largest pastry, casting a guilty look in Nan's direction.

While everyone was munching and talking, Dean sidled up to Anne-Marie and asked, "Are you the painter? May I see your drawings?"

"Of course," she answered, "but only if I can see *yours*." They headed for the stairs. "You'll be sleeping in my studio anyway, so you might as well bring your suitcase. I hope you don't object to the smell of oil paints!"

Dean was very impressed with Anne-Marie's paintings. To be honest, he didn't really understand her work; he had never seen modern art before. But he could tell there was something special, something almost primitive in her bold use of colours. He didn't know how to say that but he felt the emotion. "Wow!" was what he did say. It was enough.

He showed Anne-Marie the drawing that was going to appear in his school's brochure. The rest of the morning disappeared in deep technical discussions about dimensions and colours and the merits of oils versus watercolours. When they were summoned to lunch, Dean said, "I'm glad you're going to be my aunt," and slipped his hand into hers.

Harry and Doc Elliot came for lunch, as did Dean's mother, Doris. Doris had invited herself when she knew Dean and her mother were going to arrive that day. She had said that she wanted to see for herself that Dean was happy about things—a noble sentiment indeed, if true. Netty and Micky rather thought she was just using the opportunity for social climbing. Lunch was a simple affair of homemade asparagus soup followed by cold sliced chicken and salad. After lunch Dean played with his new sister while the adults milled around, chatting, discussing politics or local news, and generally enjoying the contentment of happily filled tummies and a day free from work stress.

Gravitt stopped by briefly about five o'clock to say hello to Dean and Nan. Micky had invited him, not Anne-Marie, so he wouldn't try to have a tête-à-tête with her, although he did hope to see her. He loved her so much! He asked Marge if he could have a quick word with Micky.

"Of course, Alex," she said. "I'm not sure where he is, but he's around somewhere."

But no one could find him. Gravitt felt his palms grow sweaty; he had that intuition that policemen get, that instinctive awareness of trouble. He tried not to let it show, but Netty noticed the stiffening of his shoulders, the tightening of the muscles around his mouth. When Gravitt began a room to room search, Netty was on his heels. But Micky was nowhere to be found. Gravitt was about to begin looking outside when Bill came in from the garden and beckoned to him. Netty unfortunately saw this.

"What is it?" she demanded. "Is it Micky? Tell me!"

Netty's voice was loud. Everyone stood still and listened. Bill turned red and clammed up. Gravitt took control.

"Please, everyone, stay here. That's an order. You too, Netty," he added as he saw the mulish set of her jaw.

"The hell you say!" She pushed her way forward.

Gravitt grabbed her arm and said, "I don't know what we will find, but I do know how easy it is to damage evidence. If you insist on coming, it will be with me." He surveyed the family until he spotted Marge. "Please keep everybody inside," he said. He then asked Dr. Winston to accompany him.

Bill led the way to the shed. Inside, lying face down on the floor with one leg tucked under his body, was Micky. His head had been nearly severed from behind and a knife was still sticking out of his neck. There was blood everywhere. Bill, not looking in the shed, apologised for adding to the mess. "I threw up," he stated baldly. "I never seen nothing like this before." Dr. Winston just managed to catch Netty as she fainted, easing her gently down to the ground. Then he too turned away to be sick.

Gravitt said, "There's no point in our going in there, he's clearly dead." He rang the station from his mobile phone and ushered the others back to the house, Bill carrying Netty.

Ha ha ha ha. Remember me? You don't know me—I don't know me. But I know you...

Chapter Thirteen

The SOCOs arrived almost immediately followed by Sergeants Bateman and Wilcox, both of whom happened to be in the station when Gravitt's call came through. They located Gravitt near the shed waiting for the photographer to complete his work and for the Scene of Crime boys to finish looking for fingerprints, footprints and other useful clues. Just as they reached him, one of the technical officers approached.

"It's a sickle, sir, not an ordinary knife. By the looks of it, he was in a kneeling position when someone came from behind and dealt one blow. It was expertly done in one sense: the blow was angled so that most of the blood erupted away from the attacker. On the other hand, one would assume the victim was meant to be completely beheaded, and the blow wasn't quite strong enough for that."

"Was the sickle sharp?" asked Gravitt.

"Oh yes, sir. Very sharp."

"Could a woman have dealt a strong enough blow? Or a boy?"

"A woman could have done it because the swing would develop force as it lowered onto the kneeling victim; but not a child. There are too many tough bones in the neck. It would take a fairly strong woman, though. More likely a man, is my guess. But that's your department,

I'm happy to say. Death would have been instantaneous; he never knew what happened to him."

"Thank God for that!" Gravitt expostulated. He was remembering stories about bygone eras when executioners were paid by the condemned to do the job properly because two or three attempts at beheading meant unbearable agony.

"There's also some protective clothing which has blood on it. There is only one set of fingerprints, and my guess is, they're the gardener's. I can check when I get back to the lab. We still have everyone's prints from the last murder."

"What is the clothing?" asked Wilcox.

"Wellingtons, overalls and an anorak."

"No gloves?" queried Gravitt.

"None that look like they were used in the murder. No blood."

"Can you give me a time of death?"

"Only roughly. I know, I know," he said when he saw the unsatisfied look on Gravitt's face. "I can give a better answer after I run some tests. For now all I can say officially is that death probably occurred between 2 and 5 pm. Unofficially I would say closer to 4.30 or 5. The blood is still tacky even where it's not very thick. Analysing the stomach contents will help to give a more accurate time of death."

Gravitt looked at Wilcox and Bateman. "We may be able to pinpoint the time by asking the right questions. We need to know when lunch ended and who was the last person to see Micky Smythe. Wilcox, you start with that, please. And get prints from Nan and Doris; we have everyone else's. Bateman, you could begin with questioning the neighbours; we mustn't forget that this may not be, after all, a domestic crime. See if you can find anybody who might have seen someone creeping along the back way. I will talk to Bill. I think I will take him for a drink, get him off the premises. If he's not where he can be seen by the family, he may talk a little more freely."

Bateman headed off towards the street and Gravitt and Wilcox went into the house accompanied by two of the SOCOs. Netty was on the sofa sobbing uncontrollably, clinging onto Marge who was also crying. Nan was holding Dean and Jenny tightly. Doris had shed her airs and graces and looked scared. Anne-Marie was shivering and staring into space, saying, "Not again. Not again. Not again."

Dr. Winston, distraught himself, was rubbing her cold hands and talking gently to her. He was saying, "Come back to us, Anne-Marie, come back to us." Harry was sitting alone, tears streaming down his face. Greta and Bill were holding onto each other. Gravitt sighed; another emotional scene.

He sent the technicians upstairs to look for any inconsistencies and gestured to Wilcox to join him in the kitchen to make strong hot tea and coffee. Greta stirred herself enough to get the brandy. Gravitt's first concern was the children, and he encouraged Dean and Jenny to take a sip of much diluted brandy. Wilcox handed a glass to Marge, suggesting that she try to get Netty to drink it. One by one the two detectives handed brandy to everyone present, like rescuers in the aftermath of an earthquake. By the time they had restored at least the façade of normality, Bateman had returned from his door to door questioning. "Nobody noticed anything out of the ordinary," he reported. "And this being Saturday, most people were at home. Some were even outdoors, and they swear no one approached this house. Bill was working in a garden three doors down and might have seen something."

Wilcox positioned himself in the middle of the room and said, "I know this is a terrible trial for you all, but I would like to ask a few questions now. He turned to Nan. "You and your grandson arrived this morning, is that right?" She nodded. "What time would that have been?"

"We caught an early train which got into Charing Cross Station just after nine-thirty. Then we took a taxi here. It didn't take long, we were here by ten."

"And we had Danish pastries and Micky introduced us to our new family," put in Dean. "Now Micky won't be my father," and he started to cry.

Netty held her hand out to Dean. "But I can still be your mother and we can live together, you, Nan, Jenny and me," she offered.

131

"We can talk about that later," Nan said firmly. "Not now. I'm taking Dean back to Frittenden immediately." Nan stood up.

"I'm afraid you can't leave just yet, Mrs. Yates. Please sit down again. These questions are for everybody." Gravitt was adamant.

Doris suddenly spoke up. "That's *my* child everybody is trying to keep. *My* child! I won't leave him in a house of murderers. How could you, Mom!" She turned to face her Mother. "How could you be so careless with him?"

"Later, Doris, not now. We'll talk about this when we're alone."

"We won't talk about it at all. Dean is my son and he will live with me from now on."

"I want to stay with Nan!" Dean screamed. "And I want Netty to be my mother! Micky didn't like you and I don't like you either!" and he threw his arms around his grandmother.

"Well *really*!" huffed Doris. "We'll see about that!"

"Please!" interjected Gravitt. "Please, all of you, please shut up. Sergeant Wilcox has some important questions to ask."

"Mr. Gravitt, nothing but nothing is as important as my child."

"Mrs. Wainthrop, if you aren't more co-operative, I will instruct Social Services to take Dean into care."

Doris opened her mouth, took one look at Gravitt's face, and closed it again. Gravitt nodded to Wilcox to resume the questioning.

"Now then," Wilcox said. "Were you all together when Dean and Mrs. Yates arrived?"

Marge answered. "No, just the immediate family was here. Harry, Doris and Elliot arrived for lunch."

"Those of you who were here at ten: were you together all the time?"

"Anne-Marie showed me some of her paintings upstairs, and I showed her some of mine," replied Dean. "She's a real artist, you know. We spent the morning talking about stuff. She knows everything!!"

The mention of her art brought Anne-Marie out of her stupor. She nodded in agreement. "Yes, that's right. We discussed proportions and colour contrasts. Oh, is it true? Is M...is Mickey really...is it...?"

Winston took her hands again. "Don't think about it, sweetheart. It's nice to see some colour return to your cheeks." He handed her the brandy. "You just sit there and sip this." Fortunately the glass was not full; her hands were shaking violently. Gravitt wanted to take her in his arms and hold her closely until she stopped shivering, but of course he couldn't do that. He realised that he was jealous of Dr. Winston's familiar manner.

Greta said, "Everyone else was in the sitting room. Bill and I also came in to meet the newcomers. Lunch was at one, like usual. I believe I told you before that lunch is at one."

"And where were you and your husband the rest of the time?"

"My wife was in the kitchen and Saturday is my day to work at the Henderson's—three houses down," Bill responded.

Bateman corroborated this. "He was there all day. Mr. Henderson had him digging a flowerbed."

Wilcox carried on with his questioning. "Was Micky with you at lunch?"

This time Netty answered. "Yes, we were all there, including Doris, Elliot and Harry. We lingered longer than usual. Well, it was a special occasion."

"What happened after lunch? Who left the table first?"

Marge said, "We all got up at the same time. We returned to the sitting room but we broke into smaller groups. I remember seeing Dean playing with Jenny. I talked with Nan for a while, and with Harry and then with Doris, but I can't honestly remember how long I was with them, or what the others were doing at the time."

"Did you happen to notice what Micky was doing?" Marge shook her head.

Netty answered. "Micky and I talked together immediately after lunch. We were thrilled with how seemingly right everything was. It was as though Nan and Dean had always been part of the family." She dropped her head into her hands and her shoulders shook with silent sobbing.

"Who else talked with Micky after lunch?"

"I did," said Dean, "and Anne-Marie did—they went upstairs together. And my mother did; my real mother, I mean."

"That's very helpful, Dean," Wilcox praised. "I don't suppose you remember who was talking to him last, do you?"

Dean screwed up his face in thought, but he couldn't remember. "I went with Netty and Jenny and Ma for a little walk, then I helped Jenny to go to sleep by telling her stories. She's not bad, for a girl."

"I spoke with him too," volunteered Harry. "He asked me how my job was going. I saw him go upstairs with Anne-Marie, but I got to talking with Dr. Winston and I never saw them come down again."

Wilcox and Gravitt looked towards Anne-Marie, who flushed. "I asked Micky to help me move a damp canvas from my studio, where Dean is staying, to my bedroom. I stayed up there to work on it a bit and I forgot about Micky. I guess I just assumed he would rejoin the party." Her face clouded and the blank stare returned to her eyes. "Doc Elliot," she pleaded hoarsely, "Is it true? Please tell me it isn't true."

"Hush, child. Don't think about it." Winston encouraged her to drink some more of the brandy.

Harry said, "That was about three o'clock or half past. Not later, because some of us gravitated into the study where the cheese and port was laid out. I don't remember seeing Micky there." No one else did either.

While this discussion was going on, Gravitt approached Bill privately. "It must have been horrible for you, finding the body. I imagine you could stand to get away from here for a while. Let me buy you a pint at the pub. Wilcox and Bateman can handle things here." Bill nodded gratefully and followed Gravitt out of the house. They walked to Hampstead High Street and managed to find a pub with somewhere to sit, quite surprising for a Saturday evening in such a popular area. Of course, it was still quite early.

It was Bill who first broached the subject in both their minds. "When Mr. James was murdered, I tried to convince myself that the murder was committed by someone outside the family," he said. "But now this! It's a dangerous house."

"You told me you've lived there since you and Greta married. Is that right?"

"Yes sir, fourteen or fifteen years now. It will be a wrench to leave, but we can't stay there any longer."

"What will you do?"

"Well sir…"

"My name is Alex."

Bill grinned. "I ain't never called a policeman by his first name before. Well, Alex, we have some savings, and what with the money Greta was left by Mr. James, I reckon we can buy a little place in the country. I'm a good labourer, I'll find some work."

"You obviously know the family very well. Can you tell me anything, anything at all, that seems out of the ordinary to you?" Gravitt saw Bill's face close up and added, "They're such nice people. I have to find the killer before anyone else gets hurt." Bill nodded. "Let's start by looking at the two victims. What similarities do they have?"

"They're both men."

"Yes. What else?"

"They have the same name."

"Yes, and they occupied the same position in the family when they were murdered." Bill looked blank. "They were both, in a sense, the head of the family."

"Rather an old-fashioned notion nowadays," countered Bill. "But true as far as it goes."

"Are there any other similarities?"

"None that I can think of. There are a lot of differences."

"Go on," encouraged Gravitt. "This is just what I need."

"Well, sir—Alex—Mr. James was in books and Mr. Micky was in music."

"But both books and music are artistic occupations. Let's go into that for a moment. Who else works in an artistic field?"

"Mrs. Netty, she's a musician. You don't suppose, I mean… sometimes having a baby can unbalance a woman. I've read that."

"Uh huh. We won't jump to conclusions, but let's look at her more closely. She wanted to move into a house of her own, didn't she." It was not really a question, and Bill stayed silent. "Who or what stopped her?"

"Mr. James liked having his family around him, and he offered them free accommodation; but he couldn't force them to stay."

"Maybe not, but money is a powerful influence. We won't rely on that as a strong motive for murder, but perhaps a factor nonetheless. Were there any other obstacles?"

"Mr. Micky didn't want to leave." Bill paused. "James and Micky didn't want them to leave the house, and they're both dead."

"Careful, Bill, don't rush to any conclusions. After all, they weren't prisoners. Besides, Micky had agreed to move to Kent; he wanted to adopt Dean."

"That would still mean living in someone else's house. If they lived with Mrs. Yates, that is."

"True."

They sipped their drinks in silence, each weighing up the pros and cons of Netty in the role of a killer. Bill added, "Mr. Micky looked like he had been executed. She might have felt that way. Trouble is, she looked really upset when she saw him and she fainted, you remember." They finished their drinks and Gravitt bought another round.

"Who else is in something to do with the arts?" picked up Gravitt.

"Miss Anne-M is, sir." Bill stared closely at Gravitt; he was as aware as everyone else that Gravitt was emotionally involved with Mr. James' youngest child. Gravitt avoided Bill's eyes.

"Yes, she's quite an artist. In what way, no matter how far-fetched it may seem, could she have resented her father?"

"Well, sir, I can see two roads here. One, he was very protective of her, too much so, I think. He didn't really give her any freedom when she was a teenager. And two, he made her give up her studio on the top floor when Mr. Micky's wife had a baby. She—Miss Anne—threw quite a tantrum about that."

"Okay, not strong motives for murder, but just as strong as Netty's. Look at your first suggestion; I wasn't around then, so I'm dependent on what you tell me. Anne-Marie is twenty-three now, no longer a teenager. Did James let her go out more as she got older?"

"Yes, though I think he was still worried about her. Mrs. Marge was always arguing that it was unnatural for a pretty young girl to stay at home on a Saturday night. Oh, Mr. James was less restrictive when she went to art school, too."

"Okay, point two: Anne-Marie must have known that her brother was planning to move to Kent with his family. She knew she could have her original studio back."

"That was the funny thing. Greta told me she overheard Miss Anne say that she didn't want to change studios again, that she wanted things to stay as they are. Were. She wanted Micky to stay."

"If she loved him so much that she didn't want him to leave, why kill him? He's gone forever now."

"Maybe she executed him because he *was* planning to leave the family. Maybe in her eyes he's not gone forever but is here forever." Bill was being deliberately provocative; he wanted to see how biased Gravitt might be.

But whatever his shortcomings might be, Gravitt was a cop, first and foremost. He said, "Okay, I hear what you say. It would seem an extreme reaction, especially as she could go visit him. She would even probably like painting a country scene or two. But it's perhaps just as valid a motive as we have for Netty."

"Although it's hard to believe she faked her grief at her brother's death," commented Bill. "She seemed really upset. Even more so than Mrs. Netty."

There was a pause while each man mulled over the idea of Anne-Marie committing such an atrocious act against her brother, and then Bill said, "Mr. Harry is in books."

"So he is. Can you think of a motive for him?"

"Only a mercenary one, and maybe jealousy. His mother, Mr. James' sister, married badly. Her husband spent money faster than they earned it. Harry might have resented the fact that this family had so much and his had so little. He was invited here for Sunday dinners, but he seldom came. Or maybe he just felt out of place surrounded by so much wealth."

"James gave him a job that he loves. Why bite the hand that feeds you?"

"Mr. James gave Harry a job, but at the bottom. Seems to me that

Harry had to prove himself more than the other workers in order to be noticed."

"But that way no one could accuse Harry of not deserving his rewards."

Bill emptied his glass. "If Harry saw it like that. He's a strange one, keeps to himself. He doesn't appear to have any mates or girlfriends. Loneliness can lead to all sorts of contorted thinking."

"As you say, loneliness can be deadly," Gravitt agreed, immediately wishing he had not used the word 'deadly.' "But greed can also be a driving force. I assume that since the required thirty days have passed, Netty receives James' share of the estate." Bill recognised that Gravitt was thinking out loud and kept his mouth shut. "Now for Marge or Anne-Marie to gain financially from Micky's death, the murder would have had to take place at least a few days ago. That's a strike against Netty. I'll have to check her accounts. I have to see if Micky left a will. Marge seems to have been within someone's sight most of the afternoon, but I need some confirmation that Anne-Marie was really in her studio. I'll need to know more about Dr. Winston and Doris. They seem unlikely, but I need to eliminate them." He glanced at his watch. "We'd better be getting back," he said to Bill. "You've been very helpful."

Chapter Fourteen

When Gravitt and Bill re-entered the house in Reddington Gardens, they found a full-blown argument going on. Doris was demanding the right to leave and she wanted to take Dean with her. Nan wished to return home and she wanted to take Dean back to Kent with her. Dean kept saying to Doris, "You're not my mother, you're not my mother!" Jenny was crying. Marge was trying to calm Jenny and Netty was trying to quieten Dean, and both women were crying themselves. Anne-Marie, Harry and Dr. Winston were looking on in amazement. Wilcox and Bateman had obviously given up trying to restore order and were letting the situation play itself out. Bill gave Gravitt a wry grin and scarpered down to his basement flat.

Gravitt reached in his pocket, found a police whistle and blew it loudly. Everybody stopped. "I've always wanted to do that," he said boyishly. The three onlookers, Anne-Marie, Harry and Winston, gave little smiles. "Now, I don't want to force anyone to stay in this house who doesn't want to be here, but I can't let any of you go very far. There's a bed and breakfast place nearby, and I suggest that you, Mrs. Yates, go there with Dean and Doris. Bateman will ring about availability." Bateman immediately went into the study to telephone before any objections could be raised. When he returned to say that rooms had been booked, Gravitt informed the three that they were not to try to leave the hotel; a detective constable would be on duty just outside.

Doris sucked in her breath sharply. "Do you mean we're under *arrest*?" she squeaked.

"The officer will be there for your protection," replied Gravitt. "But you are all suspects in a murder investigation."

"Me, too, Alex?" asked Anne-Marie.

"All of you, I'm afraid," was the answer. "DS Bateman will remain here tonight."

"Tough luck," Harry said to Doris, smirking. "You only get a constable; we get a sergeant." He turned to Gravitt and asked, "I presume I am to stay here?"

"Please. Dr. Winston, you may return home if you wish, but I would be grateful if you stayed. In case of any hysteria." Winston nodded. "I'll sleep on the sofa here in the lounge."

The telephone rang; it was for Gravitt. While Gravitt was in the study, Greta approached Marge and handed her a letter of resignation. "I'm sorry to do this, but I can't work here any longer," she explained. "I'll work out my two weeks notice but that's all."

"Oh, Greta, I'm so sorry," Marge said, throwing her arms around the faithful servant. "I can't imagine how we will cope without you!"

Anne-Marie was more vociferous. "No, Greta," she wailed. "You've been here since before I was born! You knew my mother; who will talk to me about her now? You're the only one left in the family who knew her. My childhood is being stolen from me!" and she grabbed hold of Greta's arm, rebuffing all attempts to make her let go.

Gravitt returned in time to hear Anne-Marie's outburst. His jaw gaped. Is *that* the connection between the murders? he asked himself. Is somebody carrying out the execution of those connected with Katherine Smythe? If so, would Anne-Marie be targeted as the next victim? God forbid!

Dr. Winston put his hands on Anne-Marie's shoulders and said in a calm, almost droning voice, "Now, sweetheart, that's not true. I knew your mother and so did Harry. We'll talk to you about her whenever you wish." Harry squirmed and turned red.

Here's something else to consider, thought Gravitt. Was Harry so resentful of Anne-Marie's rejection a few years ago that he wanted to make her suffer? Oh, yes, he knew about that spurned kiss. Anne-Marie had told him. If so, Harry would have to be unhinged, mentally. But then, anyone who could commit two such abominable murders was certainly deranged. And clever. Harry may not have received a university education, but he was not lacking in intelligence.

Under the doctor's gentle concern, Anne-Marie began to relax. She released Greta and went to stand in front of Gravitt. She laid her hand lightly on his cheek and said softly, "When this is all over, we can be together forever, can't we, Alex? I'm growing up fast."

His heart skipped a beat and he didn't care who was watching. "Yes, forever," he replied. "Go to bed now and try to get some sleep." He addressed himself to everyone in the room. "All of you. Try to get some sleep." To Marge he said, "Wilcox, Bateman and I will use the study for a little while. We'll try not to disturb you when we leave."

Ensconced in the study, Gravitt told his colleagues about his telephone call from the lab. "Death was between four and five in the afternoon. Micky was either kneeling, as if praying or pleading, or—more likely, I think—he was looking for something on the floor of the shed when the killer struck him from behind. That would seem to indicate that he knew his attacker and trusted him or her."

"What might he have been looking for?" queried Bateman. "Did the SOCOs find anything when they searched the shed?"

"No, nothing at all. Bill kept the shed tidy and nothing seems to have been out of place. The blood on the gardener's clothing was Micky's. I think we all anticipated that."

"The gloves?"

"They haven't turned up. Not in the shed, not in the garden, not in the house. Not in the local public bins. Not in neighbours' bins, either. They seem to have disappeared."

Gravitt told the officers about his informative chat with Bill. "Here's what we came up with; it's pretty weak in places:

"First, Netty. She wanted to move house, both James and Micky wanted her to stay in Hampstead. James called the shots financially when he was alive. Wilcox, will you look into Netty's finances, please?" Wilcox made a note. "Also, could you find out which hospital she was in when she gave birth to Jenny and see if she suffered from post-natal depression? I know, it's a long shot. Everything we've got is a long shot. Talk to her friends in the orchestra, see if she resented giving up playing to have a baby.

"Next, Anne-Marie. Her studio was shunted around by both her father and her brother when it suited them. I gather she took it hard at the time. We did quite a lot of research into her childhood after the first murder, but Bateman, please study those reports and see if we missed anything. Her father was over-protective; was her brother?" Bateman nodded. He was pleased that his superior was wise enough not to do the search on the girl himself.

"Harry," continued Gravitt. "The poor relation. Spurned by his beautiful cousin and working for his uncle in a lowly position. Was he jealous? Did he feel ill-used? How well did he know Anne-Marie's mother? Could he—or, for that matter, any of the others—be waging some sort of vendetta against Katherine's close relatives, or because of her in any way?

"That's as far as Bill and I got. There's Marge to check out for possible motives. Wilcox, you might see if Netty can be drawn out on that subject; I'll chat with Greta. I'll also look into Dr. Winston; I'll talk to his colleagues and some of his former patients."

"What about Doris and Mrs. Yates?" asked Wilcox.

"I think they're unlikely to be involved. Let's see how we get on with the family first, and then we'll tackle them.

"That covers motives. Bear in mind that both victims were male, had the same name, and were head of the family at the time of death. And both were close to Katherine. How did you get on with alibis?"

"Everybody is clear until about three, but of course we know now that the crucial time is four to five. Micky was last seen going upstairs with Anne-Marie about three, but no one saw either of them return. Of course, we know Micky came down at some point, but Anne-Marie says she stayed in her room to paint. And according to the lab people, her canvas did have fresh paint on it. That would seem to back up her story, but it's not necessarily conclusive," answered Bateman.

"And it's damned odd how this family never notices time!" exploded Wilcox. "Everyone seems to have some point during the afternoon unaccounted for. Even Greta wasn't much help. She finished washing the lunch dishes about three and then she went down to her own flat for a while. Anybody could have gone out the back door to the shed after three and not been noticed."

Chapter Fifteen

The next morning, while Gravitt was discussing the case with the Superintendent, Wilcox was carrying out his allotted tasks. A trip to Netty's accountant, fortunately the same as Micky's, provided him with copies of their Inland Revenue tax returns for the last three years. There was no shortage of money! The lack of any household expenses had indeed allowed them to accrue an extremely healthy bank balance and several long-term savings plans.

Wilcox next paid a visit to Netty's doctor, who was extremely reticent about divulging any information at first. He had to assure her that he would return with a court order if she refused to be helpful.

"Okay, Sergeant; just how much do you know about female fertility problems?" Wilcox blushed. "Do you have children yourself?"

"No, ma'am, I'm not married."

"Not that that's preclusive," Dr. Hopkins commented with only the merest hint of sarcasm in her voice. She brushed a wisp of hair from her face in the manner of Miss Piggy. But while her hair resembled the Muppet star's coiffeur in its colour and cut, there the similarity ended. Dr. Hopkins was tall and slender and quite, well, not exactly beautiful, but certainly fetching. "I presume you know next to nothing, then," she remarked resignedly. "The most common cause of infertility in women is endometriosis, but it is not the only cause. I won't bore you with the details, I doubt they would mean much to you. Suffice it to say it is a pregnancy that takes place outside the uterus. Mrs. Smythe exhibited some of the symptoms of endometriosis, painful intercourse and gastric complaints such as diarrhoea and nausea, but there was no history of similar problems in her relatives. That particular disorder does seem to run in families. There are several other diseases with more or less the same symptoms. Pelvic Inflammatory Disease, for instance. In Mrs. Smythe's case, actually, there were several things against the chances of her getting pregnant; there were abnormalities in the thyroid gland for a start, and she was under stress in both her career and her home life, all of which affect ovulation. It is quite amazing that she had a child at all, especially one which she managed to carry to completion!"

"Can you tell me the cause of the stress?"

"I gather her job with the English Philharmonia held no security, and in order to protect the foetus she gave the position up, knowing that she might not be able to get it back should the pregnancy abort. And she told me that her husband wanted children; she had not told him it was unlikely she could conceive. That preyed upon her mind a great deal."

"What about post-natal depression?"

"What about it indeed? Nobody really knows what causes it, although it is fairly common after the first baby and with those women who don't have much support from their families. Hormonal changes after birth are certainly a factor."

"How long would you expect it to last?"

"For the average woman, not very long. In Netty's case it was quite severe. She was exhausted all the time which made her feel guilty."

"Guilty? Why guilty?"

"She felt she was letting the baby down by being tired, so she insisted on taking care of it by herself to prove she was a good mother— which made her more tired. And keeping the care of the baby all to herself alienated her husband, who felt left out. It was a vicious circle."

"Could a woman commit murder because of post-natal depression?"

"Well, yes, I suppose so. But Sergeant, Mrs. Smythe looked much better the last time I saw her. She told me she was sharing the work with her husband now and that they were going to adopt a young boy. She also said they might move to the country. That doesn't sound like a woman in a murderous frame of mind to me."

Sergeant Wilcox stood up. "Thank you for your time," he said politely.

"You're welcome. Just pull the door shut behind you, please." But Wilcox continued to stand by his chair, looking at the doctor. "Is there something else, Sergeant?" she asked.

"Yes ma'am, there is." Wilcox shifted nervously. "I wondered if you'd have dinner with me this evening?"

"Why Sergeant, how nice! If I can get a babysitter at such short notice, I'd love to."

Wilcox was startled. "Oh I'm sorry," he apologised. "I saw you weren't wearing a ring and I assumed you weren't married." He fidgeted uncomfortably.

"I'm not married. I'm a single parent," she said bluntly. "Does that put you off, or does the invitation still stand?"

"Yes ma'am, please. I'm not really such an old fogy." They smiled at each other and he took her telephone number, promising to ring her later.

On the same morning, Bateman was sitting in a stuffy room studying the reports on Anne-Marie. What a little spoilt brat she had been! Probably the name calling episodes had been good for her; at least she had the gumption to fight for her right to be clever. Bateman couldn't find any holes in the reports, so he decided to go and talk with her himself. He wanted to form his own opinion of her and to ask for more details of her mother.

When he arrived at the Smythe's house, Anne-Marie was in her bedroom working on the painting that Micky had moved for her the day before. At his own suggestion, Bateman went upstairs rather than asking her to come down. He was interested in seeing her artwork. It was certainly startling! Big swirls of red and yellow covered most of the canvas, with streaks of black and grey bolting through, apparently at random. In many places the oils were applied thickly while elsewhere the paint was applied so thinly that it gave the sense of an underpainting. Bateman could see Anne-Marie's mastery, but he didn't like this picture. The longer he looked at it, the more it gripped him; and the more it gripped him, the less he liked it. The painting seemed to be looking at him, reading his thoughts. "My god, it's alive!" he breathed.

"I call it *Soul*," Anne-Marie told him. "I'm painting it for my mother and for my father and for my brother. They're all gone now, you know," and she sat on the edge of her bed and stared blankly at the painting. Bateman stood watching her, suspiciously at first and then with real pity as he saw her body beginning to tremble. He went to the door and shouted for Dr. Winston.

Winston was making himself a cup of tea when he heard Bateman's call. Not another murder! was his first thought, and he shot upstairs like a man half his age. He took in the scene immediately and put his arms around his best friend's daughter, saying, "That's right, sweetheart, let the tears come. Get it out of your system." He laid her gently down and pulled a blanket over her to keep her warm. He asked Bateman to fetch his medical bag from the study, then gave Anne-Marie a mild sedative. When she drowsed, the two men crept out.

When the tea was in front of them, Bateman asked, "Did you see that painting? It's totally scary. 'I call it *Soul*,' she said. 'I'm painting it for my mother, my father and my brother. They're all gone now.' I tell you, it sent shivers up my spine!"

"If it sent shivers up your spine, you can imagine what it's doing to her. All of her immediate blood relatives are dead, and two of them have been murdered. Recently. She's probably wondering if she'll be next."

"You've known the family for years. Do you have any idea who can have such a fierce hatred for these people?"

"Don't think I haven't racked my brains trying to think of someone or something that could have led to this! But the truth is, James was a nice man, a fair man. And the son was as good as the father."

"What about Anne-Marie? She had trouble getting along with her peers in school. Could she have made a real enemy somewhere along the line?"

"That's your job, Sergeant. Go and find out."

"Yes, I will." Bateman decided to visit all of Anne-Marie's schools. If there was anything to be found, he would find it.

It was a busy morning! While the police were out and about, Nan and Doris, too tired to yell at each other any more, were having a much overdue mother-daughter talk.

"My concern was for Dean," Nan was saying. "You remarried so quickly! He didn't have time to finish grieving for his father when suddenly his mother was gone. I'm surprised that you were ready to remarry so soon."

"Oh, Mom. I suppose I should have confided in you, but I had made up my mind what I was going to do and I knew you would try to talk me out of it." Doris looked out the window at the traffic. "I loved Greg; he was charming and full of fun. But when he was told that he would be sent to Afghanistan within the month, he changed. I mean, I know war changes—even just the threat of it—changes people, but Greg became a different person altogether. It wasn't a war he believed in. He started drinking and gambling and he hit me several times. That was bad enough in itself, but he also got us into debt. Deeply in debt." Doris began pacing around the room. "I'll never forget one day in particular; I hadn't known about the gambling at that point. The drinking I knew about, but not the gambling. Two men, two ugly brutes, came to the door looking for him. I think they were going to—what's the phrase?— do him over. Beat him up. They pushed into the house looking for Greg, and when they couldn't find him, they looked at me and one of them said, 'This time we'll settle for that ring,' and he pointed to my engagement ring, 'but tell your husband next time we'll take his wife and child.' I gave them the ring."

"Oh, Doris, I'm so sorry! I had no idea you were going through something like that. Why didn't you come to me for help? Or go to the police?"

"Greg told me not to go to the police, and I couldn't tell you. It would only have worried you and there was nothing you could do." There was an awkward silence which neither woman knew how to end. Dean, listening behind the door, was afraid to breathe. Finally Doris continued, "You accused me once of hiding Dean in the country. Well, you were spot on; I *was* hiding him. I would have asked you to keep him even if I hadn't married again. Dean's safety was everything to me. Then when Arthur proposed, it seemed a good solution to my financial problems. He paid off Greg's debts. And I have learned to love him. It may not have been the most romantic of affairs, and Arthur may not be a dashing swashbuckler, but he cares for me. He makes me happy. When he heard I was going to let Dean be adopted, he suggested we bring him home to live with us. I was surprised because I thought Arthur didn't want Dean, but apparently I was wrong. He thought I was leaving Dean with you because that's what we, you, me and Dean, wanted. He said he had been hurt, really hurt, when I wouldn't share Dean with him and so he just kept his mouth shut. Am I making any sense? I seem to be babbling. Well anyway, leaving Dean in Kent *is* what I wanted, but not because I don't love my son. I do love him. And I wasn't trying to keep Arthur out of my personal life, either. I was just so afraid those men would come back."

There was another long pause, then Nan said, "That doesn't really explain why you visited him so rarely."

"I suppose I'd better tell you the rest. You haven't heard all of it yet." Doris cleared her throat. "At first I was afraid of being followed. There was one period when I kept seeing the same dark blue Ford behind me, wherever I went. I thought, let them grab me, but not my son. And then, too, you both seemed so happy. I was jealous! Especially when Micky was with you. It was as though the three of you belonged together." Doris hesitated. "How will Dean cope with losing a second father figure? He's only a child. He shouldn't have to lose two fathers at his age."

"Well," answered Nan, "he's getting his mother back, and that ought to be some compensation." Nan raised her voice. "Come in, Dean!" she invited, throwing the door open and revealing the skulking lad. "I know you've been listening. Come in and give us your thoughts on what you've heard."

Dean looked from his Nan to his mother. "I didn't know about Pa's gambling and drinking," he said. "You never let on." He looked squarely at his mother. "Can I have music and painting lessons, and can I visit Netty and Jenny? Can Nan live with us? Will I have to change schools? I like my school. They're going to put my drawing on their new leaflet, you know."

The three of them spent the rest of the day making plans.

The Inspector and his two sergeants met briefly for a pub lunch to compare information thus far gained, then Wilcox returned to Reddington Gardens to interview Netty. She said to him, "I know you went to see my accountant this morning, Sergeant. I hope you are now convinced that I didn't murder my husband for his money. All our assets are in joint names."

"Yes, ma'am. But I'd still like to see a copy of his will, if he left one."

"Then you'll have to talk to Mr. Frederick Collins of Collins, Collins, Harris and Collins," she replied. "He deals with all our legal affairs."

"Does he also deal with Marge Smythe's legal business?"

"You'll have to ask her." Oil would have frozen on her tongue.

Wilcox, in spite of his pedantic nature, was not an insensitive man. He was hurt by her tone of voice. "Please, Mrs. Smythe—Netty—I'm not trying to harass you. I'm trying to find your husband's murderer."

"Forgive me…John. I really don't know who acts for Marge." She smiled at him. "I'm glad we're finally on a first name basis."

"Can you think of anyone who disliked your husband or wanted him out of the way? A family member? Marge, for instance?"

"Certainly not Marge. Not anyone in this house. We've all lived together for several years without killing each other. I'm sorry, but I think the police are barking up the wrong tree. The murders have to have been committed by an outsider."

"But how, then, do you explain the slow dosing of arsenic to James?" Or the decapitation of Micky in the garden shed?"

Netty covered her face at the mention her husband's gruesome killing. "It seems to me," she said, her voice muffled by her hands, "that the arsenic could have been administered by anyone at work; his secretary, for instance. The police just assumed it was in the homeopathic tablets."

"The police have talked to Smythe's secretary, of course. But you're forgetting that the arsenic which actually killed him came from the shed."

"The shed! The shed!!" Netty exploded. "Everything happened because of that God-awful shed! I'll go and destroy it before it destroys anybody else!" She ran out of the study. Wilcox was on her heels, afraid of what she might do. He caught up with her in the kitchen and held her tightly while she heaved with great dry sobs. We should have a female constable on this case, he thought. Fortunately, Dr. Winston came in to see what all the commotion was about. He extricated Netty from Wilcox's arms and walked her into the lounge, murmuring soothingly. Whew, said Wilcox to himself, dealing with women is tricky; they always seem to need to be molly coddled. He decided to ask Gravitt if they could borrow a woman officer from another precinct!

Left to himself, Wilcox telephoned Collins' office and made an appointment for four o'clock. He contacted the orchestral manager and was given the names and telephone numbers of Netty's friends. The next hour passed quickly and did not really give him anything to build a case on. Netty was apparently quite popular and was certainly concerned about leaving her job, but it had been her choice to put the pregnancy first. Resentment? Of course not! A new life has to come before a job.

Wilcox arrived at the offices of Collins, Collins, Harris and Collins in good time. Frederick Collins showed him Micky's will. It had been made a couple of months after Micky met Dean. Short and to the point, Micky left everything to his wife with only a request for her to visit Dean herself and, if she liked him, put some money aside for his education. "My wife has excellent judgement," he wrote. "She will do whatever is right."

Chapter Sixteen

Detective Sergeant Ben Bateman began his afternoon interviews with a visit to Anne-Marie's former primary school. As is the way in London's schools, many of the staff had moved on to other positions, including the Headmistress. The current Headmistress was clearly annoyed by the disruption of her very busy day and informed the detective that she had no knowledge of students from fifteen or more years ago, and anyway, if those records still existed, she, for one, certainly didn't know where they were. An enterprising secretary was more helpful and guided Bateman down to a dusty storage room in the cellar, and together they managed to find the student files for the relevant years. Unfortunately, Anne-Marie's file did not really contain the kind of information Bateman was hoping to find. Oh, it mentioned the numerous detention periods for misbehaviour, but it was all too impersonal. He was careful to thank the secretary and moved on to the next school.

He ran into an identical situation there, but he did manage to find a librarian who remembered Anne-Marie. "She was too clever to be popular with her classmates, but she didn't seem to care. She kept her nose in a book. What subjects did she read about? Art, mostly; painters and painting."

So Bateman went on to the Academy of Art. Here, Anne-Marie was remembered well. The Principal proudly showed Bateman several of Anne-Marie's works that were hanging in prominent positions around the building. "She not only has the talent required to be a great artist, she also has the intelligence. You wouldn't believe, Mr. Bateman, how much talent gets wasted because it isn't backed up with the same amount of intellect."

"You found her a good student, then?" queried Bateman. "How did she get on with the other pupils? Was she popular?"

"She never gave us any problems. And yes, I was certainly aware of her difficulties fitting in at her previous schools when I agreed to her acceptance here. But we are a specialist institution, and she had a chance to mix with others interested in the same things that concerned her. She exhibited no behavioural problems with us."

"Did she form any amorous relationships or make any serious enemies?"

"Not that I'm aware of. I wouldn't particularly know those things, in any case. Our students are all over eighteen. We do, of course, provide pastoral care when it's required, but we don't force it on anyone. Anne-Marie lived at home. I would assume that if she had needed help or advice, her family would have seen to it."

Bateman returned to Reddington Gardens and asked to see Marge. Bateman was surprised at her changed appearance. My God, she looks ten years older, he thought. She was gaunt and stooped, and her voice was weak.

"How can I help you, Sergeant?" she asked.

"I won't keep you long," Bateman assured her. "I just need to clarify something. I know you said once that you felt James was over-protective of his daughter." Marge grimaced. "Did you feel Micky was as well? Please be open with me, Mrs. Smythe. I'm trying to help you," he added as he saw her eyes glaze over.

"To tell you the truth, Sergeant, I can't see that it would have mattered much one way or the other. Micky was away quite a lot of the time."

And that was certainly true, agreed Bateman.

Alex Gravitt, finally free to do some footwork himself, started his afternoon by interviewing Harry. He decided to take a less understanding approach this time and invited Harry to come to the station.

"I thought you might like to get some real experience of crime investigation," he said. "Something more than you can learn just by reading books. Please come with me into one of the interview rooms." Gravitt had chosen the smallest and dingiest room available; there were no windows, nor indeed any air vents.

"Normally there would be two officers in here and the interview would be taped," Gravitt explained. "Are you happy to be alone with me and unrecorded?" Harry looked confused. "Call it a trial run," Gravitt suggested. "I won't be able to use anything you say in court." So Harry agreed. He trusted Alex.

Gravitt turned his back on Harry and kept silent until he heard Harry fidgeting in his seat, then suddenly the detective rounded on him and demanded, "How does it feel to be the poor relation of such a wealthy family?"

"What?" Harry was surprised by Gravitt's condescending tone.

"Oh, come off it! You were living in a run-down area and your uncle and cousins were not far away living the life of Riley. Don't tell me it didn't bug you!" As Harry gawped stupidly, Gravitt dug the knife in deeper. "You have a father who loves you so much he kicked you out. You had a mother too weak to stand up for you. A rich uncle who could have made life easy for you but who instead gave you a job at the very bottom of the firm. Don't tell me you don't resent them. *All* of them. You hate your father for his weaknesses and despised your mother for her cowardice!" Gravitt was bending over Harry menacingly. "You hated your uncle for not doing more for you. Maybe you hated him so much that you killed him!"

"Stop it!" shouted Harry, jumping up.

"*Sit down!*" Gravitt pushed Harry back into his seat. "You hated Micky because he had the opportunity to develop his talent. Maybe you killed him, too! *Shut up!*" he bellowed when Harry tried to interrupt.

"Who's next, Harry? Who else do you resent that much? Will it be Anne-Marie? Because she rejected your advances and called you ugly?"

"Hideous! She called me hideous! Not ugly. Hideous! *That* was she word she used. Hideous!" Harry burst into tears. "Yes, I do hate them! I hate them all! My father is a waste of space! He never wanted me and he has never been a father to me. My mother always did everything he said and he still treated her like crap. I'm *glad* to be living on my own. I'm *glad* I don't have to see them anymore." He cried again, then said, "But I never killed anybody. I didn't hate Uncle James. I…I loved him! He gave me a job which I like. He encouraged me to read, and I like reading." He folded his arms on the table and put his head down.

"What about Micky?"

"I don't…didn't…like him much. I did resent him. He was attractive and I'm 'hideous.' He had money and I didn't. He got a good education and I got none. But I didn't kill him."

"Anne-Marie?"

"She's a bitch! Spoilt rich kid. She doesn't care for anyone but herself." Harry sneered at Gravitt. "You'll find out!" he threatened. "And then maybe *you'll* get pulled in for murder! She's no right to be so condemning. After all, it's only a trick of fate that made her pretty and rich and me ugly—hideous—and poor. It could have been the other way around."

"Harry, how well did you know Anne-Marie's mother, Katherine?"

" 'bout as well as I knew the rest of the family in those days. Which wasn't much. Mama alienated her father when she married Dad and it wasn't until he, my grandfather that is, died that regular family relations were resumed."

"Was she nice to you?"

"I suppose so. She was always sick."

"Did you like her?"

"I guess. As I said, I didn't know her very well. She died when I was nine."

Gravitt opened the door and called for two coffees. He said to Harry,

"I want to keep you here for a few days. I can't hold you officially because I'm not making a charge. Will you stay here voluntarily?"

"But I didn't kill anybody, I really didn't!"

"Actually, Harry, I think I believe you. But you are the only man left in the Smythe family and it's possible that keeping you here may save your life."

Harry looked frightened. "I hadn't thought of that! Do you really think someone is trying to get rid of all the men in the family?"

"It's one line we're exploring," Alex replied guardedly. "And then, of course, if the killer is you, then keeping you here may save someone else's life."

"I keep saying, I never killed anyone."

Part 3
(In the Year 1976)

Penelope Smythe had a secret. She was pregnant. At least she strongly suspected that she was 'in the family way.' She had just missed her second cycle, and she never had been irregular. Besides, the home pregnancy test was positive. She wanted the baby! After all, she was getting on in years; she was thirty-two. Her problem was that she wasn't sure who the father was. She knew it was one of only two men—she wasn't *that* promiscuous, after all!—but which one?

Leonard Cousins could be the father. Leonard was a well-educated man, a dentist. He loved her, but how much did she really love him? He treated her well, frequently bringing her flowers or charming little baubles. He would make a good father. But he was also, she confessed to herself, somewhat dry and humourless. There was no magic of spontaneity.

George Franklin, on the other hand, was full of surprises. He would take her to a lecture on politics one night and dancing the next. Despite his limited education, he held a job as sports coach in a respectable secondary school. He was tall, dark and ever so handsome. He also loved her. Would he make a good father? Probably. The drawback with George was his inability to hang onto money. If he had it, he spent it. And the earnings of a schoolteacher were small! George was already thirty-five and unlikely to better his position.

The odds were that the baby was George's. Leonard was generally careful to use a condom, but there had been a couple of occasions when the passion got the better of him. Her eyes warmed at the memory. Those had been special moments!

But suppose she married Leonard and the baby looked like George? Or the other way around? Penelope shuddered. She had a vision of Leonard as a blackbird with a wide wingspan saying to her, "You cuckoo! You chose the wrong nest!"

Both men had proposed to her. Neither knew of the existence of the other, and she doubted that either would want to marry her if they did. Especially if they knew there was doubt as to the paternity of the baby. If she married quickly, she might manage to get her husband to believe the baby was premature.

George would marry her tomorrow, but Penelope knew that Leonard wanted a large wedding with all the trimmings; that would take time to arrange. She had another vision of herself waddling down the aisle nine months pregnant and before she can say, "I do" the baby pops out and says, "I am."

She picked up the phone and rang George.

Within a week Penelope and George were married. Her father, James Michael Smythe Senior, was deeply hurt and shamed by his daughter's elopement. "No member of this family has ever behaved so badly," he declared, erroneously, as it happens. "I cannot recognise you as my daughter." He was not an uncaring man; indeed his charitable works were widely acknowledged. But he lived his own life to a strict moral code and he expected the same of his family.

Penelope moved into George's bachelor flat and set about turning it into a matrimonial home. There wasn't much space, but she was a clever homemaker. After six weeks had passed, Penelope put some champagne on ice, donned her prettiest dress, and awaited George's return from rugby practice with his students.

When George arrived home and saw the special preparations, he smiled to himself. "Don't move a muscle," he ordered. "I have to wash the sweat off or you won't be able to stand the pong!" He sang as he showered; Penelope rehearsed her speech for the umpteenth time.

George poured the champagne and asked, "What shall we toast?"

"How about the new addition to the family?"

"I knew it!" George bellowed, "I knew it!" He grabbed his wife and danced her around the room making up words to the Blue Danube waltz. "I'll be a father, Dad-dy, Dad-dy. He'll look just like me, you'll see, you'll see!" Then suddenly he stopped. "What am I doing? You have to take it easy! Sit down. Here, take this cushion. We have to take care of our son."

Penelope was relieved. "How long have you known?" she asked.

"Since you asked me to marry you. Oh, Penny darling! I'd been proposing to you for months and you always said no. There had to be some reason why you suddenly changed your mind." He laughed. "I've always wanted a son. I'll teach him to play ball. He'll be the greatest rugby player that ever was!"

"He could be a girl," she reminded him.

"Then she'll be the finest tennis player that ever lived," he responded happily. "And I'll build her the best doll house in the world."

The rest of the evening passed in a pleasant haze of planning. George would put aside a little of his income each month towards a larger flat; they would need more space now two were becoming three.

Six and a half months later Penelope gave birth to a baby boy. George was over the moon. He had spent the previous months bragging to his mates about how special his baby was going to be. Now he would be able to prove it. Penelope had suggested naming it George Harold, to honour her husband's late father. George was deeply touched by this gesture.

He was surprised that the newborn baby was red and wrinkled; pictures always showed babies with round chubby faces and big smiles. Perhaps in truth all babies are ugly, George speculated. He didn't have a lot of experience in this area. And probably all babies cry as much. Oh, well, if that's what he had to endure to have a son, then he would suffer it gladly. He got used to waking up every three hours to change a nappy or warm a bottle, and it made him feel important when he discovered that he could send Harry off to sleep just by singing to him. Fatherhood is hard, thought George, but it will be worth it.

Unfortunately, Harry seemed a sickly baby. When he was only a year old, George and Penelope took their son to the doctor because of his constant crying and because of some discolouration on his elbows and neck. "He has eczema," explained the doctor, bouncing a gurgling Harry on his knee. "He cries because his skin is itchy. Look here, there's a bit of it behind his knees as well as the places you've mentioned. You will have to keep his hands in mittens, taping them to his arms so he can't get them off. That will stop him from scratching and making the pain worse. Don't be alarmed," the doctor added as he saw the look of fear in both parents' eyes. "It's very common. They say as many as one out of every five school-age children has eczema." He gave them some advice on diet and assured them that their baby was as normal as any other.

When Harry was two, George had to accept the fact that Harry was never going to be beautiful. That was his first big disappointment. His son did not even have average looks; he was decidedly unattractive.

As Harry grew older, George tried to teach him to catch a ball. No matter how gently he threw the ball, Harry would run from it, screaming. George even tried rolling it along the ground, but still Harry screamed. That was George's second big disappointment. It was obvious Harry would not be a sportsman. George was having to do some growing up of his own. He learned to take pride in his son's achievements in school, such as they were. But his disappointment was deep, especially as no second child came along to ease the pain.

And then things got worse. George, now over forty-three, lost his job. "They accused me of making advances to a couple of the students!" he told his wife.

"What! How could they do that?" exclaimed Penny, disbelievingly.

"You know those two boys—did I tell you about them?—the ones who cause so much trouble; I've put them on report a couple of times. They went and told the Headmaster I touched them sexually when there was no one watching!"

"They weren't believed, surely?"

George sat down, depressed and angry. "I don't know. The Head said he couldn't risk a scandal like that, true or not. Apparently the school is in trouble, financially, and the Head said if there was even a small hint of 'unsavoury behaviour'—his words—they would probably close."

George stood up and began pacing back and forth, a worried frown on his face. "The Head also said they want teachers with qualifications, and of course I don't have any."

"You mean, several years of organising sports so successfully count for nothing?"

"Yeah, apparently not."

Penny was indignant. "Then you're better off out of there! I think it's absolutely disgusting that the Head would take the word of two boys, especially two boys with a history of trouble making, over you. You'll find a job with nicer people."

"Not in a school, I won't." As Penny's eyes rose in question, George added softly, "The Head won't give me a reference. Says he won't take the risk. He says he won't report it to the police if I leave quietly but he won't be a party to my getting another job with teenagers."

Penny mulled this over for a while and finally asked, "George, forgive me for asking this: you didn't really touch them, did you?"

George was furious. "Thank you, dear wife. Your trust in me is moving!"

Penny apologised profusely, naturally. But it didn't escape her notice that George had not answered her question. They spent the rest of the afternoon discussing possible avenues for George's sports talent, but a few enquiries soon informed him that experience was not enough. To obtain a job as a coach in a secondary school, he needed to hold a PGCE, the recognised Teacher's Training Certificate. George had no education beyond O-levels. The gymnasiums he contacted were uninterested because his experience did not include training on all the equipment. He felt old and useless. Poor George; he had always been an optimistic man. He was not used to depression and he didn't know how to handle it.

"It's early days yet," encouraged Penelope. "It's too soon to despair. At least we have our savings to tide us over."

"Savings? What on earth are you talking about?" sneered George. His mood was turning nastier as he had to accept the fact that he was a middle-aged man without a future.

"Why, the money you've been putting aside for a new flat," Penelope reminded him. "We can use that to live on until you find some work. We can stay here a little longer."

George laughed. It was not a pretty sound. He stood up, towering over his wife. "You fool!" he shouted. "How do you think we've managed to keep *this* flat on my income? There never were any savings." Her look of disbelief angered him even more. "How easy do you think it is to support a family of three? I'll tell you. It's not easy at all! Especially when one of the family—*you!*—think you're a member of high society and lie about all day doing nothing. Well, I'm very sorry, my little chickadee," he gave her a deep bow, "but when you married me you joined the working classes." He swept his arm round to include the whole flat. "What has it all been for? What did I get when I married you? Nothing but disappointment. A son who is ugly and clumsy and a wife who is lazy. The seven worst years of my life!" He raised his hand and slapped Penelope hard on the cheek. "Why don't *you* get a job and support *me* for a change!" He walked out.

Penelope was too stunned to cry, even though her face burned where George had hit her. She thought being a mother was a full time occupation, but of course George couldn't see that. And she did recognise the truth of some of his remarks. She had never been employed in her life. She would look for a job. She reached for the local newspaper and turned to the employment section. A few telephone calls soon convinced her that she had no skills to offer. But Penelope was nothing if not resourceful. She turned to the yellow pages and read the headings. Nurseries interested her; she knew about children at least. But she had no references and no official training, and no one would consider her as suitable for a job with youngsters. Finally she rang a Laundromat and was offered a position as manageress if she could start right away. The hours allowed her time to take Harry to school and collect him later. She took it.

George did not return home that night so the next morning she left a note explaining where she was and left with Harry. The new job was strange to her, but what she didn't know the customers did, and she soon got the hang of it. By the end of her stint, she was knackered, to say the least. When she reached home that afternoon, George was watching television. She sat beside him and slipped her hand into his. "I love you," she said softly.

"Where's my dinner?" was his only response.

Thus began a new era in Penelope's life, one of drudgery and loneliness and tiredness. She took Harry to school, went to the Laundromat, collected Harry, tidied the flat, cooked the dinner, then returned to the Laundromat for the evening shift. Was she unhappy? She was too exhausted to consider it. George read the paper while he ate and if she or Harry tried to talk, George told them to shut up. If she displeased him in any way, he hit her. He used her sexually when he wanted, but you could not call it lovemaking. There was no tenderness. Every month she handed him her paycheque; never once did he say thank you.

Penelope's father died shortly after this change in her life. He had cut her out of his will. The one good result of his death was the resumption of the friendship with her brother. But she never told him of her financial straits and she never went to see him. Harry, however, did occasionally visit his uncle. It was more to avoid his father than for fondness of any of the residents at Reddington Gardens. When his uncle's wife, Katherine, died, Harry more or less stopped visiting altogether.

Three more years passed without significant change in the lives of the Franklins. Then one day…

"Mrs. Franklin, can you hear me?" Penelope opened her eyes and through her blurred vision was just able to distinguish the white jacket of a man leaning over her.

"Get it off me!" she gasped. She tried to push the weight off her chest, but her arms were too heavy.

"Get what off of you, Mrs. Franklin?" asked the paramedic. "Do you think you can swallow this pill for me? It's only aspirin."

"The tree; it's crushing me," Penelope managed to whisper before losing consciousness. She never woke up. The heart attack was sudden and severe.

George's first reaction was disbelief. When the hospital rang to inform him of his wife's coronary, he said, "She's just a lazy cow. I'll come down to the hospital and you'll see how quickly she recovers!"

"I'm afraid there's no chance of a recovery, Mr. Franklin," responded the obviously disgusted Registrar. "She's dead." Grief and shock affect people in different ways, and normally the Registrar would not have been so brutally frank. But he had seen the bruises on Penelope's body and he was under no illusion as to how they got there. "You will have to come here and make a formal identification, and you also have to make arrangements for the body," he informed George coldly.

George arranged for Penelope's cremation to take place the following week, put a notice in the local paper and rang James. All of this he did in a haze, in a feeling of unreality. When Harry returned from school, he told him, "Your mother has had a heart attack. She won't be coming home again."

"What did you do, hit her too hard?" asked Harry with all the insolence of a twelve-year-old. George raised his arm to strike his son, thought better of it, and stormed out of the flat.

He returned late that night reeking of alcohol. Noticing the picture of his wife on the mantelpiece, he picked it up and stared at it, studying her image. He felt his gorge rising, years of anger and frustration bubbling up to the surface.

"How dare you leave me!" he shouted to the photograph. "Who the hell do you think you are? You think you can get even with me by just going away, don't you? You think to put me in my place because I couldn't get a job, I know you! Always the superior being. Listen to me, you bitch! Listen to me when I'm talking to you! Stop looking at me with those accusing eyes!" He flung the photo at the fireplace where the glass shattered into a hundred tiny fragments. "You can't get along without me, I know you can't." He swallowed a sob. "You need me, do you hear? You *need* me!" Another sob escaped from his mouth. "I need you. Penny, I need you." He was crying openly now. He picked up the remains of the photo and pressed it to his heart. He fell onto the settee clutching it tightly, folded his legs under him like a baby, and bawled.

The cremation was a simple affair. The music was pre-recorded, the address given by a minister who clearly had never met Penelope Franklin. Her brother James was there, as were Micky and Anne-Marie. A few customers from the Laundromat put in an appearance. And Leonard Cousins turned up.

"So you were my rival," he introduced himself to George, who looked bewildered. "I was dating Penelope—in fact, I expected to marry her myself—when she suddenly ran off with you."

"I didn't know Penny was seeing anybody else." George was astonished.

"Oh, yes indeed, she was certainly seeing me. For all I know she was seeing other men as well." Leonard had been deeply hurt at the time and still resented the way he had been dumped. He relished this opportunity to get even with the man who stole his girlfriend. "I was surprised [ahem] at how quickly you had a child. Only a few months after your elopement, wasn't it?"

George turned red. "Just exactly what are you saying?" he demanded. "If you are trying to slander my wife at her funeral, then I have to ask you to leave."

"Okay," Leonard agreed pleasantly. "Is that your son?" He pointed at Harry. "Doesn't look much like you, does he? I'm going, I'm going!"

Leonard left as quickly as he could while retaining some dignity. Oh, that opportunity to hurt his opponent was delicious!

Leonard did more damage than he realised. George and Harry had begun to develop a cautious friendship on the loss of the woman in their lives. From this moment on, George had no time for Harry. And so, when Harry completed his A-levels and was eventually given a job by his uncle, George kicked him out. Admittedly, Harry was an adult by then; but because of his repellent looks and his poor interview technique, he had been unable to obtain a position of any sort, despite his natural intelligence, until he, in desperation, approached his Uncle James.

Part 1
(Resumed)

Chapter Seventeen

After Gravitt left the station, with Harry locked up safely for the time being, he made his way to the hotel where Nan and Doris were staying. How he dreaded this meeting! If they had argued all night, at least their voices should be hoarse; that was one consolation.

He found both of them and Dean in the hotel's sitting room. Nobody was yelling and no one was complaining. Instead there was an occasional giggle or a muffled 'Oh dear, oh dear.' Nan was the first to spot Gravitt and said delightedly, "Oh good! We have a judge!"

"What's going on?" asked Gravitt, totally puzzled.

"We're having a cow drawing competition," explained Doris.

"Is that so! Well, I used to draw a pretty mean cow myself," bragged Gravitt, who had seldom even seen a live cow and certainly never drawn one.

"Oho! Put your pencil where your mouth is!" Nan challenged, handing Gravitt drawing materials.

And so Gravitt drew his first cow. "No peeping!" he warned Dean who was stretching his neck to see his competitor's work.

"I'm finished now," he finally announced, and all turned to study Gravitt's cow.

"These must be her legs," Dean offered tenuously.

"No, that's her udder," Gravitt explained patiently.

"But the udder is supposed to be *under* the cow!" Dean protested. "Is this her head?"

"No, that's a leg."

"But this cow is all upside down!"

"Well, naturally," Gravitt agreed. "My cow got so exhausted posing for so many artists that she's collapsed in a heap!"

Of course, Dean won the competition. Gravitt made a little small talk and then asked if he might have a word with Doris. "Just routine, nothing to worry about."

Nan and Dean went upstairs.

Gravitt wasted no more time. "Were you happy about the adoption plans? For Micky to raise Dean?"

"At the time it seemed like the best thing to do."

"Why?"

"Why do you ask? It's my private business. What possible relevance can it have to Micky's murder?"

"Well, only this," replied Gravitt, deceptively sweetly. "It seems to me that a mother might want to get rid of the man who is taking her child away from her. That's a fairly plausible motive for murder."

So Doris told him about the two thugs after Greg and their threats to abduct her and her son. Gravitt listened without saying a word to the whole story, then at the end he asked, "Why the hell didn't you go to the police?"

"I was afraid to."

"Heavies like that prey on people like you. They know you won't cry for help. You should know that the police have a very high success rate with this sort of crime."

"I'll bear it in mind next time it happens," Doris replied sarcastically.

Gravitt left feeling dissatisfied. It's a shame, he thought, that Micky can't raise that child. His mother doesn't appear to have even half a brain in her head!

Gravitt had one more stop to make before he could call it a day. He went to the surgery where Winston used to see patients before retirement. He showed his ID to the receptionist and said, "I'd like to ask you a few questions about Dr. Winston. How long did he work here?"

"Oh, donkey's years, longer than me," replied the receptionist, who was certainly no spring chicken judging by the grey hair and the wrinkles.

"Were there any complaints about him from any of his patients?"

There were a few patients still waiting to see a doctor; one of them, an elderly man, broke into the discussion.

"Dr. Winston was one in a million," he announced in a loud voice that indicated partial deafness. "This surgery hasn't been the same since he retired. T'weren't that long ago he saved my life. Gall stones, I had, big 'uns, too. I'd be dead now if he hadn't put me straight in the hospital."

"You old fool," chirped up a middle-aged fat lady. "Nothing would put you six foot underground, you're too thick skinned!" The old man chuckled; this was obviously a recurring banter. The fat lady continued, "He saved my daughter's baby when her pregnancy turned painful. I don't think any other doctor would have recognised the problem so fast."

The old man was not prepared to be bested—he liked his limelight. "That's good," he said, "but I would have *died*!"

A third patient, not to be left out of the 'my sickness is worse than yours' rivalry, entered the fray. "He recognised that what I thought was 'flu was really pleurisy. If he hadn't, I wouldn't be standing here now."

The skirmish developed into a full-fledged battle. Gravitt left to the sounds of dissention:

"really big 'uns!"

"baby in the wrong position…"

"couldn't breathe…"

It was a pretty good testimonial for Dr. Winston.

173

After his meeting with the solicitor, Wilcox rang Dr. Hopkins to arrange their date. Dr. Hopkins was amused by Wilcox's formality.

"You are free to address me by my Christian name, you know," she told him.

"The problem is, " countered Wilcox, "I don't know it!"

She laughed. "Allow me to introduce myself. I'm called Lallie. I do hope you will spare me the jokes about being doolally."

"Never crossed my mind," replied Wilcox, honestly. "It is unusual; is it a family name?"

"No, it's of Latin derivation and means talkative. Apparently I was a noisy baby! And your name is...?"

"John; plain and simple. It's not even short for Jonathan. Have you managed to find a sitter for tonight?"

"Yes indeed. What do you have planned for us?"

"I rather thought we'd go for dinner at an Italian restaurant I know near the river. The food is good and the restaurant is quiet. It will give us a chance to talk and get to know each other. Shall I pick you up at seven?"

The time agreed and Lallie's address obtained, Wilcox dashed home to freshen up. He was rather nervous. He may appear to others to be pedantic and impervious to slights, but that was a safe exterior pose. Inside, he had a great deal of self doubt. He had received average grades in school and considered himself to have only average intelligence. He underrated himself in that regard. In fact, it may have been his lack of confidence which taught him to consider his words carefully before speaking; and as Netty said (however light-hearted her comment may have been at the time), shouldn't more of us be like that? His one true failing was his inability to see beyond another person's façade, to read another's emotions. He tended to accept people for who they said they were.

He showed up at Lallie's flat with half a dozen white roses. She was wearing a dark blue dress, not too tight and very feminine with its delicate embroidery across the front. "You look beautiful!" Wilcox exclaimed. "I shall be the envy of every man tonight."

Lallie may have been a talkative baby, but somewhere along the way she had also learned to be a good listener. She drew John out of his safe shell and made him feel important. He even confided to her that he liked reading TS Eliot and Keats, and that, when time permitted, he attempted to write poetry himself. He had never confessed this vice to anyone. At the end of the meal he apologised. "I'm afraid I've bored you to tears. I don't usually talk so much about myself. You should tell me to shut up."

"Next time I will do the talking, I promise. I shall have my revenge."

He took her hand. "That means you will see me again. That's good!" They smiled at each other. It was a clear night and Wilcox suggested they go for a walk on Waterloo Bridge. "I like looking down on the boats, and we can grab a coffee at the Royal Festival Hall." As they walked in contented silence, she took his arm. He thought to himself, I'm dreaming...

John

I'm in a dream. None of this is real. Any moment now I'll wake up and discover I'm at home, alone.

Look at that moon, and the stars! See how they shine, glittering, sparkling with excitement and wonder. And here I am, me, lowly man, with a dream on my arm. Any moment now I'll wake up.

There is nobody else on this earth, there is nothing else in this world. Just me, with my dream.

See how the moonlight shines on her hair! See how it changes the colour. See how her eyes reflect the stars! See the cherry red of her lips, the breath from her exquisite mouth. She is perfection. She is my dream.

Her movements are those of a gazelle, graceful and dainty. Her voice is music upon my ears. She is Venus; she is Athena, born of the wisdom of Zeus. She is a goddess. She is perfection. She is my dream come true.

Look there! See the gently swirling water beneath us. Listen to its rippling song. It is singing for us, welcoming us to infinite beauty, beckoning us to share in its glorious understanding, the swells of the waters mirroring the swelling in my heart. I'm living a dream.

"John, are you all right? John? John?" Lallie gave Wilcox's arm a gentle tug.

"What? Oh. Is something wrong?" Wilcox pulled himself back into reality.

"You were just staring at me for the longest time. What were you thinking about?"

"Nothing in particular." He paused, reluctant to lose the moment, his reveries. "This is where I come when I need to reflect on things, personal or police cases or whatever. I guess I slipped into my old habits. Sorry."

"The Smythe case has you worried, doesn't it? Is that what you were thinking about so deeply?"

"Yes," he lied. "Let's get that coffee."

They had a leisurely coffee and brandy before Wilcox drove Lallie home. At the door he asked, "Tomorrow evening?" She accepted.

Chapter Eighteen

"They've arrested Harry!" Marge exclaimed. "They've arrested Harry! Harry, of all people. I don't believe it!" It was the next morning; the day after Harry visited the police station.

Netty responded, "They must have some reason to suspect him. False arrest is a serious business. Are you sure they're not just holding him for questioning?"

"Oh, I don't know, I don't know!" Marge shook her head distractedly. "I don't know anything any more!"

"How did you find out about it?" Anne-Marie wanted to know.

"Alex Gravitt just telephoned and asked me to arrange some legal advice for him. For Harry, I mean."

"Not Frederick Collins, for God's sake!" Dr. Winston had no opinion—no repeatable opinion anyway—of the elderly solicitor.

They were all gathered in the lounge: the four women in the family, for Jenny was there as well, and Elliot Winston.

"This looks like a sorority house, or a harem!" Anne-Marie burst out. "Harry's harem. He's the only man left in the family." She started to giggle, then laughed outright; the laughter turned into tears. Winston slapped her hard to stop the hysterics. "I'm sorry," she hiccupped. "It's just such a ridiculous notion." She smiled tremulously.

"Certainly not Frederick Collins," agreed Marge, carrying on as if there had been no interruption. "In any case, he's not a criminal lawyer. Gravitt suggested I ring someone named Geoffrey Bowen. Apparently he's one of the best in the business."

"That's very decent of Gravitt," responded Winston, "telling you how to fight the police charge. Of course, he is practically one of the family now. Isn't he, Anne-Marie?" Winston was trying to lighten the mood, but Anne-Marie just ignored him.

Marge went into the study and rang Mr. Bowen. She returned to say he was going to contact the police immediately and hoped to see Harry that afternoon.

Geoffrey Bowen was everything Frederick Collins was not. He was a real life version of the good looking and successful TV criminal lawyer. A man in his early forties, his reputation was already nationwide and he was in a position to turn away clients if he didn't like them. Unlike Perry Mason, his clients were not always innocent; but they nearly always were acquitted. Bowen was an expert at finding loopholes in the law.

Upon making contact with the police, he had learned that so far no official charge had been made against Harry Franklin. Gravitt, however, asked him not to comment on that to anyone, especially to any of the Smythes, and to come to the station anyway. Bowen had a healthy respect for Gravitt and agreed. He knew the Inspector was a busy man and would not have requested a visit without good reason. Also, he had been reading about the Smythe murders in the dailies and he was frankly curious. The newspapers had been having a field day since the second murder, speculating who would be the third victim. One smart-assed tabloid suggested that the police would only solve the crime when there was just one member of the Smythe family remaining.

Inspector Gravitt greeted Bowen warmly and led him into his office. "I'm glad Marge Smythe took my advice and contacted you," he said. "This is the damnedest case I've ever seen."

"I've read about it in the papers, of course," Bowen answered, "and

I admit I'm interested in hearing more. Can you tell me what evidence you have against Franklin? And naturally I'd like to meet him before I agree to represent him."

"To tell you the truth, I don't really have enough evidence to present to the Crown Prosecution Service. I should have let him go last night. A clever solicitor," he bowed in Bowen's direction, "would no doubt have had him out of here in fifteen minutes. I'm asking that Harry—and you—allow me to keep him locked up for a week or so without pressing charges." Gravitt stared at his empty coffee cup. "Harry agreed to stay here last night and has indicated that he is willing to remain longer, but that is largely because he trusts me; I have to be careful not to take advantage of that. He doesn't have a solicitor and decided not to telephone his father, so until I rang Mrs. Smythe this morning, no one knew he was here." He cleared his throat. "To be honest, that's not entirely to my liking; I don't want Joe Public to know, but I would like his family to think we've arrested him." At Bowen's raised eyebrows he continued, "I want the family, more specifically the killer, if it's not Harry that is, to feel relaxed enough to lower his or her guard. That way perhaps they will make a mistake. I will do my best to keep it out of the papers, of course. I'm well aware that if Harry's name gets spread across the media, it will permanently blight him. People will remember his name as being connected with murder long after he's cleared. If he's innocent. It's important he understands the full implication of that."

"You'd better tell me everything, from the beginning."

"Okay. In the beginning God created James Smythe the Second. An honest man who carried on his father's publishing business. He married Katherine, who died young of pneumonia. Before she died he begat two children with her, James the Third, known as Micky, and Anne-Marie. Later in life, when he was fifty or so, he remarried. Marge, the lady who rang you, is wife number two. There were some pretty fierce feelings about this from the children, who never expected their father to tie the knot again, but she seems to have won them over. There are occasional rows, but nothing out of the ordinary. All families have disagreements from time to time."

"What did Marge gain by his death?" asked Bowen.

"Plenty of money. And two grown children still living at home, plus a daughter-in-law, and a granddaughter."

"Did she have money of her own when she married Smythe the second?"

"No. We looked into her very thoroughly, but there was nothing to implicate her. Her grief over her husband's death was genuine; I'm certain of that."

"And the two children?"

"The firstborn was Micky, a name he chose to avoid confusion with his old man. He is a musician and married another musician; they both played in the English Philharmonia. Micky inherited a substantial sum when his father died, but he also potentially lost free lodging and board. Anyway, he too has been murdered and that would seem to exonerate him of any guilt in his father's murder! His widow is his heir.

"The second child was only five when her mother died. She was pampered by her father and had nothing to gain by his death. I mean, she inherited as much as her brother, but she didn't need it any more than he did. I had better tell you now that I'm seeing her socially; no doubt some busybody will tell you."

"Is it serious?"

Gravitt ignored Bowen's question and continued, "She's also a suspect, just like the others, and Sergeant Bateman has been checking her out. I'm careful not to do it myself."

Bowen nodded. "Very wise. I must say, though: I'm surprised you haven't been sacked, messing around with a suspect!" Neither man spoke for a while as they ruminated on Gravitt's poor conduct and lucky—so far—escape. Finally Bowen asked, "Where does Harry fit in?"

"He's the poor cousin. He admitted under questioning, to me only and unofficially, that he resented the wealth and success of this branch of the family, but I was inclined to believe him when he said he was fond of his uncle. The problem is this: everyone had the opportunity and the means to commit the first murder, but no one had a motive. The only motives I can glean for the second murder are not strong, and again everyone seems to have been unobserved at some point during the time the murder was committed." Gravitt went through all the evidence with Bowen—that didn't take long!—and all the conjecturing, remembering to mention Greta and Bill, Dr. Winston, Nan and Doris. When he finished he said, "I don't think the killing has stopped. That's why I asked for you to see me before meeting Harry. I've told him that my plan is to make the family and those others concerned think the police are satisfied that he is guilty, even if we can't prove it. And, you know, he *could* be the killer."

"Why do you say that, if you've no evidence?"

"Because he carries a deep resentment for several members of the family, including Anne-Marie. If he is the culprit, then she may be next on his agenda. And if he's not the killer, then I think there's a strong chance *he* may be the next victim. I want him here for his own safety as much as anything."

"As you say, you have a personal interest. Introduce me to Harry. I have to warn you, while I have taken on board the things you have told me, I will advise him as I think is best for him."

"Of course."

Gravitt introduced Bowen to Harry and left them alone to get acquainted. Bowen wasted no time on chitchat. His tone was matter-of-fact; indeed, almost cold.

"Mr. Gravitt tells me that you understand he hasn't enough evidence against you—yet—to force you to stay here if you want to leave. Is that correct?" Harry nodded. "Are you aware that in spite of the lack of evidence, you top the list of suspects?" Again Harry nodded. "It may get into the papers." Another nod. "And knowing that, are you still prepared to stay here, locked up, for several days?"

"Yes."

"*Why?*"

Harry didn't like the way Bowen was talking to him; it seemed accusatory and insulting. His solicitor was supposed to be on his side, wasn't he? Talking to Bowen felt like talking to yet another policeman! He was tired of being treated like a subhuman being.

"Because I've nothing to hide!" he shouted back at Bowen. "They can't find evidence that doesn't exist, can they? And maybe it's safer in here while that homicidal maniac is out and about!"

"Good, good," smiled Bowen. "I'm glad to see you have some fight in you. Now let's get to work." He sat down, motioned to Harry to do the same, and pulled out pen and paper.

"There must be no pretence between us," he said. "I need to know everything about you until I can think like you. I need to know about your loves and your pet hates; about your friends and your enemies; your hobbies, hopes and fears. And I need to know all about your home life, your father and mother. And most of all I need to know about your relationship with the Smythes."

So Harry told him everything that he could think of. It was a subjective approach, of course, but then that's what Bowen expected and wanted. Harry talked about the constant pain he had—and still has—because of the eczema and asthma. He talked about the fear he had as a child, because of the pain, of being touched. He remembered his panic when his father threw a ball at him.

"He actually threw a ball *at* you? Not *to* you?"

"Well, probably to me," Harry replied sheepishly, "but that's not how I felt about it at the time. I would scream and run away, and Dad would get angry. He wanted a son who looked like Atlas, all muscle-bound, and who could play rugby like a pro. I was a big disappointment." He gave Bowen a wry look.

"Tell me about your mother. She was a Smythe, wasn't she?"

"Yes, Uncle James' sister. Her father disowned her, ostensibly because she eloped, but really I think because she got pregnant before she got married. Hardly matters nowadays, but he considered himself a pillock—oh, sorry; did I say pillock? I meant pillar, of course. He considered himself a pillar of society and was ashamed of her." Harry's eyes narrowed as he gave a sardonic grin.

Bowen ignored Harry's comment. He asked, "How did she feel about that?"

"Don't know, really. She never talked about it. You could ask Dad." Harry grinned openly.

"Ah, that sounds like a challenge!" Bowen responded. "I may take you up on that."

"Then I'm definitely staying here! It's safer!"

Bowen picked up his previous line of questioning. "So your mother lost touch with her family?"

"Yes, but after the old patriarch died she became sort of friendly again with her brother. But only from a distance; she didn't want him to know how poor we were."

"So money was a problem?"

"God yes! Dad lost his job and took his anger out on Mama. He said, since her wealthy family wouldn't help financially, she had to support us herself. He made her go to work while he watched TV. And he used to hit her, too."

Bowen digested these comments, then asked, "I understand your father kicked you out of his house. Why was that?"

"I guess 'cause we never got on well, and when Uncle gave me a job I suppose he just felt he'd had enough of me. You'll have to ask him if you want to know more. Personally, I'm glad he did." Harry made a rude gesture towards his absent father. "I found a flat in Ongar, near Uncle's firm."

"Did you actually see your father hitting your mother?"

"Yeah. I would have stopped him except," Harry cringed, "he was bigger than me." Harry looked straight at Bowen for the first time. "I was only twelve when she died, you know."

"Did you and your father get along with each other any better after her death?"

"We didn't talk to each other any more. Not since her funeral."

"Did he hit you?"

"No."

The interview over, Bowen searched out Gravitt, finding him in the police canteen seated behind—you guessed it—a coffee cup. "Well?" Gravitt asked.

"He's made up his mind to stay and seems to know what he's doing.

Do try to keep it out of the papers." Bowen fetched some tea for himself and a refill for Gravitt. When he was comfortably settled opposite the detective, he said, "Pretty dreadful life that young man has had, isn't it?"

"Is it?" Gravitt raised his head. "I know his father kicked him out, but not until he was earning a living wage." He peered closely at his friend. "What have you discovered that I don't know?"

"Now, how am I supposed to know what you don't know!" This was not said as a question and Gravitt waited for Bowen to come to the point.

"Okay, here we go. Did you know Harry's mother was disowned by Smythe the First when she ran off with George?"

"Yes. She was pregnant."

"Did you know George was violent? That he used to beat his wife?"

"Did he, by God!" Bowen had succeeded in getting Gravitt's full attention.

"And did you know George resented his son for being spotty instead of sporty?"

"Yes, but that's not surprising. He was heavily into athletic games."

"Then did you know George complained about the little good it did him to marry a woman from such a rich family when said family was selfish and unhelpful?"

"No."

"By the sound of it, he—George—used his wife as a drudge rather than look for a job himself, when his teaching career ended. He blamed her *and* her family for their poverty." Bowen paused. "It seems to me that George was full of animosity for the Smythes. *All* of them, not just his wife and child. In fact, it seems to me…"

Gravitt was already getting to his feet. "It seems to me, too!" He called back from the exit, "Thanks!"

Sergeant Wilcox was in the station, about to leave for home. He was looking forward to seeing Lallie again. Gravitt said, "Come with me!" Wilcox started to remonstrate but Gravitt said, "Now. Come with me!" He followed.

In the car, Gravitt explained. "We're going to visit George Franklin,

Harry's father. He seems to hold a grudge against the Smythes." Gravitt
sighed. "It will probably lead nowhere, but damn it to hell! It's time
things went right for us. We're overdue for some success!"

Chapter Nineteen

Gravitt and Wilcox pulled up outside the rundown block of flats in Cricklewood that housed George's tenement. Cricklewood, in its dim past, had been full of trees: pine, oak, and even Yew groves. But at the turn of the twentieth century the railroad came to stay, Cricklewood became industrialised, and the bulk of the already thinned trees came down. Bentley cars, Smith's crisps and the Halifax Bomber were all born in Cricklewood, making it an important area in the history of London. The promise of jobs for labourers encouraged an influx of Irish immigrants, and even today the area remains largely Irish.

Many of the original terraced houses still stand but a large proportion are now divided into flats and bedsits. George's flat was in a fairly new and rather inauspicious square block containing at least a dozen other apartments, all exactly alike. The entry phone system was not functioning, but fortunately the main door was wedged ajar. Gravitt and Wilcox made their way to the top floor and knocked on George's door.

"Who is it?" shouted a man's voice.

"Police, Mr. Franklin. Would you mind opening the door, please?"

There was the sound of shuffling and the door opened the two inches allowed by the chain. George peered out, buckling his belt at the same time. "You got some ID?" he asked. Gravitt held up his photocard for

George to study. "Got to be careful these days, you never know who might be lurking around." George smiled and opened the door. "Come in, won't you?"

The flat was not just untidy, it was a mess. A tornado could not have made it more dishevelled. George saw the look of amusement on Gravitt's face as he entered and the contrasting look of disgust on Wilcox's visage. For the first time since his wife's death he was embarrassed by his living arrangements. "Sorry," he mumbled. "I wasn't expecting company." He picked up old newspapers and clothes and threw them into the bedroom. "Have a seat, do." He fidgeted nervously and offered, "I, er, I've got coffee on the go; there's always coffee. No tea, I'm afraid. Would you like a coffee?" They accepted and George went into the kitchen, where he could be heard washing cups. Wilcox took the opportunity to step into the hall and telephone Lallie.

"I'm going to be late," he apologised. "Something's come up. Police business. Better have dinner without me."

She could hear the disappointment in his voice. "Don't worry," she reassured him. "Policing must be like doctoring: a round- the- clock occupation."

"I'll give you a ring when I'm done, and maybe we can still nip out for a drink."

"No can do. I'll have to let the sitter go," she replied. "But we can have something here if you don't mind slumming it."

"You don't know what slumming is until you've been where I am now!" expostulated Wilcox, his voice quivering with emotion.

Finally the three men were seated. "Is this about Harry?" George queried.

"Are you concerned about Harry?" asked Gravitt.

"Of course I am! I read the papers. As you can see," he added wryly, indicating the newspapers strewn about the flat. "He works for old man Smythe's publishing house, doesn't he? That puts him in the middle of a murder enquiry, doesn't it?"

Gravitt found himself getting irritated with this man who seemed so ready to accept his son's involvement with a murder case. Almost as annoying was Franklin's habit of finishing every other statement with a question. He asked George, "Do you think Harry is capable of murder, Mr. Franklin?"

"Well, I don't know," George mused. "I guess most of us could kill if the circumstances were right, don't you think?"

"And what exactly would the 'right circumstances' be?" Wilcox asked.

"Uh, I've never thought about it. I reckon they'd be different for different people, don't you?" The officers said nothing to this; they just waited. The lingering silence made George feel uncomfortable. "I mean," he stumbled on, "Some men could kill for money, maybe some could kill for love."

"What do you think Harry could kill for?"

"Well, I don't really know. Now I think about it, I can't imagine him killing for anything, can you? I don't think he'd have the guts."

"So you think it takes guts to kill?"

"Hey, what *is* this? I'm sure you didn't come here to philosophise on what makes a man murderous!" George was beginning to feel suspicious.

"Not really; but it's always nice to learn how people think." Gravitt was placating. "How long has it been since you last saw your son?"

"Quite a while. I don't think he's been around since he moved out."

"Do you talk regularly on the 'phone?"

"No." George looked from one policeman to the other and said, "It's no secret that we don't get along, is it."

"So you would be unable to provide him with an alibi for the Smythe murders, is that right? Not for either murder?"

"No, I don't suppose I could. But really, you know, murder is not Harry's kind of thing."

"What is his 'kind of thing'?"

"Books. Whenever he gets upset he buries his head in books. He finds fantasy better than real life."

"Mr. Franklin, I understand that your wife's family disapproved of your marriage to Penelope. Can you comment on that?"

"What's to say? They were rich folk with rich folk's conceits. We eloped instead of marrying with all the trimmings." He smiled. "We *enjoyed* our private ceremony. None of this 'how do you do, Madam; so charmed to meet you, sir' crap for us. We were wed in a registry office and then we danced the night away." When George smiled and his eyes softened; it was easy to see why Penelope had found him attractive. He still had charm, in spite of his much-expanded waistline and thinning hair, now grey.

"I know that Penelope was pregnant when she married you. Forgive this intrusion into your private life, but did you marry her only because you felt honour-bound to do so?"

"I'm damned if see any reason why I should answer such a nosy question, but I will. I married Penelope because she was the only woman for me."

"Yet you beat her."

"I beg your pardon?"

"I said, if your wife was the only woman for you, why did you beat her? Have you struck other women?"

"I don't know what you're talking about."

"Come now, Mr. Franklin. You were seen hitting her."

"Harry, the shite! What's he been saying?"

"How did your wife die, Franklin?" Gravitt's voice was hard.

"She died of natural causes. A heart attack. At work, not here. The hospital rang and told me she'd had a coronary."

"I understand you resented Penelope's family and her father in particular for not helping you financially."

"My feelings are none of your business."

"Please think back to the first murder. How did you learn of it?"

"I read about it in the papers."

"What were you doing at the time?"

"God knows!"

"Perhaps you don't understand me, Franklin. I'm asking if you can provide me with an alibi. Not for Harry; for yourself."

George was scared. He wrung his hands in consternation. "How do I know, after all this time? I sit here in this flat day after day, one day running into the next and all of them pretty much the same."

"Do you work?"

"No. I was a sports trainer when I was younger. I got laid off a few years back. I'm nearly sixty-two now." George hoped they would be satisfied with that explanation. God forbid they should know about his disgraceful departure from the world of education!

"How do you pay the rent?"

"Dole money, and I get a little income from the insurance company."

"Tell me about that please. The insurance income."

"It's nothing much, just a policy I had for Penny and me. An annuity for the last survivor."

Gravitt and Wilcox looked at each other. They stood up and Wilcox said, "Mr. George Franklin, I'd like to take you in to the station for questioning regarding the murder of James Michael Smythe, that you may have contributed to the death of the aforementioned..." and as Wilcox talked, George's mouth gaped wider and wider.

"But you...I mean, you can't...I didn't..."

"Let's go!" demanded Gravitt. As George backed away, Gravitt said, "Put the cuffs on him, John."

"Just a minute! Just a minute!" George expostulated. "Please don't put those things on me! Please! I'll answer all your questions, I swear. I beg you! I can't bear having my arms pulled back. See, I've got a bad shoulder—torn ligament in my left shoulder—and the pain is terrible." George was almost crying. "Can't we talk here? Please?"

Gravitt sighed. "Can you provide medical proof of a bad shoulder?"

"Yes, yes. Look, here's my prescription for painkillers, and here's my doctor's 'phone number; I'll just write it down for you. The surgery's closed at this hour, of course, but that's not my fault, is it?"

"Actually, I may be able to help here, sir," Wilcox suggested to Gravitt. "My lady friend is a doctor. I could ring her, she's at home now."

"Do that, do that!" urged Franklin. "Use my 'phone."

Wilcox picked up the receiver. "Lallie? John...No, I'm not free yet...I have a medical question...What can you tell me about torn ligaments?...Yes...In the shoulder...Is that so!...Thank you." He hung up.

"She says the shoulder is a ball and socket joint which is held together by something called the rotator cuff muscles. As near as I understand it, these muscles don't like it when you raise your arms above your head and they sometimes stretch. It's usually a sporting injury, and it can be very painful."

"Yeah, but I was lucky," George babbled. "Throughout my entire coaching days I suffered nothing, no injuries, no problems at all. Then maybe three, four weeks ago I decide to go swimming, to lose some weight you know, and bang! Just like that, my arm goes bad." He shook his head at the anomaly of it all.

"Sergeant, do you mind taking notes?"

"No sir. But I haven't any paper." He shrugged at Gravitt's frown and added, "I was on my way home when you grabbed me to come here." George found a note pad and handed it to Wilcox.

Gravitt began the interview. "How well did you know Penelope's brother, the second James Michael Smythe?"

"Hardly at all. Oh, we met occasionally when I stopped by her house to pick her up, but we never did more than exchange the time of day."

"Did he approve of your dating his sister?"

"I don't know why not. I mean, why wouldn't he? It wasn't his place to approve or disapprove, anyway. The old man was still alive then. Although I hardly ever met him, either."

"You were courting Smythe's only daughter, and you were never invited to meet the family? Wasn't that a bit strange?"

"Maybe it was, but she wasn't a young girl when we met. She must have been pushing thirty."

"I imagine you and Mrs. Franklin expected to receive a legacy of some sort when her father died." George said nothing. "Please answer the question."

"Oh, sorry; I didn't realise it was a question. It's all so long ago now, Inspector, isn't it? Penny always said if he left her anything, she'd refuse it. She was as stubborn as her old man!"

"But you?"

"Well, yes, I guess I did expect a little windfall. We could certainly have used the money."

"And you can honestly say that the prospect of a little windfall was not a factor in your choice of a wife?" Gravitt was sceptical and he let his tone of voice convey that message.

"I told you before, I loved her. She was pretty and charming."

Gravitt decided not to push the point. Yet. "Did you know Smythe Two's wife, Marge?"

"No, I knew his first wife Katherine. Not very well, if you know what mean. But I knew her. She had time on her hands because she was quite frail and couldn't do any heavy work, so now and then I would go up to see her while Penny was getting ready for our date."

Gravitt and Wilcox were leaning forward, intensely interested. This might give them a clue to the murders, if there was a vendetta against Katherine's nearest and dearest. Inspector Gravitt said in a still, unemotional voice, "I'd like you to tell me about those visits, in your own words please. Take your time."

"Well, I can't see why it should interest you, but I'm a lonely old man now and I don't get around much with this arm, do I. Would you like another coffee?" George didn't wait for their answer, filling their cups anyway.

"Now let's see," he began. "As I said, it was all a long time ago. Katherine was quite a beauty, if you like the fragile kind of girl. She was a smart cookie and no matter what was wrong with her physically, mentally she was sharp as they come. Chatting with her was always interesting: one time you saw her she might be in a funning mood, the next time you saw her she might be deadly serious."

"Did she get along with the people around her? Family and friends?" Wilcox interspersed, regretting it immediately as Gravitt scowled at him for interrupting. George, however, failed to notice this little by-play. He was in full swing, immersed in his recollections.

"Everyone seemed to like her, as far as I could tell. But her sickly spells weren't very often then. Penny and I went out together for almost two years before we married, and Micky was just a baby. After we married, I never saw Katherine again." George looked up. "What else do you want to know?"

"I want to know if you have any idea who might have hated Katherine or held a grudge against her or been jealous of her."

"Nobody, as far as I am aware."

"Do you know Greta and Bill, the housekeeper and her husband?"

"No."

"You must have felt some hostility towards the members of the family when they refused to recognise your marriage."

"You bet I did!" George exploded. "All high and mighty they were, too good for a mere footballer like me with no book learning. Old man Smythe could have made life easier for us—for his daughter—but he was too blooming selfish! Too hoity-toity! I went to see him once, at his office, to ask him to lend us a little something to tide us over the rough patch when I lost my job. I mean, I have to tell you, I didn't *want* to beg for help, and it was a *loan* I asked for, not a gift! He said no. I pointed out that his only daughter had taken a demeaning job in a Laundromat, and do you know what he said to me? He said it wasn't *his* fault Penny had married beneath her station and he saw no reason why he should be forced to pay for her mistakes. And then a year later he dies and can you believe it, he's gone and cut her out of his will! The bastard!"

"Why didn't you contest the will?" Gravitt wanted to know.

"That's *exactly* what I wanted to do. But Penny wouldn't hear of it. Said she wouldn't lower herself to that level; said she had too much self-respect to beg; said she wouldn't let her father see her crawl. She said she'd rather starve. And we damn near *did* starve, too!"

Gravitt suggested, "So you hit her to teach her a lesson and you made her go out to work to support you." His voice was steady and his face blank, but under the mask he was seething with anger.

George crumpled. "I loved her," he cried. "I always loved her. I was so mixed up inside. Penny said she loved me, she said she was protecting my self-respect; but what she really did was make me ashamed to be me. She...she *belittled* me. She even, with no job experience at all, managed to find work when I couldn't."

"Perhaps because she wasn't too proud to accept menial labour."

George nodded. "I know, I know. I can see that now. But it's too late, isn't it? She's gone and left me here all alone." There was a long silence. Finally George continued, "but she was no saint herself, that's for sure. She married me, letting me believe I was the only man in her life and that it was me that got her pregnant. And all the time she was seeing someone else and it was probably *him* who gave her a child. She used me to raise another man's bastard. That wasn't very nice of her, was it?"

Gravitt and Wilcox were stunned by this revelation. Wilcox asked, "Are you saying Harry's not your child?" George nodded. "How do you know this?"

So George told them about the funeral and the appearance of Leonard. "He was a cocky sod, just went to Penny's funeral to see the mug who raised his bastard son. I told him, if he was going to slander my wife at her funeral, he'd have to leave." Gravitt asked if George had told Harry about this.

"No, what's the point? The damage was already done. Although he might have overheard some of what was said." George remembered turning to walk away from Leonard and being surprised to see Harry standing nearby.

"And so you kicked Harry out," summed up Gravitt.

"Kicked him out?" George repeated. "It's true, I did ask Harry to leave, but not then. Not for a long time. Not until he got a secure job, and that wasn't until he was in his mid-twenties."

Gravitt asked for details of Penny's death, which hospital had accepted her body and the date of her death and then brought the interview to a close. He advised George not to leave London without notifying the police. Once in the car he said, "Somehow I keep getting the wrong end of the stick about George kicking Harry out of his home. If Harry was employed and in his twenties, you can't exactly accuse George of neglect."

Wilcox picked up on another point. "If Harry did overhear the conversation between George and Leonard, it might have laid a seed of distaste for his mother's duplicity and eventually for the Smythes in general. Perhaps this distaste festered over the years. Harry might have started thinking how much nicer his life could have been if his Mum had married the other man." He paused, then added, "Feelings like that might have warped as time distorted memory, as it always does; and maybe Harry is doing away with the whole family, one by one, trying to get even with them for his wretched childhood."

"John!" Gravitt exclaimed. "Do you know what you're doing?" Wilcox looked baffled and reminded his boss to keep his eyes on the road. "You're *theorising*, John, *theorising*. Where's my matter-of-fact, stick to the facts only, right hand man?" Wilcox was glad it was dark; he could feel himself blushing. And Gravitt had the insensitivity to continue this line. "Is this what your new lady is doing to you? Turning you into a philosopher?"

Wilcox squirmed in his seat while the Inspector drove on in silence, an amused smile on his lips. Finally he said, "I've got it bad. Can't think what's happening to me since I got involved with this case. For a while I thought I was falling for one of the family—like you, sir!—and then I met Netty's doctor. She's beautiful!"

"Damn!" Gravitt suddenly interjected. "I forgot to ask George about the joint life insurance policy he had with his wife. I'll have to set Bateman on to it tomorrow." It was an abrupt end to their intimate discussion; and just as well, thought Wilcox. He had almost confessed his taste for poetry, and that would certainly have been an indiscretion he would regret. But the brief moment of confidence also had an effect on Gravitt. He decided it was time to move his own relationship forward. He would suggest to his Anushka that they get engaged.

"Of course, that same conversation between George and Leonard also increases the odds for George to be the killer," Wilcox said, "if you don't mind my theorising a bit more. To learn that your son is not your son is a pretty hard nut to swallow. He could be carrying a grudge against the Smythes."

"You're absolutely right," agreed Gravitt. "And maybe we'd better talk to Leonard tomorrow as well. He could be hiding some pretty nasty feelings."

Chapter Twenty

The first thing Wilcox did when he reached his car was to ring Lallie. "I'm sorry tonight was a bust," he apologised, "but I do happen to be in front of an off-license. May I invite you to have a glass of champagne with me at the Palais Lallie?"

She laughed. "Come on over. I'll get the glasses ready"

Lallie was waiting in the doorway when he arrived, her tall sinuous figure framed by the soft glow from the lamplight behind her. His heart beat a little faster. Lallie ushered John into the sitting room where she had set out glasses and an ice bucket.

"Have you eaten?" she asked.

John shook his head. "No time for it."

"The doctor in me has to say, no food, no alcohol. Wait here." She returned with a thick roast beef sandwich stuffed with lettuce and dripping with mayonnaise.

"You spoil me," he said, gratefully accepting the sandwich. He had been afraid that his stomach would make loud rumbling noises. He was licking his fingers and succumbing to a feeling of well-being when he heard the patter of soft footsteps.

"I'm scared, Mummy," said a small sleepy voice. "Will you tell me a story?"

"John, I'd like you to meet my daughter Susie. Susie, this is John." Lallie turned to her daughter. "John is a policeman," she told her.

"Gosh! Do you catch bad people?"

"If I can." Naturally Susie wanted to hear one of John's stories and she led him to her room. Half an hour went by, and Lallie wondered why she heard no sounds from her daughter's bedroom. She peeped through the doorway and only just managed to stop herself from laughing out loud at the scene before her. John was propped on the edge of the bed, his back against the headboard. His right arm was wrapped around Susie, who was leaning on his chest. And both were sound asleep. Lallie extricated her daughter from John's arm and put her to bed, then gently shook John.

"Sshh," she warned, putting her finger over her mouth, and they tiptoed out. "I'm glad you like my child!" she giggled. "I'll have to be careful! Six years old and already she's stealing my boyfriends!"

John smiled self-consciously. "I'm sorry," he said contritely. "This was not at all what I planned for tonight. I wanted to wine you and dine you and fill your pretty ears with compliments. So what happens? I have to work late, *you* end up feeding *me* and then I fall asleep." He shook his head. "You probably don't want to see me again."

"Oh, no, John. You're wrong about that. I do want to see you again. Very much so."

John took her in his arms. He held her gently, tenderly, not squeezing or crushing her to him, just enjoying the warmth of her body, the knowledge that he would be able to hold her tomorrow and the day after and the day after that...

When Alex reached his flat that evening, there was no message on his answer-phone from his beloved. His disappointment was deep. He thought to himself, what will happen if we get married? Will I sleep in a separate room waiting for her to decide when we should see each other? No way! He reached for the 'phone and rang her. To his delight she picked up the receiver herself.

"Oh, Alex, I'm so glad you called! I've missed you terribly. Have you just finished working?"

"Yes, I went to see Harry's father. Is it too late for us to have a drink together?"

"Not at all. You're tired and I'm not, so you stay put and I'll catch a taxi. See you in half an hour," and she rang off.

By the time Anne-Marie arrived, Gravitt had grabbed a bite to eat and he, too, had bought champagne for his lady love—although he owned nothing as glamorous as an ice bucket. Gravitt put some Bach on the CD player and dimmed the lights. Anne-Marie noticed these preparations as soon as she walked through his door, and she felt a little nervous. Was he going to propose? Part of her fluttered with excitement but another part was fearful. How should she handle it? What should she say?

If Anne-Marie was nervous, then Alex Gravitt was a total mess! His heart was beating so loudly it drowned the music. His hands shook violently when he tried to uncork the bottle. Anne-Marie thought, we both look like we suffer from St. Vitus' Dance, and she started to giggle. At first, this shocked Alex, but then he, too, saw the funny side and attempted a nervous laugh. Soon they were both laughing outright, although it has to be admitted there was a hysterical edge to the mirth. Eventually Alex succeeded in removing the cork and poured the bubbly. Then he said, "I believe I'm supposed to get on my knees.

"My dearest Anne-Marie, I think…"

"Stop!" Anne-Marie demanded. Gravitt quit breathing. She was going to reject him! "Not like that. You're supposed to propose to Anushka, not Anne-Marie. It's Anushka you love. You named her—me. You created her—me. It's the name you gave me. When I'm with you, I'm Anushka. When we're together we're Alex and Anushka."

Gravitt was touched. He'd had no idea how much his pet name meant to her. Suddenly he understood the depth of this realisation, the importance of it. And with this realisation came also the weight of responsibility. His Anushka was already dependent on him. Should he go on with his proposal? And as he mulled these things, he realised just how emotionally involved he had become. He loved her! He carried on with his proposal, but this time there was no nervous trembling, no hesitation in his voice. He was ready to accept this responsibility and all it entailed.

"My dearest Anushka, I have loved you almost from the first moment we met. I'm only a policeman and I don't have a lot to offer you, materially. But I have a heart which I do offer you, a heart full of love. Please tell me you'll marry me." He reached in his pocket and pulled out a ring. It was only a small diamond, but Anushka thought it the most beautiful ring she had ever seen. She held out her hand and he slipped it on her finger.

"Yes," she breathed. She could hardly speak. "Oh, yes!"

Their lovemaking was different that night, slow and leisurely. Anushka stayed for the whole of the night and Alex drove her home the next morning. Life is wonderful for those who love!

Marge greeted Anne-Marie at the door with relief. She had been looking for her stepdaughter for over an hour and had panicked when she realised Anne-Marie had not slept in her bed. "Thank God!" she exclaimed. "I was just about to ring the police!"

Anne-Marie thought that was hilarious. When she could control her giggles, she explained, "I've been in police custody all night. Look!" She held out her left hand, angling it so that the little gemstone sparkled. "I'm going to be in police custody the rest of my life!"

"Darling, that's wonderful! How I wish your father could be here, I know he would be pleased." The mention of James sobered the gay mood. Marge continued, "I think we should have some kind of celebration, don't you? Just family, under the circumstances. I'm sure that's what James would have wanted."

"Do you think it's okay? It's only three days since Micky…since he was…I mean, I feel guilty being happy when, well, you know…"

Marge put her arms around Anne-Marie. "I know what you're trying to say, and I understand completely. But both James and Micky would want you to enjoy this very special event in your life. And, trite as it is to say it, life does go on. Let's put our heads together and see what ideas we can come up with."

The two women decided that Netty should be brought into the discussion. That Tuesday morning there was almost an air of normality in the beautiful house in Reddington Gardens which had so recently been the scene of so much tragedy. Tears were interspersed with smiles. Netty still felt Gravitt was too experienced for Anne-Marie, but she kept her mouth shut. They had all aged considerably in the last few weeks! At least, Netty thought to herself, the more time Anne-Marie spends with Alex, the less time she will be here, and in danger.

The Smythe women decided the dinner should be only for the immediate family plus Doc Elliot (who was almost family) and Gravitt. What about Alex's parents, asked Marge—and suddenly Anne-Marie realised she knew nothing about Alex's family. Did he even have a brother or sister?

"The problem is," Netty interrupted, her eyes filling with moisture, "we can plan this dinner but we can't choose a date. Not until we know when Micky's funeral is." The police had not yet released his body.

They all sat quietly, remembering their grief. An occasional sniff was the only sound. Finally Marge said, "I'll put the kettle on." Dinner plans were forgotten.

While celebratory dinner plans were being made and dropped, Gravitt was at the station organising his murder team. He sent DS Bateman to see George and get a copy of the insurance policy; he was instructed to follow through with any necessary action, such as contacting the insurance company, should it seem appropriate. DS Wilcox was sent to the hospital where Penelope Franklin died in the unlikely event there were still records available. Gravitt spent an hour with his Superintendent going through the police reports in some detail. And Geoffrey Bowen rang Marge and arranged to see her later that morning.

Detective Sergeant Benjamin Bateman was looking forward to meeting George Franklin. He'd read the report of the interview with interest and George sounded like a marvel of contradiction: he claimed he loved his wife yet he beat her; he claimed she was the only woman for him, yet it was almost as if he punished her for marrying him. Bateman, who fancied himself an amateur psychologist, felt that George probably suffered from a heavy dose of self-hatred. Could George, Bateman wondered, have reached the bottom of his self-detestation and now have turned his hatred onto his wife's family? Killing them off, one at a time?

George had been advised that DS Bateman would be calling on him and had tidied his flat. Well, at least he had thrown away the old newspapers and removed the dirty underwear. "I can't manage a hoover with this arm," he apologised.

"I'm just here to pick up the insurance policy," responded Bateman. "I'm not a health inspector!" He refused the offer of coffee but regretted that he could find no other excuse to linger. He wished he had been at George's interview. He sat in his car studying the policy and decided it offered little if any incentive for murder. The yearly income was too small really to be of interest at all, and he wondered what had inspired George to buy it. Had Bateman stayed for a drink, he might have learned that George arranged for this policy on the birth of his son. It was all he could afford, but he meant for his wife to know, should anything happen to him, that he loved her.

Bowen stood on the doorstep of the Smythe residence and looked with pleasure at the well-maintained property displaying some of the finest workmanship of the Victorian era. Greta let him in.

"Hello, are you Marge Smythe?" he asked.

"No, sir, but if you will just step inside, I'll fetch her." Greta returned and invited Bowen to join the family in the sitting room.

"Hello, Mr. Bowen," Marge shook his hand. "Let me introduce you to my daughter-in-law, Netty," Bowen nodded, "and my stepdaughter Anne-Marie." Bowen was interested in meeting Gravitt's inamorata.

Yes, I can understand his infatuation, he thought to himself; she is quite lovely. However, he felt her face lacked the personality and interest of the other women.

"I'm sorry to intrude at such a sad time," Bowen apologised, "and I'm grateful that you have agreed to see me. As you know, I'm representing Harold Franklin."

"Has he actually been charged with…with…you know…" Anne-Marie bumbled. "Murder," she blurted out.

"So far he is officially 'helping the police with their enquiries,' " Bowen hedged, remembering that Inspector Gravitt wanted the family to believe the police felt Harry was guilty, "but it looks bad for him."

"Harry is a member of this family and we will do what we can to help him," Netty offered. "But if he's guilty then he can go to hell!"

Marge gestured Bowen to a chair and handed him a cup of tea. "Do you want to see us separately?" she asked.

"Heavens, no," Bowen reassured her. "I'm not the police. A general discussion will be fine."

Marge, as the newest family member present, wasn't much help. She offered the information that Harry only occasionally accepted the standing offer to come for Sunday dinner, and that he had spoken very movingly at James' funeral.

"That's good to know. Generally did he seem to be fond of his uncle?" Bowen recalled that Gravitt had thought so.

"To be honest, Mr. Bowen, I doubt if any of us can comment on that. We didn't see them together very often. You might do better to ask that question at the publishing house," Netty suggested.

"You and Micky and Anne-Marie are much the same age as Harry, aren't you? Do you ever socialise together?"

Bowen looked first at Anne-Marie, who shuddered. "Not if I can help it," she stated firmly. "I think he's gauche!"

Bowen looked at her thoughtfully before turning to Netty, who replied, "I met Harry after I married Micky so I never knew him as a child. I don't really know how well Micky knew him." She started to cry. "We were very busy in the orchestra, and then with our daughter." Netty reached for a tissue only to discover the box was empty. Bowen handed her his handkerchief, giving her hand a comforting squeeze at the same time.

"I'm terribly sorry to ask you to talk to me about these things during this time of bereavement. I wouldn't normally intrude, but a criminal charge against Harry seems imminent, and I need as much information as I can get." He smiled, and both Netty and Anne-Marie responded to the sudden feeling of warmth generated by its magnetic quality—a courtroom wile that had worked on many a jury. They told Bowen anything they could think of, which wasn't much. Anne-Marie confided the story of the attempted kiss, and even implied, wonder of wonders, that she had been too harsh; it was, after all, just a kiss. Bowen took his leave, satisfied that while no one there could say anything to help Harry, neither could they damage his case.

Wilcox had no luck at the hospital; Mrs. Franklin's heart attack was too long ago. Using his initiative, he went to the library and searched out back issues of the newspapers until he found the obituary for Penelope Franklin. It held no surprises, but he photocopied it anyway.

The three detectives met again at the station later that morning and set off to call on Leonard Cousins. Bateman wasn't scheduled to go along, but he managed to worm his way in by promising to do all the note taking. This was the most interesting case ever to come his way!

Leonard was a year or two older than George but had more hair and less waist. He had a reasonably optimistic nature but was lacking in quick wit. He answered the door with a big smile on his face which blanched a little when he saw not the expected two but three policemen. "Cor, I must be important!" he exclaimed.

"We just want to ask a couple of questions and then we'll get out of your hair," assured Gravitt.

"At least let me hand around coffees," insisted Leonard.

"No thanks, not for me, anyway." Wilcox's and Bateman's jaws dropped open. Their beloved boss, the biggest coffee addict of their acquaintance, turning down coffee? Wilcox felt compelled to decline as well. Bateman didn't mind, he preferred tea anyway.

"I'd like you to tell me of your relationship with Penelope Franklin, please. In your own words." Gravitt glared meaningfully at Wilcox, who had the grace to look properly chastised and vowed to himself to keep his mouth shut no matter what.

"I assume you're here because of the murders. I can't imagine how I can help, but I'll just talk and you can stop me when it all gets too boring.

"I met Penelope Smythe, as she was then, at church and we went out together for nearly two years. I asked her to marry me—repeatedly— but while she never said yes, neither did she say no. We were intimate with each other, if you know what I mean, and I fully expected that we would eventually marry. Then suddenly she ran off with another man. End of story."

"Did you know she was seeing Franklin at the same time as you?"

"Certainly not! I would have dropped her immediately."

"Instead of which, she dropped you."

Leonard flushed. "As you say."

"You must have been very hurt."

"My pride was hurt, yes."

"Have you ever married?"

"No."

"Why did you go to her funeral?"

"Two reasons, Inspector: one, to pay my respects to the only woman I ever loved; two, to see the man who took her away from me."

"And to see your child?"

"What! *My* child! No way!"

"That's not what you told George Franklin."

A mischievous, almost malevolent look swept briefly over Leonard's face and then vanished. "All's fair in love and war, so it's said. I always used a condom, Inspector. There's no way that kid was mine."

"Well, let me tell you how much damage you did at the funeral. George never spoke to his son again. Harry grew up lonely and unloved." Gravitt stood up.

"That's not *my* problem, is it?"

Gravitt was angry. "No matter how penurious Penelope's life was, and no matter how hard she had to work for a living, she certainly chose the better man for her husband. You, sir, are a first-class bastard!" He walked out, Wilcox and Bateman on his tail.

"Damn his boots!" Gravitt said when they were outside Leonard's apartment building.

Wilcox caught Bateman's eye and nodded towards a pub on the corner, and together they steered Gravitt, still cursing, inside. Bateman went to the bar while Wilcox herded Gravitt into a corner seat. When the beers were on the table Wilcox began, "What's wrong, Alex? It's not like you to blow up at a ninny like that."

Gravitt took his time to answer. "That poor woman; two suitors and both of them selfish twits. Excuse me, I think I'm going to be sick." He went into the men's toilet. When he didn't return, Wilcox went looking for him. Gravitt was leaning against a washbasin, sweat pouring from his face. Wilcox guided him out and he and Bateman practically carried him to the car. In the fresh air he perked up a bit.

"Sorry, chaps," he apologised. "I'm okay now. It was stuffy in there." But he let them drive him home. He slept the rest of the day and all through the night, and the following morning he felt much better. He really was letting this case get to him!

While Gravitt slept, Bateman began a search of Alex's kitchen, looking in jars and food containers, even breaking open an egg. Wilcox asked him what he hoped to find. "I'm not sure," Bateman replied. "My sister's husband got a bad case of food poisoning once, and he was sweating just the way Alex is. It occurred to me that Alex might have eaten something that was off, something that is poisoning him." But they found nothing amiss aside from an unopened pint of sour milk.

Chapter Twenty-one

Surprised at finding he suddenly had a free afternoon, Wilcox rang Lallie in the hope that she, too, might not be working.

"I finish at three," Lallie said, "and then I have to collect Susie from school."

"Let me meet you both at the school and take you to the zoo. Would Susie like that?"

"Is there such a thing as a six-year-old child who doesn't like going to the zoo?" She gave him the address.

Susie was thrilled. "Can we see the monkeys and the giraffes? And the tigers?"

"We can see it all sweetheart; as much as you want."

"Oh, boy! Only I don't want to see the snakes. I don't like snakes. They're slimy."

"Oh, that's a disappointment!" Wilcox responded. "The snake house is my favourite place."

Susie's face fell. "Oh, well…*You* could go in while Mummy and I wait outside!"

Wilcox chuckled. "I'll tell you what," he suggested. "I can visit the snake house on my next trip."

They set off towards the monkeys, Susie flitting hither and thither while Wilcox and Lallie walked hand in hand, enjoying the child's awe of and love for the animals.

"Your daughter is beautiful," he said. "Like a princess in a fairytale."

"Be careful, John. She can also be very naughty," cautioned Lallie. But it was too late; John had already slipped into a poetic haze, loving this small girl as though she were his own daughter.

Though she was not created by my loins, he thought, yet she grows in my heart. Her running excitement is choreography to a Liszt piano sonata.

"John, that's beautiful!"

"What? Oh my God, did I say that out loud?"

"I'm afraid so!" Lallie smiled. "Are all policemen romantic dreamers like you?"

Wilcox looked shamefaced and diffident. He turned to face his lady friend. "Lallie," he said, "we're in a zoo surrounded by funny looking animals and even funnier looking people. Can you think of a more romantic place to fall in love?"

Lallie blushed. "Next thing you know, you'll be asking for permission to go out with my daughter!"

Wilcox laughed. He was happy.

They saw the monkeys, giraffes, tigers, elephants ("Oooh, they're so *big*!" breathed Susie) and much more. Susie petted the Shetland ponies and thought the zebra looked like a Jaillbird; well, Jailhorse actually! Wilcox decided that what they all needed after indulging the animals in so much people watching was a big strawberry milkshake. Is it any wonder that Susie slipped her hand in his and said, "I love you. I wish I could see you every day."

Lallie threw up her arms in mock horror. "I'm finished," she moaned. "Ousted by own daughter!"

Wilcox drove them home and arranged to come back for Lallie at eight, "to make up for last night." He went home, showered, and made reservations on a floating restaurant moored on the Thames.

He whistled when he saw her that evening. She had been lovely on their first date, but tonight she was royalty. Her hair was piled high on her head and she was wearing a deep purple dress elegant in its simplicity. "I c-can't believe you're going out with me!" he stuttered. "You take my breath away!"

When their meal was served, Wilcox asked Lallie if she minded telling him about Susie's father.

"Not at all, John. I was living with someone, a man called Pete. We were very much in love—or at least I thought we were. I expected to marry him and so I wasn't particularly careful about contraception. Then, when I became pregnant, he informed me that he had a wife and two children. He told me to get rid of the baby or he would disappear. I didn't and he did. I've never regretted my decision."

"You shouldn't have been treated like that!"

"Perhaps it was my own fault. I never actually *asked* him if he were married. And he never actually proposed." She was silent for a moment and then asked, "Are you married, John? I know you said you weren't when we first met, but was it true? I don't want Susie to get hurt."

"No, I'm not. I wouldn't treat a woman like that, especially one I love." They finished the meal in silence, each aware of where they were headed, each a little afraid, each expectant.

"Let's go somewhere else for coffee," Wilcox suggested.

"I make a pretty good brew." So they went to Lallie's house and let the sitter go. An old movie was showing on channel five and they snuggled up to watch it.

"I meant it, you know. What I said in the restaurant."

"When you said, so casually…"

"When I said I love you." John placed his hands on her cheeks and tilted her head towards him. He kissed her tenderly, ever so tenderly, as if he were being careful not to damage a soft rose. "I don't want to hurt you or Susie, so we'll take it gently, one step at a time. And we'll let what happens, happen." He noticed that she was looking at him quizzically and became worried. "Have I done something wrong already? Moved too fast?"

"No, John dearest; you're just being yourself: a natural born optimist." He looked puzzled. "All these arrangements you're making: shouldn't you find out first what my feelings for you are?"

He was crushed. "You don't love me! I felt sure…"

Lallie put her hand on his mouth to shut him up. "Just ask me, John. Just ask me if I love you." She removed her hand so he could talk.

He whispered, "Do you love me, Lallie?" Fear showed in his eyes and his voice trembled. "Do you think you could learn to love me?"

Lallie said, softly, "You were right; I do love you. But I'm not porcelain; I'm not fragile. I'm a woman. I have intelligence and I expect to give as much as I take. I don't want to be worshipped. I want to be loved. Physically as well as emotionally."

John Wilcox was a little slow on the uptake, but eventually he understood. He stayed the night.

Chapter Twenty-two

Early on the Wednesday morning Geoffrey Bowen rang Netty. He felt she might be able to tell him more about Micky's relationship with Harry if only he could get her away from the other family members and out of the house that held so much death.

"I would like to talk with you some more," he explained, "but I have to go to Kent. I wondered if I could coerce you into going with me? It would help me if I could pick your memory a bit and I thought you might like to get away from your nightmares for a few hours." Netty was hesitant but gave in when Bowen agreed they could make a short visit to Frittenden.

When he picked her up, she said, "I can't imagine what more I can tell you, but I'm grateful for the opportunity to see Dean and Nan."

"Well, you could start by telling me how you met Micky and we can try to work backwards. You were married for several years and you must have shared confidences and anecdotes from your childhood."

"I'm willing to give it a go, but I honestly don't think Micky ever mentioned Harry."

They drove in silence for a while before Netty started her reminiscing. "We met in the orchestra," she volunteered. "We used to have wonderful discussions about Serialism." She realised that Bowen was looking blank and added, "It's a compositional technique, a way of structuring the music." Netty laughed. "Micky was so intense! He could never tell when his leg was being pulled. Anyway, we hit it off like a house afire and he started bringing me little gifts; just small things like a book on Schönberg with a pressed rose petal in the middle." She reached for a tissue and stopped talking while she recovered her self-control.

"We became an item. Our friends were placing bets on how soon we would marry."

"What sorts of things did you talk about? I don't mean the personal things of course. Did you tell your husband about your childhood?"

Netty

I was an only child. My father was Jewish, a banker, and my mother was Irish Protestant. Mummy was a secretary in Father's bank and he found her an indispensable workmate. So he married her. Well, that's the way they tell this story, but it is always accompanied by a wink and a nod, so one assumes he found her indispensable in other ways as well.

When I was five I was taken to a violin recital. My father was dubious about taking such a young child to a long and possibly boring event, and no wonder! It's difficult to keep still at that age. But I was enthralled and immediately started begging for a violin. I responded well to my teacher and raced through the graded examinations with top marks.

My parents shared an all-consuming relationship that left little room for a third party. I'm sure they loved me, and certainly they were proud of me, but I often felt I was in the way. When they asked me if I wanted to go to boarding school, I jumped at the chance. Oh, don't get me wrong: I was not lonely; I wasn't neglected and I had lots of friends.

Girls at boarding schools reputedly have opportunities to meet young men, but that wasn't so in my case. The school I chose—because of its fine musical reputation—was quite isolated. I never learned the art of flirtation or dalliance. I had a terrible crush on my violin teacher and married him. In spite of our age difference—twenty-four years—it was a good marriage.

Micky was my first experience with a man of my own age. We made so many mistakes! Oh, Micky, if only we could wipe away those mistakes! I really did love you!

Bowen was silent while Netty fought to bring her tears under control. He pulled up outside a small café and said, "Let's stop for a hot drink," not giving her an opportunity to object. When they were settled with tea and buns in front of them, he asked, "Music must take more time than other professions in the learning; did Micky have a similarly isolated situation?"

"No, I don't think so. He never left home to study." She put down the Danish pastry she had absentmindedly nibbled. "I think his childhood worries were greater than mine, though. His mother was very ill."

"I didn't know that," lied Bowen. He wanted her to talk to him about Micky's youth in her own, unprompted, way.

"Micky said he can't remember her ever being strong. She died when he was only twelve. He took it badly, her death. The whole family did, including Anne-Marie although she was too young to realise what death is. Even Harry was affected." She looked straight at Bowen. "You were right, I do remember Micky talking about Harry. I gather Katherine died round about the same time as Micky's grandfather—I don't remember the dates, but I think the grandfather must have died first, because Harry was at Katherine's funeral." Netty paused to drink some tea. "Micky said he—Micky—couldn't stop crying at his mum's funeral, and Harry taunted him for being a cry-baby. They exchanged a few blows. But I don't think you can make too much of that, Geoffrey; they were just children being as cruel as children often are."

"Do you think Harry resented the fact that his cousins had so much and he had so little?"

"I'm afraid I can't answer that question."

They made small talk for the rest of the drive to Frittenden. So far Bowen had learned nothing to help Harry's defence, but neither had he uncovered any damaging facts. He was looking forward to meeting Micky's adopted family.

It's easy to see why Micky adored him, Bowen thought upon meeting Dean. He enjoyed Dean's company and conversation and also Nan's cooking, and the afternoon slipped by all too quickly. As neither Nan nor Dean had known Harry, and as Micky apparently never talked to them about his cousin, Bowen was able to relax and delight in the unseasonably warm weather in the country. On the return journey that afternoon Netty suddenly asked, "What was the errand you said you had to do here in Kent?"

"Get you away from Reddington Gardens," replied Bowen enigmatically. Netty peered at him suspiciously but he kept a straight face and she wisely dropped the subject.

Chapter Twenty-three

Gravitt rose from his sickbed on Wednesday morning and listened to his 'phone messages. There was one from Wilcox and another from Bateman, both enquiring about his health. And there were four from his fiancée. She said she would like to see him; she loved him; did he regret their engagement? And finally, tears at his lack of response. He rang her immediately.

"Oh, Alex, I've been so worried! Have you been so busy you couldn't even give me a quick ring?"

"I'm sorry, Anushka; I was in bed with some kind of bug, and to be honest I simply didn't have the energy to make a call."

"I don't really mean to make a fuss. It's just that so many people around me have died, and I...I was afraid that you...that someone...that something might have happened to you!"

Alex was contrite. "I didn't mean to worry you, my love," he said. "It was just a passing thing, nothing to get upset about."

"Well, you must let me nurse you back to health. Come for dinner tonight here at the house, and afterwards we can play doctors and nurses," she offered.

Gravitt decided, when he got off the 'phone, that his first port of call had better be the station, particularly the Murder Incident Room, to see what, if any, progress had been made. He found DS Wilcox there, studying notes.

"What did you do yesterday afternoon, John?" he asked.

Wilcox looked embarrassed. "Well, I couldn't think what's left to be done that hasn't been attended to," he squirmed. "We seem to have followed every avenue."

"So what, then, did you do?"

"I, er, I went to the zoo." Wilcox wished he were anywhere other than the Incident Room crowded with junior officers, all looking on with amusement.

"You went to the *zoo*?" exploded Gravitt. "The *zoo*? And just how did that help you in solving this case?"

Wilcox turned red as a beetroot. "Well, er, I couldn't come up with any new approaches, and I, er, thought a break might help me think better."

"And did it?" No, sir.

Gravitt turned to the room and spoke to the assembled men and women. "Now listen to me, all of you. This case is the most elusive one to come our way, but you don't solve difficult cases by giving up. If you can't find a new approach, then you rehash the old ground. And you keep doing it until someone or something breaks." He turned back to face Wilcox. "We'll swap jobs today. Wilcox, you interview Harry. Bateman—I won't ask you how you spent yesterday afternoon—you interview George Franklin. I'll talk with Netty and Greta. We'll meet back here at twelve."

A very much-humbled Sergeant Wilcox headed towards the cells. He reminded Harry who he was, saying, "I'm sure you're tired of being asked the same questions, but let's see if we can come up with something new, shall we?" Harry nodded glumly. "Before I begin the tape," continued Wilcox, "are you comfortable enough in your cell? Is there anything you'd like?"

Harry replied, "I'm bored. I want to leave now."

"I thought you had agreed with Inspector Gravitt to stay for a full week. Police protection, and such."

"Well, I did, but I can change my mind, can't I?" Harry sneered. "Nobody can make me stay here, you've got nothing on me."

"We would rather like to save your life." Wilcox paused for a moment. "Perhaps the prison library might have some books that would interest you."

Harry's face lit up. "Could you contact the publishing house and get them to let me have the book I'm meant to be working on? I could read it here and not fall behind. That's assuming they haven't fired me—?" He dropped the end of his comment as it struck him that he might not still have a job.

"I gather they have a high regard for your work," soothed the Sergeant. "I think DS Bateman has indicated to your manager that you are helping us, sort of undercover, so to speak. They have no reason to think you've been arrested."

Harry was happier, but not totally satisfied. "I still want out in a day or so," he insisted.

Wilcox assured him that he would inform DI Gravitt and started the tape. "I'd like to go over some of your personal details again, Harry. I'd specifically like to talk about your mother's funeral." Harry lifted his eyebrows but kept his mouth shut. "Was it a fancy funeral?"

"Nah, we were poor. It was cheap."

"Who was there? Try to answer as fully as you can, I know you were young."

"I'd like to know why you want to know. I can't see how it's relevant."

"Call it a gut feeling," answered Wilcox, thereby breaking his personal golden rule of policing: Never Trust a Gut Feeling. He had gob-smacked himself. "Let's have coffee," he suggested, and shouted for a PC to bring the jug. That settled, Harry picked up the thread.

"My father was there, of course, and a few people I didn't know. I think they were from the Laundromat. Uncle James, Micky and Anne-Marie went. A little late to show an interest in Mama, if you ask me. Maybe if they'd cared earlier she wouldn't have had a heart attack."

"And maybe if this, and maybe if that. Who knows? The world is full of maybes," Wilcox rejoined. "Do you remember seeing another man? Someone who talked to your father at the end of the ceremony? About your father's age."

Harry flushed. "Yeah. Do you know who he was?"

"The question is, do *you* know who he was? I see by the look on your face that you do."

"Well, not exactly. I overheard some of the conversation between him and my father, but I didn't hear it all. He said he had planned to marry Mama." Harry looked out of the window before adding, "I didn't understand it at the time, but he seemed to be saying Dad wasn't really my father." Harry looked at Wilcox. "Is that man my father?"

"No, he isn't. George is your father. He was someone your mother jilted almost at the altar, and he went to the funeral to get his revenge."

"Dad hardly ever spoke to me after that. Why? Did *he* think that other man was my father? Did he think he'd been suckered into raising someone else's child?"

"I believe so." He saw that Harry was getting angry and hurriedly continued. "You have a lot to think about, Harry." Wilcox turned off the tape machine. "If it's any consolation, Inspector Gravitt tore a shred off him; called him a bastard and told him Penelope married the better man. In fact, DI Gravitt got so angry that it made him ill. Truly ill, throwing up and all."

"This is not Gravitt's fight, it's mine. I want to see that man; I'll tear more than a shred off him!"

"Use your brain, lad. It's not your fight either. Oh, I don't deny you suffered because of it! But the fight belongs to George. You're a grown man now. Take my advice and look to the future; you can change the future. You can't change the past."

Wilcox stayed chatting with Harry for another hour, making sure he was calmed down before leaving him alone. He learned nothing new that would help the case. As he departed, he said he would contact the publishing house immediately for his—Harry's—next assignment. Harry thanked him.

Meanwhile Detective Sergeant Bateman was on his way to see George Franklin. This time no appointment had been made in advance, but Bateman felt sure that if George's arm were as bad as he claimed, he would be at home. And he was. But he was not alone. A skimpily clad woman came to the door.

"Who is it?" called George from the bedroom.

"Dunno, it's a man I never seen before." Bateman held up his warrant card. "It's the fuzz," she added.

George appeared, dressed except for his shoes. "Sorry, mate," he apologised. "You caught me at an awkward moment." He turned to his companion, saying, "Time for you to get lost, sweetie." He held the door open for her. "One of my neighbours," he explained to Bateman, a lopsided grin on his face.

"I'm returning your insurance policy," said the sergeant. "It's not big enough to be of much interest."

"Thank you. Was there something else?" George waited at the door.

"Yes. I'd rather like to go through your previous statement with you."

"Then you'd better come in and sit down," George offered, obviously deciding to be gracious after all. Well, better late than not at all, thought Bateman.

"Was there something in particular that concerned you?" George queried. "It can't be too serious, if you've come on your own!"

"I'd like to start with Penelope Franklin's funeral. I was wondering why you had her cremated instead of buried."

"It's because that's what I thought she'd like, if she had been in a position to state a preference. Her family always opted for cremation, didn't they?"

"Did they?"

"Yes, they did. That's what I said, isn't it?"

Bateman, like Gravitt, found George's manner of speaking irritating. "Tell me about meeting Leonard Cousins at the funeral."

"Who? Oh, Penny's boyfriend? I told all that to the other policemen who came here."

"Yes, I know. I have your statement with me, ready for you to read and sign. But first I'd like to hear about the incident from your own lips."

So George told the story again. There were no appreciable differences. Leonard had approached him after the ceremony, said he'd been sleeping with Penny before her marriage, and indicated that Harry wasn't George's son. While Leonard hadn't exactly claimed Harry for his own child, he did point out that Harry and George bore no physical resemblance to each other. "You know," George said at the end, "I've been thinking about this a lot since yesterday's visit, and it seems to me that Penny's other lover—Leonard?—did a great injustice not only to me but also to Harry. He might at least have coughed up some child support for his son. God knows *I* didn't have the wherewithal to support a family!"

Bateman had difficulty controlling the surge of loathing that welled up for this small-minded little man. He couldn't refrain from saying, "Well, sir, it looks like Harry really is your son and not Leonard's."

"How do you know? Have you carried out a DNA test?"

"The police only use DNA testing to solve a crime. We're not interested in paternity problems." Bateman wasn't about to tell George that the murderer had been too clever to leave behind even a hair that might be traceable. "We interviewed Mr. Cousins and he was adamant that he always took precautionary measures. He was quite convincing. Aren't you glad you don't have to return twenty years or so worth of child support payments?" Bateman couldn't hide the sneer in his voice.

"Okay, Sergeant. I can tell you don't like me. I am what I am, and ever since Penny died I've believed she foisted another man's child on me. I'm used to feeling resentment. Wouldn't you? Do you have children?" Bateman nodded. "How would you like it if you suddenly learned one of them was not really yours?"

"I think, Mr. Franklin, that I would try to remember it wasn't the child's fault."

George mulled this over. "You're obviously a better man than me, Bateman. Perhaps I will visit Harry this afternoon. Have you asked him what he overheard Leonard saying that day?"

"He seems to have realised there was doubt about his parentage. If you are serious about visiting him, we have him at the station. Oh, he's not under arrest," he added as he saw George's eyebrows rise. "He's in protective care."

George was silent as he digested this information. "Does that mean you think Harry's in danger?"

"We think every member of the immediate family is potentially in danger. The killer has not yet been apprehended. Now, just run your eyes over your statement, and then I'll ask you to sign it."

"Yes, all right. But first I'd like to know if you're also keeping the girl, Anne-Marie, in protective custody. She's more immediate family than Harry."

"We're keeping a close eye on her, but we think it may be significant that both murder victims have been male. Harry's the only remaining male blood relative."

"God yes!" exploded George. "If it's a vendetta, and it sounds like it is, keep Harry somewhere safe!" He signed the statement and Bateman took his leave.

Of course, Gravitt had no luck seeing Netty. He hadn't realised that Bowen had driven her to Kent. Instead he had a quick word with Greta.

"Are you still planning to leave here?" he asked her.

"Yes sir," she replied firmly. "This used to be such a happy house, but now it's sad. And frightening, too. Suppose this man killer goes after my Bill? I couldn't stand it if anything happened to him!"

"Have you found somewhere to go yet?"

"Bill and me, we've found a cottage in Sussex that's just right for us. It needs some work, but my Bill can do it."

"Greta, I'm sorry to keep asking you the same questions, but you're in a very special position here, in this household. Everyone trusts you and confides in you, and I keep thinking that if I can only find the right question, you probably have the answer."

Greta flushed with pleasure. "I'm sure I don't know about that! I've enjoyed working and living here, too, until this present trouble. But I don't know more than I've already told you."

"Have you noticed anybody's manner, or behaviour changing? Especially since Micky's death?"

"No, sir. Except everyone's scared, looking over their shoulder, like. Except Anne-Marie, who doesn't know whether to cry with grief or sing with happiness. Because of her engagement to you, I mean. Forgive me, I should have offered my best wishes already."

"Thank you, Greta. I'm a lucky man."

"She's a lucky woman, if I'm not being too bold to say so. You're a fine young man. I gather you're eating here tonight. Anne-Marie said you need fattening up, so I've got a rib roast for the main course."

Gravitt laughed. "It sounds wonderful! Will you keep your eyes peeled for me?"

This settled, Gravitt went looking for Marge. He found her in the study going through the month's bills.

"My dear Alex," she said, rising to her feet. "Apparently you have decided it isn't enough for me to be one of your prime suspects; now I am to become your mother-in-law. Well, Mr. Detective Inspector Alex Gravitt, I have to confess that I am delighted! At least something good has come out of all this horror." She kissed him on the cheek. "Are you any nearer to solving this—these murders?"

"Every day we make a little more progress," he answered. "But it's a tedious business."

"How is Harry?" Doing fine. "Is he guilty?" Unknown. "When is he likely to be released?" He's free to go whenever he wishes.

"I think we've swapped places!" smiled Gravitt. "You're asking the questions instead of me."

"Oh, I do apologise. I've been trying to find some way to restore normality, or at least the appearance of it. Your and Anne-Marie's engagement should be celebrated somehow, but of course no one wants a party at this time. I thought maybe I'd invite a few people for dinner Friday evening, if you're free."

Alex thought about it for a moment, then said, "I think that's a very good idea; very good indeed. Do you mind if I decide the guest list?"

If she was surprised, Marge had the good breeding not to show it. She picked up pen and paper and said, "Tell me."

"You, Anne-Marie, and Netty. Could you send Jenny to a friend's house for the evening?"

"I expect so."

"Doctor Winston, Harry. George? I'm not sure about him, I'll have to think about it. Me, of course. And someone to help me, either Sergeant Wilcox or possibly Geoffrey Bowen."

"Why not both?"

"If you don't mind, that would be ideal."

"Are we laying a trap?"

"Oh goodness, no," lied Gravitt. "I just don't want to forget anyone, you understand; it could cause ill-feelings."

"Yes, I can see that perfectly." Marge smiled conspiratorially.

"In fact, I'd like Greta and Bill to join us. Perhaps in that case we shouldn't have a dinner. Snacks and drinks would be best. Varied snacks, like spicy Tortilla chips and humus. Eatables with a strong flavour."

"I've got the picture," agreed Marge. "And I can say the choice of snacks was entirely my decision."

"Wasn't it?" They smiled.

"There's one more thing you can help me with, if you will. Get a tape measure and show me the open bottles of spirits, the decanted brandies." Marge did that and together they measured the height of liquid in the bottles. Marge made a note of the amounts and tucked the paper and tape measure behind a book. "We can slip in here from time to time and see if the amounts suddenly show an increase," she said. "But what about the food?"

"I guess we'll have to risk that. Try not to open any packets until the last minute. I'll bring Bowen with me, early, and he can hang around the kitchen."

Gravitt made his way back to the station where he found Wilcox and Bateman already waiting for him. They reported the results of their morning's work, Wilcox informing the others that Harry wanted to go home. Bateman protested, saying that George might visit his son that afternoon and it would be a shame, if reconciliation was in the air, to spoil it. "I'll talk to Harry in a bit," offered Gravitt, "but I have to tell you what's happening on Friday." He told them about the planned party. Bateman immediately said, "I want to go." Gravitt agreed. Wilcox said, "It sounds dangerous to me." Gravitt again agreed but added, "It might be that nothing happens at all."

When he went to the cells, Gravitt discovered that Harry already had a visitor. Harry and George were so deep in conversation that neither noticed the arrival of the Inspector. "I don't want to interrupt," Gravitt said pleasantly. "I've just come from Reddington Gardens and Marge asked me to extend an invitation to you, Harry. You are invited for drinks Friday evening. It's to make official my engagement to Anne-Marie. Under the circumstances a party isn't possible, so this will be just family and a few of my friends. I hope you will come."

Harry was flabbergasted. "Well, what do you know!" he burst out. "Thank you, sir. Thank you." Harry indicated his father. "Have you met my Dad? He came to see me. He's been here for an hour or more."

"Yes, we've met. You're welcome to come on Friday as well, Mr. Franklin."

"No, no, thanks anyway. They're Harry's relations on his mother's side. Anyway, I'm not getting about very easily yet. Another time." Gravitt made a mental note to put a tail on George for Friday night.

"Is it okay if I go home tomorrow morning?" asked Harry. "I'd like to get into some clean clothes."

"Of course. I'll tell them at the desk." Gravit left.

The afternoon passed without incident. The Superintendent popped by the Incident Room for an update, took one look at Gravitt and commented on his pallor and the dark circles under his eyes.

"I haven't been feeling very well, sir," Gravitt explained. "It's this case. I wish I had some proof of something!"

"Particularly worried about one of the suspects, are you?" Gravitt nodded, only mildly surprised that the Super knew of his relationship with Anne-Marie. "Afraid she'll be the next victim?"

Gravitt nodded again. "God yes!" he erupted. "She could easily be next on the list. Her or Harry, they seem the most likely. I've got suspicions, but nothing really tangible that points to the killer!" He sat down, dropping his head in his hands. "Some cop I am! I can't even find a homicidal madman who commits the most atrocious and outrageous murders." He told his Superior about the planned party.

"What are you hoping to achieve at Friday's get-together?"

"I thought that if the killer is developing a taste for blood, he or she might find the situation irresistible. The other murders happened at family gatherings."

"Hmm, yes," murmured the Super. "It could be very dangerous."

"It's dangerous doing nothing. And anyway, nothing may come of it; the killer might not rise to the bait. But at least it's taking some action!"

"You will need your wits about you on Friday. My advice is, take the rest of the day off. Take tomorrow off too. Whatever you do, make sure you're in good form on Friday. I don't have to tell you what the publicity will do to us if there's another killing, especially if it takes place in the presence of several policemen!"

The Super's last statement was not designed to make Gravitt feel better. Before going home he called Wilcox and Bateman in for a meeting. "Time for some slog work," he said. "Take each individual statement for the second murder and draw up a comparison chart. Dates and times where possible. Then do your best to draw up a chronological chart combining everyone's statements. Then take the charts we did for the first murder and compare them. Note any similarities or diametrically opposed comments or actions. After you've done that, show the whole mess to a detective constable who hasn't been involved with this case. Get a fresh viewpoint. You can reach me at home if there are any problems."

Alex Gravitt went home. He poured himself a small whiskey and soda and turned on the telly. Daytime television shows were not his idea of entertainment, but in spite of the boredom of quiz programmes and the worsening knot in his stomach, he fell asleep.

Harry left the cells at midday on Thursday. He rang the publishing house, thanking them for the book and making sure his job was safe. Then he went into town and bought himself a suit for the gathering. It wouldn't do to turn up in jeans!

On Thursday Anne-Marie also went into the West End to buy a dress, asking Marge and Netty to accompany her. The three women agreed that they need not wear black on this occasion. Marge found a pretty little number in dark grey which was perfect for showing off the ruby brooch given to her by her husband. Anne-Marie chose a dark blue dress of mid-calf length. With her good taste she decided to wear only a gold locket, an engagement present, by way of jewellery and, of course, her engagement ring. Even Netty indulged herself by purchasing a dress in a deep mauve colour. The three of them had a pleasant day, giggling as they sneaked out and back into the house via the back alley in order to avoid the few die-hard newspaper men still hanging around the front entrance.

That day Doc Elliot received his invitation with concern. It wasn't the partying that bothered him; he was a great believer in taking life forward and not dwelling on life's heartbreaks. But it had occurred to him, as it had to Gravitt, that this would provide an opportunity for more mischief. He packed his medical bag to take with him.

Chapter Twenty-Four

Friday was one of those beautiful days you sometimes get in England: warm and balmy with bright sunshine even though it may snow tomorrow. The women made sure there were enough ashtrays scattered around for the men. Greta was hijacked and forced to wear eye make-up while Marge piled her—Greta's—hair on top of her—Greta's—head, leaving a few wisps dangling sexily. "Bill will divorce me!" complained Greta; but secretly she was pleased. It had been a long time since she had dolled herself up. It felt good. And when the women took Greta downstairs to show her off to Bill, he was stunned. He blurted out, "If I wasn't already married to you, I would ask you to be my wife!" Everyone clapped.

Gravitt arrived early, as promised, with Bowen in tow. The detective realised at once that things were not going to go as planned. Marge had got caught up in the transformation of Greta and forgot to keep an eye on the food, and Bill, trying to be helpful, had opened the bags of snacks and put the humus and dips in bowls. Everything was sitting on the kitchen table where anyone could get to it, even someone from outside the house. Bummer! thought Gravitt.

He took Bowen into the study and checked the levels of drink in the decanters. At least they appeared not to have been touched. They went back into the kitchen, and after making sure there were plenty of bottles in the fridge, managed to find an ice bucket, and pulled out a bottle ready for opening.

Harry was the next to arrive, followed closely by Wilcox and Bateman. Doc Elliot came in last, carrying his medical bag. The doctor saw three policemen and a lawyer eyeing his bag suspiciously and gave a huge grin. "I came straight from seeing a patient," he fibbed. "I'll just put my case in the study." Bateman wandered over to the study as well. "Good, good," Elliot enthused. "Though I'm not sure I really feel much safer!"

The women made their entry, which was no less spectacular for all its planning. Anne-Marie led the way, followed by Marge, Netty and Greta. They glittered in their finery. But it was Greta who stole the show; no one recognised her. She felt proud!

Bill opened the champagne and Greta poured it into glasses, handing them around. Gravitt said, "I believe the honour of the first toast goes to me. To my wonderful wife-to-be and to all the beautiful women in the Smythe household."

"Hear, hear!" agreed all.

Harry surprised everyone by claiming the right to give the second toast. "May my cousin find happiness as her new future unfolds." He looked at Anne-Marie and continued, "I believe you have found the right man for you."

Anne-Marie blushed and said sweetly, "Thank you, Harry. I hope our childhood squabbles are forgotten."

As the evening progressed, the assembled company broke into smaller groups. Bowen took the opportunity to speak with Netty. "I enjoyed meeting your friends in Kent," he said. "May I go with you again sometime?"

She looked at him doubtfully. "What am I to understand by that request, Mr. Bowen?"

Geoffrey smiled. "Take it at face value," he said. "I'm not hitting on you, but I did enjoy the day immensely and would like to repeat it. That's all there is to it. And my name is Geoff."

The evening passed pleasantly. A second bottle of champagne was opened, and then a third and a fourth. Anne-Marie slipped her hand into

Gravitt's and asked him to walk with her in the garden. Gravitt glanced around the room, deciding everything was okay. Bowen and Netty had been joined by Harry and Marge. Sergeant Bateman was talking with Doc Elliot, Greta and Bill. Sergeant Wilcox was out of sight, but he was probably checking the bottles in the study. Gravitt stepped outside with his fiancée.

"It's such a lovely evening," Anne-Marie said softly, "and I haven't seen much of you this week. I've missed you!"

"I've missed you, Anushka, just as much—no, more!" Gravitt responded, pulling her towards him and spilling his champagne in the process. "Damn! Why didn't I leave my glass inside?"

Anne-Marie giggled. "There's a small table just inside the kitchen," she informed him. "Why don't you bring it out—and some more bubbles, too? I'll hold your glass for you."

While Gravitt was obeying the edicts of his love, Anne-Marie fiddled with her locket, apparently admiring it. Wilcox, unknown to her, was standing in the shadows watching her. He had slipped out to get a little fresh air and felt it too awkward to appear now, so he stayed put.

Gravitt found the table and an abandoned but partially full bottle of pink champagne and returned. He topped up his glass. "A little private toast," he said, "and a promise. I vow I will spend the rest of my life making you happy!" They drank.

"I can't think what's wrong with me," Gravitt complained, dropping his glass, which shattered into a hundred pieces, and knocking the table over. He put his hands to his head. "I feel drunk; know I haven't drunk that much." His words slurred and he started to fall over, white froth appearing in his mouth.

Wilcox jumped forward, shouting "Doctor Winston! Hurry! He caught Gravitt before he fell and laid him down gently.

Winston appeared with his medical bag. "There's no time to waste!" he explained. "I have to assume it's arsenic." He injected Gravitt with a large dose of dimercaporal.

"It's in her locket!" Wilcox announced, pointing to Anne-Marie. "I noticed she was touching it just before Alex took ill, but I couldn't see exactly what she was doing."

Bateman approached Anne-Marie and said, "I'll take that, if you don't mind."

"But there's nothing in it," she protested. "I don't even know how it opens! Why are you looking at me like that? I'm going to marry Alex; I wouldn't hurt him." She was crying. "Is he going to be all right?"

Bateman took the locket and opened it carefully. There were traces of white powder. He said to the doctor, "It looks like arsenic to me."

Wilcox saw red. "I swear to God, you little trollop," he barked at Anne-Marie, "if he dies you'll stay locked up for the rest of your life!"

"But…but I didn't do this!"

Yes you did!

"No I didn't!"

Are you sure?

"Who are you?"

Ha, ha, ha. That's for me to know and you to find out!

Everyone was standing in the garden listening to Anne-Marie. One moment her face was beautiful, the next it was grotesque with hatred. The sound of an approaching ambulance could be heard in the distance.

"What is your name?"

My name is Anne-Marie.

"Then…then who am I?"

You? You're nobody. You were known as Anushka.

"I have a right to be myself!"

You? You have no rights at all. I will kill you.

Anne-Marie put her hands around her neck and squeezed hard, falling to her knees. Her face turned red, then purple. Bateman grabbed her arms but she had the paranormal strength of lunacy. Bowen leapt to

233

help and together he and Bateman managed to get her to release her throat. The ambulance men, having been advised by Harry when he dialled nine-nine-nine, arrived with a straightjacket.

"But who are you?"

I am the chosen one. To me is given all power.

I am the one who destroys that which you love.

I am the one born in your painting 'Soul.' You created me. You released me.

Don't you know me yet? I am the Bringer of Death. I will be your death.

Chapter Twenty-Five

In spite of the lack of hard evidence, Anne-Marie was charged with the murders of James Smythe the Second and James Smythe the Third and the attempted murder of DI Alex Gravitt; while she waits for her trial, she is being held in a hospital for the criminally insane where her mental health is being assessed. She has been provisionally diagnosed as suffering from Dissociative Identity Disorder, better known to the layman as Split Personality. The prognosis is poor. As Anushka, she constantly protests her innocence. As Anne-Marie, she rages and accuses Anushka of all kinds of atrocities.

Alex spent a week in hospital recovering from arsenic poisoning. Had it not been for the prompt action of Sergeant Wilcox and the foresight of Doctor Elliot Winston, he would have died—as his father, Commander Gravitt, pointed out, once Alex was out of danger.

Although the Commander ordered him to report to the station as soon as he was released from the hospital, Alex had something else to do first. He went to the mental hospital to visit Anne-Marie. Before he was allowed to see her, the Medical Officer responsible for new admittances invited Alex to step into his office for a 'little chat.'

The psychiatrist's office was covered with papers, and at fist glance you would have wondered about a doctor who kept such messy records; but Alex's policeman's eye was quick to realise there was an order about the litter. He felt sure the MO would be able to find any report he wanted.

"I thought perhaps I had better prepare you a little," warned the MO. "Anne-Marie's moods vary widely depending on which personality is present. She's on quite a hefty dose of tranquillisers—as much as we dare to give her—so don't be surprised if you should find her rather unresponsive."

"Is that how DID is treated? With drugs?" Alex queried.

"No, certainly not." The MO was shocked by this question. "We would prefer not to use medication at all, but her stronger side was not letting her weaker self rest; she was beginning to hallucinate from lack of sleep. She has enough problems without that one as well, poor child. We will be treating her with psychotherapy."

"What are the chances of recovery?"

"I'd rather not answer that just yet. People *do* occasionally learn to balance more than one personality, but I don't want to raise your expectations." The MO cleared his throat. "So far only two personalities have emerged, but this can change."

"What would have caused her to develop this condition?"

"It can be brought on by mental trauma or it can be hereditary; I gather the latter is probably the case in this instance. I'm told her mother had spells of forgetfulness, or 'waking faints.' How can I explain this simply? Quite often the first personality doesn't know the second personality is there, so when the second one is dominant, the first is in a state of black-out. In Anne-Marie's case the two personalities seem to be able to communicate with each other, at least to some extent."

"May I see her now?"

The MO showed Alex to a small cell. "I'll be right outside in case she gets too excited," he offered. The room was as small as a gaol cell, which of course is exactly what it was. There was a barred window with no curtain, a bed with no sheet and no loose items she could use to harm herself or another. The walls were padded. God, how depressing! thought Alex.

"Oh Alex!" She held out her arms when she saw him and he moved forward to take her hands. "They're trying to tell me I poisoned you. I told them I couldn't do anything like that to you. I told them we're going to be married. Now you're here, you can tell them too. You'll tell them, won't you Alex? You'll tell them, and they'll let me go home. I want to go home."

Alex clasped her to his heart. "Yes," he croaked, "I'll tell them. But it may take a while. You'll have to be patient."

"I think they're trying to turn you against me. I know that's what they're trying to do! Are they succeeding, Alex? Do you hate me too?"

"No, no, my sweetness. They can't stop me from loving you. No one can change that." Alex kissed her on the nose and smiled tenderly. He had been shocked when he first laid eyes on her, here in the hospital. Her beautiful hair was uncombed and matted, and her hospital gown was blotched with old food stains. "Are you being looked after?" he asked her. "Do they help you brush your hair, let you have a bath, things like that?"

"Do I look awful? There's no mirror in here. I refuse to have a shower because they insist on someone being with me." Anne-Marie began to tremble and her voice rose. "*She's* going to kill me! *She* wants to take you away from me!"

The Medical Officer and two male nurses entered quickly. As he was being hurried away by the MO, Alex could hear Anne-Marie's voice shouting obscenities. It was awful.

Alex wanted to get away from this depressing environment as quickly as possible. Even his appointment with his father and the Superintendent couldn't be as depressing as the meeting he had just experienced with his fiancée.

On the other hand, he could be wrong.

The first person he encountered at the station was DS Wilcox. In actual fact, this was not an accident; Wilcox had been apprised by the hospital of Gravitt's release and had been waiting around for two and a half hours. He felt the first face Gravitt saw at the station should be a friendly one.

"It's good to see you on your feet!" Wilcox exclaimed. "I've missed you; we all have."

"Tell me something, John," requested Gravitt. "How much press coverage has there been about this case? Especially my involvement." He looked sheepishly at his friend. "No one would let me see a newspaper while I was ill." He noticed Wilcox's reticence and added, "Please don't hold anything back. I'm about to see the Commander, and the more I know, the better I can handle things."

"Yup, I can see that. Well, sir, there's been a lot about it in the papers, a lot. You have been hung, drawn and quartered by the press, and the whole structure of the police force is being called in question. The only good report was an interview with Mrs. Smythe. Marge, that is. She said you'd risked your life trying to save the family and she believed they'd all be dead if it weren't for you."

"Thanks, John. Here we go then," and he took the lift to the top floor where his father and the Superintendent were waiting.

"Alex. How are you feeling?" asked the Super.

"Nervous, sir." Alex glanced at his father and quickly looked away.

"I should think you are!" exploded the Commander. "Just what in hell did you think you were doing, getting physically involved with a suspect? You know it's forbidden!" The Commander was a fit man of fifty-four, but just at this moment he looked like he was having a heart attack. His face was purple with anger and his hands shook. "Do you know what the publicity has been like? The Commissioner has been on the 'phone every day! Every bloody day!"

"I'm sorry, sir. At the time it seemed the only way of solving the crimes."

"What!" shouted the Commander in a voice that must have been heard throughout the whole building. "Since when has bedding a suspect been an acceptable method of police detection?"

Alex's face grew rigid and suddenly he looked remarkably like his father. "If I would be allowed to say something?" he suggested coldly, and waited for his father to sit down. "The case was getting nowhere. Smythe Two was murdered without motive. It wasn't a crime of passion. It wasn't a crime committed for financial gain. No one hated him. It was senseless, totally senseless. We wasted a long time trying to make sense of a senseless crime. I had to get into someone's head, but at first I wasn't sure whose. I'm no psychologist, but it seemed to me that Anne-Marie and Micky were the two moodiest members of the family, with Harry a close third. Anne-Marie threw herself at me and I took the opportunity to get closer to her, to see how she thinks. Oh, I won't say I had any personal objection to 'bedding' her, as you put it," he added, curling his lip in a sneer.

The Super cut in, saying, "Are you aware that information obtained in such an unorthodox manner would hardly be admissible in court?"

"Yes, certainly. But I also knew there was going to be a second murder, I felt it in my bones. And it seemed more important to try and stop another killing than to do nothing because the evidence was inadmissible." Alex paused. "And there *was* another killing, and I wasn't quick enough to stop it." He sat down and closed his eyes. "That was why I arranged the engagement party; the first two homicides occurred during family gatherings. I hoped the party would be too appealing for the murderer to resist. Catch them in action." He opened his eyes and glared at his father. "Which we did."

"Well, Alex, I will try to save your career, but I'm not at all sure I can," said the Commander, not without sympathy in his voice. "I might be able to transfer you to a desk job, perhaps in a different venue, out of London, you know."

"Let me save you the trouble," Alex answered. "I quit." He stood up and turned to leave. As he reached the door, the Super asked, "Just one more question, Alex, if you don't mind." Alex looked at him and raised his eyebrows. "If the killer had turned out to be someone else, not Anne-Marie: wouldn't that have placed you in an awkward situation?"

"Then it would have been my problem, not yours!" Alex walked out. He went down to his own desk on the ground floor and cleared it, most of his papers going into the dustbin. Wilcox looked on wondering if an offer to help would be appreciated or resented. "What will you do now, sir?" he finally asked.

"In the long term? I don't know. Maybe I'll go into business as a private investigator. At least the pay ought to be better! Right now I'm going to get stinking drunk. Care to come for a drink?"

"Sure. Maybe if you open that PI agency, I'll join you."

They left the station together and headed for the nearest pub. After downing a couple of whiskeys, Alex realised that several of the patrons were watching him and whispering to each other. "God, I forgot this place is the police local. Let's get out of here!" He grabbed Wilcox by the arm and pulled him to the exit. All eyes immediately turned away, feigning indifference. At the door, Alex whirled round suddenly—sure enough, the eyes were upon him again—and said, "I just want to let you all know I wasn't fired. I quit." He took a deep bow, accepted the smattering of applause, and left.

They made a proper crawl of it, a drink here, a drink there. Wilcox, mindful of still being a policeman, drank halves to Gravitt's pints, but he knew he was drinking rather too much. They ended up at a pub in Soho which boasted an opening time until midnight. Gravitt was pretty well paralytic by this time and was becoming maudlin.

"I love solving crimes," he confessed. "It's the only work that gives me true satisfaction. D'you know what the Commander suggested? 'I can get you a desk job,' that's what he said!" He banged his fist on the table. "Can you imagine that? *Me*, in a desk job?" Gravitt shook his head in disbelief. After a brief interval he put his hand on Wilcox's arm. "We've both changed a lot, John; this case has got to us both." Wilcox nodded at the veracity and deep insight of this remark. "I don't know how I would have coped without you beside me, John. It's friends like you and Geoff that make life bearable." Gravitt lowered his head into his hands, his shoulders sagging in sorrow. "And I love my father, John. I love the old bastard, I really do. He was putting his own neck on the line, offering me any kind of job. He was so proud of me when I qualified for this position. I've let him down, John; I've disappointed him. And I've let you down, and Ben Bateman. But I had to quit, you know, I had to. I couldn't embarrass my father like that."

Wilcox made soothing noises and tried to change the subject, but Gravitt wasn't ready to let go of his remorse. It would certainly be true to say he was thoroughly enjoying his bout of self-pity!

"Anne-Marie," he almost whispered, "my little Anushka. How can she be so ill?" A tear fell onto Gravitt's cheek. "I really loved her, John. I love her now. Did I tell you I went to see her today? She asked me to take her home, and I couldn't. She asked me to help her, and I was unable to, John; I was helpless! It made me feel impotent." Gravitt held his hands over his eyes to hide the tears. Finally controlling himself, he exclaimed—more loudly than he meant to—"Damn them all. The Smythe family is certainly cursed!"

At the mention of the word 'Smythe,' two men joined them, one saying, "You've been following that case in the papers too? That Inspector's got a good job! I bet he gets to screw a lot of women, but that blonde girl! I wouldn't mind giving her one myself!" He nudged his companion and they laughed licentiously.

Gravitt threw his bitter in the man's face. Preferring to drink beer rather than wear it, the man quite naturally lost his temper. Unfortunately, those two men had a lot of friends in the pub to encourage them, whereas Gravitt and Wilcox had none. The man sporting the bitter on his face grabbed Gravitt by the lapels, hauled him to his feet and planted a firm uppercut on his jaw. The crowd cheered. Wilcox floored him with one punch to the chin. "That's for you, beer-face!" he snarled. There was booing. "The same for you?" he asked the other man. Although he would never have admitted it, Wilcox was enjoying himself. His eyes gleamed with the pleasure of finding an outlet for his pent-up emotions. The crowd moved back to leave more space between it and the four antagonists, and police sirens could be heard approaching. Wilcox snatched Gravitt from the grip of the second man and couldn't resist hissing to the onlookers, in his best James Cagney voice, "You dirty rats! You called the cops!" Then he and his boss fled quickly before the uniformed police arrived.

Wilcox dropped Gravitt off at his flat at half past twelve. As you can imagine, Gravitt wasn't pleased when the 'phone rang at eight the next morning. He pulled the pillow over his head and tried to ignore the incessant ringing, but it wouldn't go away. Eventually the answering machine clicked into operation. His father's voice boomed loudly into the room. "Alex, it's Dad. Pick up the phone. It's urgent."

Gravitt groaned. His head hurt, and what had happened to his jaw? He felt his teeth with his tongue; one of them was decidedly loose. Slowly memories of the night before returned, and he groaned again.

Thank God Wilcox had got him out of the pub before the police arrived! Is that why his father was ringing? Had someone recognised him and reported his ignominious behaviour? At least they couldn't fire him!

The 'phone rang again and this time Gravitt managed to stumble over to the cursed instrument. "Dad?" he rasped.

"You sound awful."

"I feel awful."

"Hangover? No doubt you deserve it. Get down here right away."

"Where's 'here'?"

"Damn it Alex, don't be obtuse! Get down to the station *now!*"

"No thank you. I quit, remember? I'm going back to bed."

"Get down here now or I will come and get you myself! We need you."

"Why? What's happened?"

"We've arrested the wrong person."

"Huh? What are you talking about?"

"There's been another murder. Marge Smythe is dead."

Alex was aware of two equally strong but conflicting emotions. He felt chagrin as the realisation dawned on him that a killer was still loose and active; and he felt joy in knowing that his sweetheart was not guilty of the abominable murders. As he had done the previous day, he chose to take a circuitous route to the station—one that went past the mental institution. He hoped that being told she had not committed a crime might help Anne-Marie to an early recovery.

As he pulled up in front of the hospital, the Medical Officer came rushing out to meet him. "I've been trying to telephone you," he said. "Please step into my office."

"Is there a new development?" asked Alex. "Is Anne-Marie all right?" There was that horrid feeling again, the same as he had suffered just before Mickey's death. He could barely breathe.

"No, I'm afraid not. I'm sorry to have to tell you that Miss Smythe managed, in spite of all our fail-safe measures, to commit suicide." The

MO waited for an outburst of grief or anger or disbelief; when it didn't come, he continued. "She strangled herself with a ribbon." He paused again, watching for some reaction, but sill there was none. "We don't know how she got hold of ribbon; she had two visitors yesterday evening, Mrs. Vanessa Smythe and Mr. Franklin. Harry Franklin, that is. They both brought chocolates, but of course we checked, as always, to ensure that no presents are wrapped with anything that could be potentially dangerous."

Gravitt sat as if turned to stone. Little by little he realised he could hear someone moaning, whimpering, and he was shocked as he realised the sounds were emanating from his own mouth. The doctor was holding a glass of water to his lips and he drank deeply of the cool liquid. After a few minutes he managed to utter hoarsely, "It's all so unnecessary, so pointless; she was not guilty of murdering her father and brother. She may have been mentally ill, and who knows? Maybe she was capable of murder; but she hadn't done it, not this time." He faced the doctor. "There's been another death. Her stepmother."

"My God! The poor child punished herself for someone else's crimes!"

"I'd like to see her, please."

The MO was reluctant. "I don't recommend it," he protested. "It's better you remember her as she was."

"I want to see her." Alex rose to his feet.

"You don't understand," the MO insisted. "Death by strangulation is not a pretty sight."

Alex lost his temper. He grabbed the MO by his lapels, pulled him close and shouted into his face, "I'm a fucking policeman, you twit! I've seen more horrid deaths than you can even imagine! I want to see her *now*, and while I'm there you can ring Sergeant Wilcox at the station and give him details on time and manner of death, who visited her yesterday, and how often medical staff checked on her. And tell Wilcox to send the SOCOs. This should have been reported immediately. *All* unnatural deaths have to be reported. You have a lot of explaining to do. This is *supposed* to be a secure institution!"

The MO, recognising Gravitt's grief, held his tongue. He had been trying to reach the Inspector all morning.

Taken at last to Anne-Marie's cell, Alex looked down at the figure covered by a white sheet. He removed the shroud and his heart broke. This once beautiful face, with its fetching nose tilted slightly to the left, was blue and distorted. The eyes bulged from their sockets and the tongue protruded. There was a thin red mark around her neck and a ribbon was hanging loose from the window bars. A chair was lying on it side. Where had that come from? It had not been there the day before. Alex took her hand, still warm, and placed it against his cheek. He remembered the first time they were together; she had placed her hand on his cheek then…

Alex

You said my name, and my name became a sigh on the gentle caress of your breath. You held my hand, and my hand accepted the hesitant promises of intimacy. You kissed my lips, and I loved you, then, now and forever.

You were an oasis of beauty in a desert of disfiguration. You warmed the ice of the frozen Antarctic with your smile. You melted my heart. Oh, Anushka! Why did you leave me? Did you not know how much I need you?

I always knew you would never harm me. I never believed that you poisoned me. I promise you, the world will know it too! You have my heart's pledge on that. But I wish you had chosen to remain with me! I love you so much!

May you find peace at last.

At the station Alex went straight to the Incident Room where he found a haggard-looking Sergeant Wilcox waiting for him. "I'm sorry to hear about your fiancée," he offered.

"You know?"

"The MO rang, as you told him to. The SOCOs should be there by now, under the direction of Inspector Haywood."

"You're off the case?"

"The Commander said as this is a suicide it's not part of our murder investigation. That's what he *said*, but I got the impression the MO complained that you threatened him."

"What rubbish! I merely reminded him that not reporting a suicide immediately is a criminal offence. Anyway, I had a good look around while I was there. I'll tell you about it later. Right now you and Bateman can help me most by lending me your grey matter. Let's start this business again from scratch. Something keeps niggling at me but I can't pinpoint it."

So began three solid days of reviewing reports, evidence, motives and alibis, of brainstorming and of dreaming up the wildest scenarios. They kipped at the station and sent junior officers out to fetch food.

"There's something there, if only I can grab it," Gravitt kept repeating.

"I can't spot any discrepancies," Bateman complained on the morning of the third day.

"Discrepancies!" shouted Gravitt. "That's it!"

"But where?" questioned Wilcox.

"The cheese dish!" Blank faces gawped at him. "You know, the first murder. I remember thinking, how could a clever killer—and he or she was clever, clever enough to almost get away with slow poisoning—how could such a person leave the cheese dish unwashed?"

"Because it wasn't important?" Bateman couldn't see that it mattered a toss.

"Think man, think! A meticulous and careful person, leaving a clue just lying around? Unlikely, if he could help it."

"I'm with you!" Wilcox sat up straight. "He didn't remove it because he didn't have the opportunity."

"Which means…?" encouraged Gravitt.

"He wasn't at the dinner with the family! Otherwise he could have remained behind long enough to rinse it out, when everyone rushed upstairs to check on James."

"Assuming you're right—and I'm not convinced," Bateman argued, "that leaves only Harry. Everyone else was there."

"And his father, George, and possibly Leonard." That was Wilcox being pedantic and thorough. "Or the man in the street."

"The man in the street only if he knew of the back alley," corrected Gravitt. "Unless he had a key, the killer would have had to enter the house through the back door. It was open. At least I think it was. Greta will know. But speaking of Harry," Gravitt mused out loud, "he lied to us. He must have, because he said he didn't know there was a garden shed; but he *must* have known! He visited the house off and on since before Katherine died, and while it's true that you can't see the shed from the house, the garden is not all that big. Don't you think it's odd that a boy of eight or nine didn't explore the garden?"

"But he *is* odd!" countered Bateman.

"He was also excruciatingly shy," responded Wilcox. "Where better to escape from people than in the garden? Let's go through his file again."

"We know Harry read at least one book on chemistry as well as a couple of other science books," said Gravitt, checking Harry's first interview. "He also admitted to some knowledge of criminal investigation procedures."

"But he appeared not to know about the attempted slow killing of James!" exclaimed Bateman, following this remark with a blush as the two senior officers grinned at him. "Of course, he would take that attitude if he were guilty."

Gravitt suggested comparing these facts with George and Leonard's situation.

"Leonard is a dentist; he must know something about drugs. But George?" questioned Wilcox.

"George taught sports, but it was at a school. He may have visited the library or sat in on a science lecture occasionally," put in Bateman.

Gravitt started a comparison chart. "In order of likelihood," he wrote. "Cheese dish: (1) Harry (2) George (3) Leonard. Knowledge of poisons: (1) Harry (2) Leonard (3) George. Knowledge of shed: (1) Harry only. Knowledge of existence of rat poison in shed: (1) Harry only. Opportunity: (1) Harry. Others, unknown."

"I'll do motives," offered Wilcox. "(1) Harry—hatred, jealousy. Possibly monetary." As Bateman lifted his eyebrows in surprise Wilcox explained, "In the beginning money didn't seem a likely motive for Harry, but with so many of the family dying he probably stands to inherit a tidy sum. (2) George—hatred, but defused by time. He wouldn't inherit anything, so not money. (3) Leonard—no motive, really."

"There's another loose end," added Gravitt. "Now that we know Anne-Marie didn't commit the crimes, who tried to frame her? Who gave her a locket containing arsenic? And who slipped a length of ribbon to her in the hospital?"

"What about Bill?" asked Bateman. "He knew of the shed and the rat poison and he had the opportunity."

"No motive," said Gravitt and Wilcox at the same time. "And no opportunity for the second murder or for giving Anne-Marie the ribbon," finished Wilcox.

Someone had to break the news of Anne-Marie's suicide to Netty, and it was decided that Wilcox was the obvious choice because he and Netty were on a first-name relationship. "Not my idea!" the Sergeant declared emphatically.

When Wilcox informed Netty of her sister in law's demise, she said nothing. Her face was blank and her eyes unfocussed. Wilcox was worried. He took both her hands in his giant paws and asked urgently, "Netty, did you understand me?" She didn't move. He gave her a shake and finally she seemed to return to reality. "Johnny," she whispered. "When is it my turn?"

He held her tightly and said, "Never! We're going to make an arrest this afternoon." Still no tears came to wash away the shock. "Netty, I have to ask you something." He felt her stiffen. "Do you remember the locket Anne-Marie was wearing at her engagement party?" She nodded. "Was it a present?"

She looked at him for the first time. "Does it matter now?" she asked. "It was a present from Harry. Anne-Marie was so happy! She said it showed that he had forgiven her for being rude to him a few years ago."

Wilcox stayed with her for a while, chatting about inconsequential things, trying to help her bear her losses. He asked after Jenny and was told she was staying at a friend's house, "Where there's laughter." He promised to visit her again in the morning.

Harry was picked up for questioning and formally charged. He had means, motive and opportunity, and even the services of the great Geoffrey Bowen failed to save him. Harry never admitted to any of the crimes, but the jury had no doubts. He was sentenced to life imprisonment with a recommendation from the judge that he receive no remand for good behaviour. "You are totally heartless, an embarrassment to the human race," the judge said, in his summing up.

Epilogue

Netty Smythe sat on the antique sofa in the richly decorated lounge of the beautiful house in Reddington Gardens, watching the news on the large, wide screen television. She was alone except for her daughter who was playing with her dolls. Netty was a wealthy woman now.

The news was full of the Smythe murder case. Netty watched it closely, not missing a word. The media branded Harry as the Abominable Murderer. At the end of the news report she switched off the TV and continued to sit, staring blindly at the set. Slowly her mouth began to stretch and a smile formed on her lips. She started to laugh.

Printed in the United States
44005LVS00003B/190-210